AF439794

"I'M A MONSTER, KERES."

"OH, BUT DARLING, I WOULDN'T WANT
YOU ANY OTHER WAY."

Blood of Two crowns
book two of hallowed fates

Mareina is now Atratus' future queen and a goddess of the underworld while being mated to two males who hate each other. When she finds herself forced to make a heartbreaking decision that forces her away but ultimately saves her mates, Nakoa and Malekai are forced to work together to get her back.

This book features the following tropes:

Fated Mates
Why Choose/Reverse Harem
Enemies to Lovers
Friends to Lovers
Bromance
Trauma Healing
villain redemption
Found Family
LGBTQ Rep (w/ spicy scenes)
Political Intrigue
Gods, Vampires, Fae, & more
Kink & Spice Galore

"There is but one mast that will not bow or break beneath the ever-changing winds of your emotion, and you must allow all other emotion to pass over you like the current upon your wings."

I held my breath as his smile stretched until it split and revealed the fangs framing a radiant smile.

"Love."

BLOOD OF TWO CROWNS

A SPICY FATED MATES, WHY CHOOSE ROMANCE
ABOUT HEALING & REDEMPTION

HALLOWED FATES
BOOK TWO

CHIARA FORESTIERI

ILLUSTRATED BY
KUSH B (@KUSHB_ ON X/TWITTER)

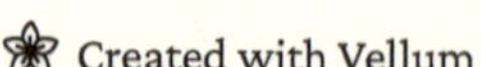 Created with Vellum

TRIGGER WARNINGS

This book is a 'relatively' dark fantasy. On a scale 1-5 on the darkness level, I'd say it's perhaps a 2.5. Are you going to cry? Probably.

And, as per usual, if you find any of the below triggering, **please**, do not read this book. I beg of you. Please? Please. Please DO NOT read this book if you find ANY of these trigger warnings upsetting.

Be gentle with yourself and your mental health.

Ends on somewhat of a Cliffhanger (not nearly as intense as the last one)
Explicit NSFW art at the end of the book
Bondage
Blood Play
Explicit Language
Graphic Scenes Depicting Sexual Acts
Torture, Gore, & Violence
Mention of Trauma
Mention of Suicidal Feelings
Recovery from Substance Abuse
Mention of genocide (historically within this fictional world)

If you find all of that palatable in your literature, you'll do just fine with the rest. Let's leave some mystery between us, shall we? :)

REMEMBER...

THE VERSION OF YOURSELF YOU ASPIRE TO BE EXISTS ON THE OTHER SIDE OF A BRIDGE THAT ONLY YOU CAN CROSS.

THE BAD NEWS:
THE BRIDGE IS ON FIRE.
IT'S PEPPERED WITH NAILS AND SHARDS OF GLASS.
AND IT'S LITTERED WITH DEMONS OF EVERY KIND (MOSTLY JUST THE ONES IN YOUR HEAD).

THE GOOD NEWS:
YOU HAVE WINGS.
YOU ONLY HAVE TO LOOK AWAY FROM THE BRIDGE TO SEE THAT THEY'RE THERE.

LOVE YOU.

— CHIARA XO

GLOSSARY

Arcanum *(ark-cah-num)*
A creature manifested only in spirit that imbues the being bound to, and marked by, them with additional powers. A rare gift from *Akash,* though only the arcanum chooses who it binds itself to

Archestratim *(ark-eh-strah-tum)*
an immensely powerful winged immortal from one of the divine realms

Anim Gemla *(ah-neem-gehm-lah)*
the Aurialingan term for *soulbound.*

Kailuma *(kaey-looh-mah)*
Mors' favorite secluded beach in all of Avernus.

Katadamna Kaza *(kah-tah-dahm-nah kah-zah)*
An aurealingan phrase, literally translating to *damn the cost.*

Omnisseras *(ohm-nee-seras)*
an ancient race of primals from the Ouranissa realm.

Olana Kah'hei *(oh-lah-nah kah-hey)*
Kalohani for 'chosen family'

Dream Leaf

a plant medicine, usually smoked or brewed as a tea, used to induce feelings of euphoria, deepen sleep, and enhance dreams

Kahlohani Islands

An archipelago in the majestic Kahlohani Sea that lies south of the Atratusian continent that is renowned for its fearsome tribal warriors

Ku'kāne *(koo—hah—nay)*

Kahlohani for 'my son'

Lohane thili *(low-hah-nay-thee-lee)*

Kahlohani for *soulbound*

Maha Loha *(may-hah-low-hah)*

Kahlohani for 'my love'

Maha Mo'ina Li'ili

(mah-hah moh-ee-nah lee-ee-lee)

Kahlohani for 'my little nightmare'

Mare Nerum

(mah-reh neh-room)

The 'Black Sea' in Vassileo (a hell realm)

Nephilim *(neff-eh-lim)*

an immensely powerful winged immortal from a divine realm that guards the hell realms. Distinguishable from other *seraphi* races by their horns, tail, and armor (the dark plating often found on their brow, chest, legs, and back).

Ouvelleet *(ou-veh-leet)*

A town south of Bastrina, just beyond The Sentient Forest.

Poa Hanei *(po-uh-hah-nei)*

Kahlohani for 'soulmate'

Protus Archestratim

(proh-tuhs ark-eh-strah-tim)

Chief Archangel

Syfaro Vescor

(see-fah-roh vez-core)

a soul-eating demon

Sanguinati *(sang — gweh—nah—tee)*—an immortal being

sustained by blood similar to the traditional 'vampire' but is not hindered by sunlight, is not allergic to silver, and will not die by a simple wooden stake to the heart

Seraphi Ousia *(seh- raff—ee—Oo—see—uh)*—Fragments of resting divine spirits

Seraphi *(seh-raff-ee)*

a broader term for beings and deities originally from one of the higher realms, such as the *Nephilim*

Syntrifa (seen-treef-fah)

The aurealingan term for fated mate

Tessari mú *(tess-ah-ri-moo)*

An aurealingan term of endearment meaning *my treasure*

Wielder

any individual or entity capable of wielding magic.

Yatól *(yah-tohll)*

A northern province with a harsh and extreme climate that possesses mountains, dense forests, and a sprawling desert

Vassileo

(vass-eh-lay-oh)

A realm consisting of multiple 'living' and 'after death' hell realms

ONE

MALEKAI

"Thank you for coming." I infused every bit of urgent gratitude into those words. Miroslav hesitated, his gaze warily flitting between Mareina and me before shaking his head in resignation. "Where is it that you'd like me to take you?"

"Mors' Temple."

Miroslav's brow furrowed.

"For what? To beg him not to take her life? Her life force is strong."

Forcing my expression to remain neutral, I silently deliberated just how much to disclose. Of all people, I'd have assumed he'd know Mors is her father. Erring on the side of caution, I merely tugged at Mareina's sleeve to reveal Mors' sigil. The inverted torch with wings symbolizing the extinguishing of life and the liberation of the soul.

"She bears his mark. Surely, he will know something."

Miroslav's brows pinched before relaxing in resignation. Wordlessly, he extended his hand.

My heart leapt with relief as I turned scooping Mareina off the bed, into my arms. Miroslav laid his palm on my shoulder, and a breath later, we were standing in front of Mors's temple.

"Send one of his acolytes when you're ready if she still hasn't woken."

Miroslav's eyes dipped to Mareina, his stoic features briefly belying his concern.

"Thank you, again."

The male nodded silvery eyes burning with that piercing know-ingness as he hesitated to leave.

"Zurie's guest... Thalia. I do not trust her. I cannot read her as I do others. She is something... *Other*... And even more unsettling, she wasn't in a single one of my visions. I do not believe she is what or who she claims to be."

Wariness crept in, but it only further cemented my decision to bring Mareina back to Avernus. "I will speak with her."

Miroslav's expression darkened. "Do not interrogate the female. We do not need to make any more enemies. Especially ones as powerful as her."

Impatience was making my fucking skin crawl. "I have no inten-tion of making enemies. Believe it or not, I'm actually quite good at making *friends*."

Miroslav hardly seemed reassured, but Mareina didn't have time for this. If I determined Thalia was in any way a threat to Mareina, I would have my beast devour her whole.

I turned on my heel only for Miroslav's hand to shoot out and grab my arm. "Malekai, the path that you all have chosen doesn't guarantee—

I shook my head, not wanting to be reminded of his *predictions*.

"It doesn't matter. I will always do what is best for Mareina."

Understanding filled his gaze before he folded away. "I hope it is enough."

With Mareina still in my arms, one of the large doors to the temple swung ajar. I stepped inside, the space cool and dimly lit with the same flickering fire-lit torches as when Mareina and I had been here, little more than a day ago.

One of Mors' shadowy, hooded *Pharalaki* hovered a few feet

away. It turned and drifted down the hallway leading to the hidden doorway of Mors' realm. Avernus.

It seemed to be in a rush because I practically had to jog to keep up with it. When it revealed the doorway, I made my way down the steps alone.

The only light illuminating the stone stairwell was the distant glow of Avernus' threshold. As I stepped through, three suns showed brightly in the sky - one large, two small. Silken grasses of vibrant green undulated against a summery breeze. At first sight, Mors' house looked exactly the same as before.

As we approached, an unfamiliar winged male stepped outside of Mors' house, standing even larger than my six feet eight inches. He bore dark grey wings tucked tightly against his back and an even darker set of stormy grey eyes. Long alabaster hair reached past his dark, broad shoulders.

"There's a spare room you can stay in. Watch out for the broken pots and door splinters. I'll have it taken care of shortly."

Dread tightened my chest as I took in the sight of the obliterated door and my boots crunched against shards of clay pots. "What the hells happened?"

"Keres happened," he called back as he turned down a hallway.

Mors' sister?

Sunshine poured into the floor to ceiling, darkly wood framed windows lining the left wall of the hallway to reveal a spectacular view of the fields and mountains in the distance. Elaborate tapestries and paintings hung from the opposite wall between doors. The male disappeared, stepping into a room at the end of the hall. As I stepped inside, he turned to face me from the center of the large, spare bedroom decorated in neutral tones of linen and terracotta.

There was a stillness to the house and a distinct lack of energy that told me something was wrong.

"Where is Mors?"

The male's face became stricken with emotion as he gestured vaguely at the bed, the covers already peeled back. "Gone."

My heart stalled in my chest as I carefully laid Mareina on the bed. "Gone as in… Busy with work? On vacation? Or…"

"As in Keres murdered Soteira, somehow persuaded Mors to drink from The River Oblivion, and dumped him on some beach in the Bellorum realm. *Nippies Piss Thilis* or something like that."

What in the fuck.

"Do you mean *Nissi Tis Pillis?*"

The male waved an unconcerned hand again as he scrubbed the other down his face, emotion welling in his eyes.

"That."

"And who are you, exactly?"

The male drew in a shuddering breath, his palm still covering his face, voice cracking with barely restrained emotion.

"Lathrimos."

I tucked Mareina beneath the covers as he sidled next to me to stare down at her. "Somnus already told me you might be coming."

"… Mors' brother?"

Lathrimos' lip quivered as he nodded in affirmation.

"Is he here?"

Lathrimos shook his head, taking shaky breaths to calm himself.

Fuck me.

I wasn't the best at handling emotional upset. Unless it was for Mareina. I'd had my fair share of mental breakdowns, but it had always, thankfully, been in private. *Or with Mareina.*

Tension knotted in my chest as I deliberated whether or not to try and soothe the male. I settled for clapping him on the back.

"Well, he's not dead, at least."

A choked sob broke free, and Lathrimos threw his arms around me, crushing me against his chest. It was a bizarre and highly emasculating sensation.

"There, there…," I managed awkwardly, whilst patting him on the back as I settled in to hug him.

"*He was my best friend,*" Lathrimos sobbed, hiccuping.

"... He'll be back. Nissi Tis Pillis isn't that far from Atratus. Maybe I can find him and bring him back."

Lathrimos heaved a shuddering sigh as he finally straightened, swiping away the evidence of his emotion.

"He's not there. Somnus went and got him. And it'd be pointless anyway. The River Oblivion wiped his memory completely. He won't remember me or our thousands of years worth of memories, let alone his entire realm. Thankfully, the effect isn't permanent for a god. We just have to wait for his memories to return."

"How long will that take?"

Lathrimos shrugged, chin wobbling as though it were the crumbling cornerstone of his emotional foundation.

"Years. Maybe even decades. Who knows? This has never happened before, as far as I know."

My eyes drifted back to Mareina.

"Do you know what she needs? How to heal her? Make her wake up?"

Lathrimos only threw her a cursory glance, making my hackles rise. "She'll be fine. She just... Her soul is tied to this realm. Being outside of it is draining."

"She's lived her entire life outside of this realm."

"She's a goddess. Not a mortal. It won't kill her not to be here, but she certainly won't be at full power if she doesn't spend significant time here."

Mareina was already, inarguably, one of the most powerful beings in Atratus. We'd fought in a war together. I'd witnessed her power and fury in all its jaw-dropping glory.

How much more powerful could she get?

The thought made my beast growl his excitement.

"Not to mention, she needs to be here. Especially with Mors being... *indisposed.* The entire realm will disintegrate without at least one of them here."

His words yanked my gaze back to his.

"What?"

The male looked at me like I'd just sprouted a few extra heads.

"Just as it is with any other god, the realm is tied to their life force. They sustain it. Just as a tree requires soil and rain. Without those things, the tree will gradually wither away and die."

"How long can she or Mors be gone for before that starts to happen?"

Lathrimos furrowed his brow thoughtfully, scratching his bristly beard. "It wouldn't happen overnight. It would take perhaps years, but it would be an inevitability without them."

How the shit is Mareina supposed to rule a kingdom and *an entire realm?*

"I mean, you didn't plan on going anywhere, did you?"

I huffed a laugh."You'd literally have to kill me."

Lathrimos gave me an appreciative smirk. "That'd be no small feat, killing a creature like you."

I stilled with apprehension. In my 200-plus years of existence, I hadn't revealed my true nature to a single soul. I had only ever allowed myself to shift when my beast became most desperate and well away from any prying eyes. It was too great a risk of potentially being seen. My kind was a distant and tragic memory in this realm.

"Gift of an Archestratim. Discernment. You can't lie, hide, or glamor anything from us. It's a curse at times. The truth is often a burden."

TWO

NAKOA

Zurie's lips curled into a smug grin. As if she *weren't* covered in dungeon grime and wearing a palladium collar. "I'll make a bargain with you. Vow to bring me no harm, allow me to continue living in my palace and maintain access to my coffers, and in exchange, I'll assist you in ruling Atratus, provide a smooth transition for you in becoming King, *and* I'll introduce you to your father."

How delusional can one person be?

Turning on my heel, I strode towards the exit. Zurie shrieked in protest behind me.

"Wait! You can't keep me here!"

Glancing over my shoulder, I stopped in the doorway, where my beloved and loyal *olana kah'hei* waited for me. Thalia remained notably out of sight. "I can. You are no longer a Queen, and the sooner you accept that, the easier your sorry life will be *if* I decide to let you live."

The heavy dungeon door slammed shut with an ominous finality. Thalia strode closely beside me as we made our way back into the palace's northern wing. Though she said nothing, something inside me prickled with unease at her closeness. I didn't trust her. The more time I spent in her presence, the more certain I became of that. Even if my Knowingness had gone silent again. Probably to spite me after my *altercation* with Mareina.

You tried to kill her, it hissed.

Guilt and anger warred within me. Her betrayal was something that I wasn't entirely sure I would be able to ever forget. Forgive one day, yes. We had a kingdom to rule together, after all. But forget? No.

Not to mention, I couldn't help but resent the fact she was with that blonde fae fucker.

A piercing burn seared my fingers, dragging my gaze to my hands. My newly grown claws lengthened to beastly proportions. Blood trickled to the floor, leaving a trail behind us as we walked back to my rooms.

Fuck.

How would the people of Atratus accept me as a monster?

I'd spent my whole life glamoring away my wings, tail, and solid black eyes. I'd dreamed of one day being able to live freely without having to hide my true form. Just as my nightmares had foretold, I'd become something even more terrifying to behold. The feathers of my wings had vanished and become membranous like a bat's. Black, stone-hard plating had risen from bone and pierced the skin on either side of my brow like a dark crown adorning my black, gazelle-like horns.

I looked like a demon.

But I was tired of hiding.

Monster or not, Mareina and Atratus will *accept me.*

Val and Lokus walked beside me, flicking me concerned glances before locking eyes briefly with the rest of my *olana kah'hei.*

Val silently *willed* a handkerchief into his hand and passed it to me.

"Fuck me, mate. Are you alright?" Lokus asked.

Pomona smacked him on the back of the head.

"Yes... Fine."

Lokus gave me a bored look. "Fine?"

"Lay off it, ya cunt," Val growled in warning.

"Fuck off. He needs to talk about it. The male's been through—

"Yes. *Fine,*" I snapped, my patience for bickering nonexistent, "I'm just adjusting."

Lokus heaved a sigh. "Right. Well, on that note, I'm gonna go find a brothel, see if anyone's feeling adventurous—

I narrowed my eyes at him. "You do realize there are about a hundred reasons why you can't do that?"

"Can't or shouldn't?"

"*Can't.* It's not like you can *fold* out of the palace. What the fuck are you gonna do? Walk out the front door? We're not even supposed to be here. What're her guards going to—

"I'll take him to Zurie's harem."

I shifted to look at Thalia, who smirked when I raised a brow.

"What? A girl has needs. And the guards won't bat an eye at me... or your pretty friend." Thalia's gaze flicked to Lokus, scrutinizing him. "Zurie and I spent copious amounts of time there together already."

My eyes narrowed. *Did this female fuck my birth mother?*

I wasn't entirely sure I felt about that.

"And Zurie is in the habit of sharing her harem?"

Thalia shrugged. "I won't deny that she's a recluse and hasn't had many visitors since your father, but as I said, her guards have seen me many times. If one of her guards say anything, I'll just say that I brought him from my own harem."

My eyes darted to Lokus to find him grinning. "I'm gonna lose my mind if I have to stay quarantined in this dusty-ass wing of the palace, brother."

Growling, I continued the long walk to my bedroom. "Thalia can *fold* a few of them to your room. Offer them a vow of silence in exchange for their freedom. Pay them handsomely enough to start a new life. And if this causes us any trouble, I will fucking castrate you."

The hairs on my arms rose as a distantly familiar magic swept into the room, dragging my eyes open. I'd fallen asleep in the bathing pool of my new bed chamber.

Miroslav.

"Your soulbound is unwell."

Anger and sadness returned to me with a merciless weight.

"She will live?"

"Yes."

"Malekai is with her?"

A pause.

"Yes."

My jaw clenched so hard, a tooth cracked. Thank fuck it would grow back. It wasn't the first time. I spat out the shard into the bathwater, watching it sink beneath the clear surface to the darkest blue tile floor.

"Well then, she has no need of me."

"*Wrong.*"

Silence settled heavily between us, his presence behind me felt like a ominous cloud. I just wanted to bathe in peace. Finally, I twisted to look at him. His silver-white gaze was unsettling as ever.

"Isn't *my mother* waiting for you to return or something?"

My mother.

Another spear of betrayal lanced through me.

She still had my precious babies, Peanut and Bellona. Their absence, especially now, was enough to choke me. It was nearly on the tip of my tongue to ask Miroslav to fold them here, but it wouldn't be fair to keep them trapped indoors, and the ruckus of canines would draw far too much attention. Thankfully, Pumpkin was safely tucked away in the stables due to the considerate male before me.

Miroslav's gaze became scornful. Or was that pity in his eyes?

Either way, it had some strange emotion suddenly clogging my throat.

"The first time I saw you, you were no larger than the palms of my hands."

Oh, fuck.

My mind may not have known where he was going with this, but something in my soul did. Emotion fisted my throat with an unforgiving grip.

"Just after Zurie gave birth to you..."

"Do you know who my father is?"

"Yes. And no I cannot take you to him. Only Zurie has the power to do that."

"How did Leilani become my mother?"

"I took you to her."

"Why did she get rid of me?"

Miroslav's gaze softened. That was *definitely* pity in his eyes.

"That is a discussion you need to have with Zurie."

Dread sank like an anvil in my gut. Even with my petulant Knowingness ignoring me, I knew that the truth I needed to learn would not be a welcome one.

"Your mother, Leilani, loves you the same as if you had been born of her blood, Nakoa. Let *nothing* dissuade you from that fact."

I shifted to face away from him as some foreign sensation began to burn my eyes.

"You would do well to remember that it is because of her that you are even half the male you are. One day, you will learn just how much you truly owe her."

The burning in my eyes swelled until saline streamed down my cheeks. Quickly wiping them away, I drew in a calming breath to quell the overwhelming tide of emotion.

"Why, exactly, have you come?"

"Two reasons. One, Thalia is not to be trusted. She hides her power, and I cannot enter her mind, nor am I able to gaze upon her past, present, or future potentialities. When I attempt to scry even her father, there is a block. The only beings powerful enough to evade my magic and my sight are *the gods*."

"That doesn't include the descendants of demiurges?"

Miroslav frowned. "I certainly wouldn't think so, not after so many generations... but I cannot be sure."

I heaved a sigh, sinking further into the bathing pool.

"And what is the other matter of urgency?"

"Your *soulbound* needs you," he pressed.

As his words settled in a crushing weight settled on my chest. *"Wrong."*

Footsteps sounded behind me until Miroslav stood in front of me, gaze searing into mine like white hot coals, as I failed to *will* my ebon eyes to stop leaking water.

"Whether you're willing to admit it or not doesn't change the fact that your souls are entwined. You are weakened without one another. You will *need* each other if either of you plan to survive what is to come."

Having no argument, I knew when to remain silent.

"I suggest you learn to see things from beyond your own narrow perspective and find forgiveness somewhere in that heart of yours before it is too late. Karma and fate are not synonymous entities, Nakoa. If you do not cherish the *soulbound Akash* has gifted you with, you shouldn't be surprised when she is stolen from you. "

CHAPTER

THREE

MAREINA

Waking up beside Malekai was the second-best thing to ever happen to me. Handsome features slack, his peaceful expression lent a certain lightness that I'd never witnessed in him. Laying beside Malekai like this, dressed only in one of his shirts, with his delicious heat pouring into me and his bare, broad and thickly muscled chest winking me in the face had me slick with desire.

Even my magic was writhing—both inside me and around me. Around us. Dark red tendrils whispered over his skin like they were trying to lick him. Taste him.

Willfully pushing away all thoughts of recent violence and turmoil, I was choosing to focus on the gift at hand. After all this time, I was finally lying beside the male I loved, revelling in his glorious presence. Perhaps it made me unforgivably selfish, but not only was I desensitized to death, I had spent my entire life forsaking the desires of my heart and, thus, my happiness. I refused to let it pass me by any longer.

Simply staring at him beside me in bed caused this *thing* to wind tighter between us as if physically pulling me closer to him. Urging me to press my lips to his. For my hands to caress the thick, formidable length of his cock pressing against my abdomen and hip.

His sea salt and embers scent seemed to thicken in the air. My hips squirmed as my core clenched with need for him. A soft, low rumble purred from his chest as his hips shifted forward to drive closer to mine. My breath caught at the same moment his eyes popped open wide with shock.

Large hands gripped me with brutal strength as he shifted me onto my back and straddled me, burying his face in my neck. *"Oh praise fuck, Mareina."*

Emotion swelled in my chest, my hands sliding up the scarred plane of his back as he drew away slightly, concern pinching his brows. A tendril of dark golden hair hung over his perfectly arched brow.

"Are you ok?"

"Couldn't be better."

"What do you remember?"

My throat worked as memories flashed through my mind of Nakoa, seemingly blinded by his anger at my betrayal and his attempt to kill me. Of nearly killing my own soulbound. Stabbing Zurie. Of my father's bother, Somnus, giving me the news about my father drinking from the River Oblivion and now having no memory of me. Of something happening to my mother because of Keres, my father's sister. Though he hadn't given me any details.

"Everything. And nothing I care to remember."

The heat radiating from him felt hot enough to brand me. That burning embers scent of his further intensified and I swore I could faintly smell smoke.

My heart pounded as he leaned forward on one elbow, and his free hand possessively gripped my jaw. "You have no fucking idea how worried I was."

My heart squeezed even as my arousal burned brighter, eliminating whatever restraint I had on my emotions *and* my body. Drawing my legs out from between his, I wrapped them around his narrow waist. Instantly my hips rose, slicking my entrance against his cock and turning my words breathless. "Thank you for taking care of me."

He growled, body tensing as the hand on my jaw coasted over my neck before fisting a handful of my hair. Something dark flickered beyond the turquoise depths of his gaze, further confirming that staring back at me was someone or something I had only caught the briefest glimpses of before and had ignored. His voice was little more than an animalistic growl. *"You belong to me, Mareina."*

My heart soared as his lips met mine in a bruising kiss. At the warm, almost cinnamon-y taste of him—oddly similar to my venom. My fingers carded through his hair and roved over his thickly muscled shoulders. My nails dug into him with the need to hold him closer. "I want you to mark me as yours," I murmured against his lips.

He growled low, the heat of his body stoking higher alongside the intensifying prickle of his magic, making the hairs of my body stand on end. It felt like the way the shifting of someone's form was described.

"My venom isn't like yours. It will hurt, Mareina."

"If it's yours, I want it."

Before I could dwell any further on it, Malekai gripped the bottom hem of the shirt I was wearing and tore it in half. The heat of his gaze, like a flame, licked up every inch of me. Of my bared breasts and—

Akash almighty.

I sat up on my elbows to peer down at the inky, blood-red snake marking the space between my breasts and upper abdomen. *It moved,* slithering around one breast before curling around the other and re-settling itself between them. Watching me with sentient, intelligent eyes. *All three of them.*

"Arcanum."

I didn't know what exactly that was, but I couldn't bring myself to care enough at the moment to ask. My sole focus, need, and desire were currently wrapped in the cage of my legs. *Where he belonged.*

Malekai's hands engulfed my waist as his lips parted, and his fangs sank into the plush flesh of my left breast. A searing heat *burned* my veins, tearing a whimper from my throat. Blinding pain burst through me that sent my nails carving crescents into his flesh. The warmth of his blood blossomed at my fingertips, stoking my hunger.

His hands cupped my breasts, teasing my nipples as his venom continued to seep into my veins. A delicious, sharp curl of pleasure that I felt in my clit eased the pain of his bite and drew a soft moan from my lips. His throat worked on a single swallow before he pulled away and sank his fangs into my other breast. Gradually, the pain was replaced by a tingling heat. His cock began to steadily stroke over my clit, stealing keening noises from me. Malekai's tongue laved at the wounds of the twin marks before diverting his ministrations to the tender peaks of my breasts.

I pushed away the sensation of guilt and anger rising in my chest. Guilt at how I knew this would wound Nakoa. Anger that he'd marked me against my will. Desperate to drown out the pain, my hips thrust in tandem against Malekai's cock, already leaking his seed on my abdomen. His hands trembled as his grip returned to my waist, tightening to the point of bruising.

The sight of my blood on his mouth was nearly my undoing. I licked a stripe across his lower lip and stole it between my teeth. The action drew a rumbling growl from his throat. His hand slipped between my legs before he licked my arousal from his fingers.

"Have I always made you this wet, *tessari mú?*"

"*Always.*"

Malekai sat back on his heels, gripping me by my hips and lifted my pussy to his face. I let out a yelp of surprise, now upside down. He growled his satisfaction, inhaling my scent deeply once more before his tongue licked me from entrance to clit where he wrapped his lips around the aching bud and *sucked.*

"Look at this beautiful fucking pussy. So tight and pink and sopping wet for me."

My hands gripped the solid muscle of his thighs as he proceeded to feast upon me like a starved beast clutching its prey to its hungry mouth. The wet, slick, sucking noises filling the room between my soft cries and Malekai's growls were a sweet symphony.

He rewarded me by slipping two fingers into my entrance and curling them against that sensitive, shallow spot inside me. Malekai's fingers pressed firmly against it—nearly to the point of pain—stroking in tandem with the ministrations of his mouth. The action was demanding and ruthless—bearing no concern for the noises it drew from me or the way it made my body tremble.

Less than a minute had passed when liquid heat gushed from me. My words became unintelligible as I writhed in his hands. Malekai continued to devour me, gently guiding my body down from my climax and licking up my mess before laying me back down on the bed beneath him.

Malekai gripped his tremendous length in his fist, giving it a steady stroke. It was nearly the length of my forearm, perhaps 9 or 10 inches, thicker than my wrist and curved ever-so-slightly upwards. Pearlescent pre-cum leaked from the slit of his thickly flared crown and dripped onto my clit where he rubbed it in, making my pussy spasm with need again.

"I'm gonna fuck you til you bleed, *tessari mú.* You might wanna hold onto something."

His promise stole my breath. "You swear?"

A luminous grin split his face as he gave me a dark chuckle and aligned his cock with my entrance.

"Since the day I laid eyes on you, Mareina, you have possessed me. My heart, my soul, my mind—my cock. It's all yours."

I braced my palms on the headboard above me as he pressed the broad head of his cock to my entrance. My core spasmed at the demanding stretch. *"Oh, fuck... Malekai."*

Malekai groaned, tipping his head back as he hissed a curse, and his hips gradually slid forward inch by inch.

"Tell me who this pussy belongs to, Mareina."

"*You*. She belongs to *you*."

Bracing himself on one elbow, he brought his lips near mine, grazing against them with every uttered word. "I love you, Mareina Kalini. In this life and all our lives to come."

His words were punctuated by the meeting of our hips as he settled fully inside me. The ache and pain of his length and girth gradually ebbed. Something intangible but no less visceral seemed to lock between us.

Emotion stung my eyes, and I drew my fingers over the apples of his cheeks. "In this life, and all our lives to come. When Akash returns us to Source, my soul will always seek yours."

Malekai's eyes glistened before he captured my lips as he withdrew to the tip, only to slide home.

Tingling energy rose, lighting up my entire body in waves. My head spun, and the entire world narrowed down to just the two of us. Salty tears slipped from the corners of my eyes to chase our lips as I poured the last century's worth of emotion into our kiss.

Malekai's voice dropped to a growl.

"*I'm so fucking angry you kept this from me for so long.*"

"I wanna spend the rest of my life making it up to you."

Taking in the gravity of my words, emotion flickered in his eyes as his strokes slowed. "I would do it all over again if I had to, Mareina. If I had to pay in blood, every second of time I got to spend with you, I'd let *Akash* bleed me dry, and when I died, I would beg to reincarnate so I could do it all over again if it meant that I would be beside you."

My breath hitched with emotion that made my eyes burn. "*Katadamna kaza.*"

Malekai's strokes gentled as he held my gaze, fingers slipping between mine. "*Katadamna kaza, tessari mú... Ad thanátou kae sora.*"

To death and beyond.

Malekai sat back on his heels, gripping me by my upper thighs as his strokes turned unforgiving. Sucking on his cheeks, he let a ball of spit land directly on my clit. Caressing it in teasing circles as his half-lidded gaze took me in, briefly dipping back to where we were joined.

My moans stuttered as that tingling energy built anew, and I began to slam my hips in counter to his. *"Oh, fuck, Malekai... I'm gonna cum again..."*

Malekai gave a deep hum of pleasure, taking his time as his strokes steadily picked up their pace, the caress of his thumb upon my clit never faltering. "I'm gonna fill this pretty pussy up with my cum, and I want you to steal every drop."

Merely the image those words gave me inspired another orgasm to rise. *"Gods, yes. Please."*

Malekai leaned over me again, taking my jaw between thumb and forefinger. *"Open."*

I eagerly followed his direction, opening my mouth and extending my tongue. Malekai rewarded me with a ball of spit. I greedily swallowed, and my orgasm erupted, dragging a breathy cry from my throat as my writhing against him increased. My nails dug into the flesh of his thighs. "I've never seen anything more beautiful than the way you come undone for me. The way your cunt needily grips my cock."

As soon as my orgasm waned, Malekai took hold of my legs, laying them to one side. His strokes slowed but remained deep.

"On your knees, Kalini."

My mouth went dry as my belly swooped with anticipation as I shifted to present my backside to him. Malekai gave a deep hum of pleasure as he alternated between gripping and caressing the generous flesh of my ass before moving to stand at the foot of the bed. Gripping me by my hips, he yanked me to the edge and knelt behind me, taking fistfuls of my ass in his hands as he proceeded to devour every inch of me.

"Fuck, Malekai!"

He growled from behind me, delivering a swift smack to the

globe of my ass. "I've lost count of how many times I've fantasized about claiming this pussy, Mareina. How about you be a good girl and make it up to me?"

Malekai rose, sweeping his cock through my wet folds and over my clit. Weaving an arm around my waist, he fisted my hair to bring me flush against his front before dipping his head to nip at my ear lobe. "Do you trust me?"

"With my life."

I felt his fangs against the curve of my neck as his lips parted in a smile. "I want my name on your flesh and yours upon mine. Would you like that, *tessari mú?*"

I nodded, throat working on a swallow. "More than just about anything."

Malekai growled his pleasure, folding my arms behind my back. His fangs sank into the curve of my neck as he caressed the ache between my thighs by sliding his cock through my folds. More of his venom flowed into me before he withdrew his fangs and took my folded arms in one of his large hands, leaning back to watch as he pounded into me. When his cock began to harden further, his thrusts turned slow and deep as if edging himself back from orgasm.

"I want it where you can always see it," he murmured against my neck before turning me around to lay me back on the bed. "So you never forget who you belong to." He punctuated the words with a wink that I swore I felt in my clit. "It'll need to be deep, but stop me if it hurts too much, ok, sweetheart?"

I nodded eagerly. *No way in all the hells would I stop him.*

Malekai *willed* his dagger into his hand. The blade parted the flesh of my wrist like a knife through butter, but the pounding, swelling of my heart drowned out the pain. My blood trickled onto my belly between us.

"I love you," I whispered.

"In this life and every life to come, *tessari mú.*"

His magic, like burnished gold, flared, weaving itself into the wound. My heart squeezed with so much love it fucking hurt. He'd carved his name in cursive. In moments, my skin was already knit-ting back together. All that remained was a pink scar in the shape of his name.

He pressed a kiss to the mark before flipping the dagger with practiced ease to pass it to me by the handle. "Choose your canvas."

My eyes roved up and down his body. *Fuck me.* He was so beau-tiful it hurt. There was already a bounty of scars, but now, it seemed obvious my name was the one thing missing. Pressing the dagger flat on the bed, I leg-swept him and pinned him beneath me. Malekai's face lit up as a husky laugh rumbled from his chest, and I pressed the tip of the blade directly above his heart. His grin broadened. "Perfection."

I lifted my hips, sliding down his still-hard length before pinching the blade between my fingers like a quill. "I can't promise it'll be as pretty as yours, Theikos."

He gave me a devilish grin, gripping another fistful of my ass. "As long as it's legible so everyone knows to whom I belong."

Malekai's blood spilled over his chest as I began to carve my name over his heart. I wasn't remotely surprised when I felt his cock harden further inside of me.

As I finished carving the last letter, the crimson tendrils of my magic poured into the wound. Malekai gripped me to the point of bruising as he lifted his hips and began to slide in and out of me. The dagger fell from my hand onto the bed as I succumbed to our pleasure.

Malekai rolled, pinning me beneath him again. I licked a stripe up the side of his neck before sinking my fangs into his flesh. The effect of my venom was immediate. I cried out in ecstasy from around my mouthful as Malekai growled, and his thrusts turned brutal again. After allowing myself several gulps, I released him as another orgasm began to rise, making my core grip his length like a fist.

Malekai gave a dark chuckle, slowing his strokes. He licked my throat and nipped me hard before murmuring in my ear. "Greedy thing. You'll have to earn the rest of your orgasms."

He pulled out of me and stood beside the bed. "Back on your knees, Kalini." With a heavy-lidded gaze, he grinned down at me with purely masculine satisfaction—blood streaking his chest, abdomen, and cock from the mark I'd adorned his chest—as I knelt at his feet, eager to worship at the altar of his proud length. Holding his gaze, I caressed the needy peaks of my breasts, pinching them as I extended my tongue and licked a slow, vertical stripe up his length. A dark grin parted my lips. "You'll let me cum if I'm a good girl?"

Malekai's gaze darkened further, growling deeply as he wrapped his hand around a fistful of my hair, baring my throat to him. "You wanna be my good girl, Mareina?"

I moaned my affirmation from around the head of his cock. With anyone else, this kind of thing would make me want to gut them like a pig, but with him, I was *living* for it.

His grip on my hair tightened. "I want your words."

I licked my lips in eager anticipation as I held his gaze. "I'll be a good girl. Just for you."

He gave a grunt of approval while the look he gave me practically promised violence. "Swallow every drop of this cum, and let's see how good you are at begging."

I hummed my pleasure as I took the hard, silky length of him and began to stroke him in tandem with the ministrations of my mouth. Precum blossomed on my tongue, spurring my efforts. My hands stroked him in tandem with the ministrations of my mouth, and Malekai's hips began to thrust in counter to my movements. "*Fuck, Mareina.* This is the only place my cock belongs. Your gorgeous mouth, voluptuous ass, and this beautiful, needy cunt."

I whimpered my agreement, pulling back to take a breath. Lavishing his cock with open-mouthed kisses from base to head as I held his gaze. My words were filled with adoration. "*So fucking perfect.*"

I descended his length, taking as much as I could into the back of my throat. Not nearly his entirety, but I vowed to one day be able to. Malekai held my head by my hair as he pumped into my throat, filling the air with vulgar wet noises that stoked my arousal. Saliva leaked from the corners of my mouth, dripping down my neck and chest. Slicking my hands over the mess, I caressed it over my breasts and teased my nipples.

Malekai groaned at the sight. "Fuck, Mareina... All of this is for me?'

Emotion streaked my cheeks, and my voice turned breathy with reverence. "All for you, Malekai."

Rotating my palm in a gentle twisting motion over his crown whilst stroking down the rest of him, Malekai began to fuck my hands, and he forced my gaze back up to his by gripping my throat. "Beg me for my cum, *tessari mú.*"

I held his gaze, pouring a lifetime's worth of all the love and desire I had for this male, all while licking, sucking, and kissing my way up his length.

"Please, Malekai. I need all of you. I need your heart. Your soul. Your mind. Your body and your perfect cock, along with every drop of cum you have to give. I need you like I need the air in my lungs."

Malekai's eyes glistened as his jaw flexed. He released my hair and scooped me up off the floor in one swift motion to spread me out beneath him on the bed. My legs parted, and as I looked between us, I saw the blood coating my thighs. A breathy moan punched out of me as he slid back inside me.

"Mine," Malekai growled as he thrust with deep, firm strokes. My eyes held his as I breathed my reply. *"Yours."*

His thumb returned to my clit, already drenched with my arousal and blood, making another orgasm rise, soft and tingling. My back arched, and my nails dug into his powerful thighs. Malekai's hips stuttered as he filled me with liquid heat. *"Li Saro, Mareina."* I love you. *"In this life and the next."*

"I love you in every life, Malekai."

His strokes gentled, and his eyes dipped to where we were joined.

I could feel his cum seeping out of me. "Look how perfect you are, filled with my cock, my cum, and my blood."

He withdrew from me briefly to push his leaking cum back inside. Satisfied his seed was where it should be, he leaned in close, brushing his lips against mine. "Marry me, Mareina."

My breath caught, and the sweeping motion of my fingertips along his back stilled. When I hesitated, vulnerability flashed across his face. "... Considering everything that's transpired over the last several days, this may not be the best timing, but—

"Yes."

My eyes burned with sweet relief, the threat of my emotion escaping. Malekai pulled back slightly to catch my expression. A watery grin perched on my lips. *"Yes."*

Malekai's expression hardened as though trying to quell his own emotion. "Yes, you'll marry me?"

I nodded, too much emotion clogging my throat to speak.

Malekai's eyes glistened as they searched mine before his mouth captured mine, and his arms came around me to scoop me into his lap. *"My wife."*

CHAPTER

FOUR

NAKOA

My sleep had been fitful and when I finally woke, it was to a sharp pain in my chest. *In mine and Mareina's tether.* Something had changed, and intuitively, even without my Knowingness, I knew what it was. Anger seared my veins. For her increasing number of betrayals. At *him* because he had dared to claim what rightfully belonged to me. The other half of my soul.

Most of all, I was furious at myself because I knew that no matter how I tried to ignore the fact, I knew that she had bonded with another male because of how I'd treated her. Miroslav's words echoed in my mind.

"If you do not cherish the soulbound Akash has gifted you with, you shouldn't be surprised when she is stolen from you."

Before jealousy and despair could consume me, I forced myself from the bed, slipping on trousers and a shirt. The halls of the palace's mostly abandoned north wing were blessedly empty as I made my way to my *mother's* dungeon cell.

A vision overtook me, making me stumble and the world tilted.

Peanut and Bellona ran past me, barking happily and tails wagging as they rushed into the open arms of a kneeling, smiling Mareina.

25

The sight stole my breath like a fist, crushing my lungs.

I could feel both the joy and love of my future and the anguish of my present self, poisoning it.

Mareina's eyes lifted to mine, her expression stuttering for a moment. Her mouth formed words that disappeared like smoke in the wind—

The vision disappeared, and I realized I'd stopped in the middle of the hallway. Thalia's head tilted as she studied me with keen interest. "Does that happen often?"

I gave a noncommittal grunt and resumed our journey down the hallway.

"You're having visions, no?"

At my silence, she continued, unperturbed by my rudeness. "I used to know someone who had them."

My eyes finally slid to hers for a moment. Her expression took on a sudden hardness as though pained by a memory. "And?"

Her frown deepens. "And they're dead."

"... That is not what I meant."

Her eyes flicked to mine, annoyed. "You really don't make it easy for someone to like you, ya know. I thought we were trying to be allies."

A tiny pang of guilt knotted in my chest. "I suppose I'm not very good at... *this.*"

Thalia gave me a scrutinizing smirk before clapping me on the back with the strength of an ogre. "Nor am I... Now, let's get you to your mother, *petulant prince.*"

My eyes narrowed, even if a corner of my mouth quirked. "I am not petulant."

She huffed a laugh. "Prickly? Ah, yes. That suits. *Little...*" Thalia's eyes gave me a cursory side-eye "... The *behemoth prickly prince...*"

I hummed in consideration. "Hmmm... doesn't have quite the same ring to it."

Thalia rolled her eyes, grinning. "Shall I add petty? Persnickety? *Punctilious?*"

I snorted. "You just taught me a new word."

Thalia chuckled, shaking her head as we arrived in the dungeons. At my hesitation, Thalia arched a brow. "So what happened with your friend if you don't mind me asking?"

Sadness flickered on her face. "She said that the outcomes sometimes changed. Nothing was guaranteed. It all depended on our decisions and choices. Something about lessons and repeating them endlessly until we actually learn them."

Anxiety tightened in my chest. I could only pray that somehow, someway, Mareina and I would *swiftly* learn whatever lessons needed so that we could have love between us one day, as it had appeared in my vision.

Thalia turned away, continuing down the dungeon's steps. "Come on... This place gives me the creeps."

Admittedly, the female was charming, but even without Miroslav's warning of Thalia, which had been gradually working its way deeper into my mind, she had been keenly obliging when it came to opening my mother's dungeon door, and it had only made me that much more distrusting of her.

How the fuck did she know how to open these doors hidden and sealed by magic?

As if reading my mind, she wiggled her dainty fingers at me to display a plain, unsuspecting ring. "It's a family heirloom; cuts through wards." She pressed a hand against the wall glamoring Zurie's cell door, and that strange ephemeral barrier appeared with glowing runes. Thalia pushed the door open a crack before winking at me and turning on her heel to leave.

"What happened with the harem?"

Thalia hesitated for a moment, shifting to look back at me. "They were eager to please and even more eager to be free. Most of them anyway. A few of them requested to stay, but they still vowed their silence."

"Stay for what? Loyalty to Zurie?"

Thalia shook her head. "I don't think so, no. I think they were just afraid to go back to wherever they came from."

"Even after you offered to give them the coin they needed to start over?"

Thalia's brows pinched, frowning. "Money can't always solve the problem."

I grunted, neither in agreement nor descent. "Maybe. But that sounds an awful lot like something only someone who's never known poverty would say, princess."

Something dark flashed behind Thalia's eyes. In the next moment, it disappeared, swiftly replaced with a condescending smile that had me seeing her with new eyes. I tugged at my Knowingness, but it remained silent.

"Well then, by all means, oh great and mighty King, why don't you try and see if all the money you've just stolen will heal them from a lifetime of—

"*Shut you're fucking mouths*. Grating on my last fucking nerve, and I have a godsdamned migraine," Zurie called out from inside the dungeon. Her voice was unusually raspy, as though raw from screaming and crying.

I pushed open the door fully to find she'd remained just where I'd left her, sprawled out on the dungeon floor. Only now...

Mother of fuck, is she dying?

Zurie managed to roll red eyes that she strained to recover from the back of her head. Her voice was little more than a croak. *"Aetra."*

Realization washed over me. Of course, she would experience withdrawals after half a fucking lifetime on the stuff.

Thalia stepped forward to gain a closer look, something like actual concern twisting her features. *"Oh, Zurie..."*

Zurie's face hardened into a spiteful glare. "Why would you even bother in pretending to care?"

Thalia frowned, holding Zurie's gaze for too long to be meaningless before silently turning and striding away.

I gave Zurie a pitying shake of my head. Her eyes squeezed shut as if swallowing back pain before she managed to speak again. "You've come to make your vow?"

I couldn't help but huff a sardonic laugh. "I've come for you to introduce me to my father."

"As soon as you vow what we've agreed upon, plus a supply of aetra."

"Truly, your delusion knows no bounds."

Her doll-like features slackened with numbness. "I prefer the term *optimism,* Your Majesty."

Her retort *nearly* made me laugh. "Get up."

She pursed her lips, haughty despite being covered in blood and filth and *dying.* "And why exactly would I do this without your vow?"

"Because, for some reason, you chose to give me away the moment you gave birth to me."

Her expression faltered at my words. "Only if you give me aetra. You don't have to give me anything else. Just the aetra."

Fucking hells. This female was willing to sacrifice everything just for aetra. I squatted down beside her, studying her features... Our similarities. Something like compassion twisted in my chest as I took in her desperate state, softening my words, infusing a calm in my voice that I didn't feel. Based on tone alone, one would think I was murmuring platitudes and reassurances to her.

"I am going to raze and burn the fields of aetra on every Kahlo-hani Island. I'm going to ban it across Atratus. You will never touch aetra again."

Silence stretched between us as she held my gaze and took in the truth of my words. Resignation settled on her expression.

"I don't want to be here anymore."

"... The dungeon?"

"Here as in... Alive. In this realm."

"So because you can't have aetra anymore, you'd rather die and go to a hell realm?"

She gave a bitter laugh. "Darling, this *is* hell."

I glanced around the dungeon. As far as dungeons went, it wasn't all that bad. I'd experienced far worse. For one, there weren't even any rats. I fucking *hated* rats, thanks to the handful of prisons I'd spent time in.

And she hadn't even been tortured yet.

"If you think withdrawals from aetra and a little solitude in a dungeon are the worst form of suffering imaginable, then you've led a very privileged life."

Zurie rolled over, giving me her back. "Oh, I'm well aware. If you think this is my first time in this dungeon, you'd also be wrong."

My Knowingness whispered the very words I'd spoken to Mareina only a week ago. *Truly, monsters are made, not born.*

I couldn't help but wonder what this world had done to this twisted creature that had made her so grotesquely inhumane.

However, at this particular moment, I didn't have the time or patience to ponder it.

I permitted a minuscule tendril of my magic to slip through the barriers of flesh and bone, seizing her lungs and drawing the air from them. A prickle of guilt wound through me as I watched her ribs spasm, trying and failing to breathe. After a few moments, she rolled over, clawing at her chest and throat. Her brow hardened with anger and anguish as she held my gaze.

"If you think I'll let you die this easily, you're gravely mistaken. I will spend every fucking moment here beside you in this *hell,* torturing you until you bring me to my father. The fact that *this* is hell to you shows me just how fucking privileged and sheltered you are."

Her struggle slowed, eyes rolling in the back of her head.

Ohhhh, no, you don't.

Zurie gasped for air, coughing and wheezing to catch her breath.

"How are we feeling now? Agreeable?"

Zurie glared up at me, but I'd inflicted enough torture over the years to recognize my enemies' bitter submission.

"I want out of this dungeon. I want my room back. And I want your word that no harm will come to me."

I tilted my head, holding her sharp, crystalline gaze.

"I owe you nothing, Zurie. Either you do as you're told, or you will discover methods of torture that will have you begging for Mors to rescue you."

I turned, striding back towards the door. The sound of rustling behind me the evidence of her persuasion. Rather than travelling down the hallway that led *out* of the dungeon, she led us deeper into it, towards a circular room with an arched doorway. A shaft of sunlight poured into the center of the room where a dais lay. Runes lay carved into the floor, and the closer we drew, the more powerful the hum of magic became. The hairs on the back of my neck stood on end.

"You remind me so much of him," Zurie murmured with surprising softness.

My heart began to thump a nervous beat. I'd dreamed my entire life of meeting my father. And to think, he'd been in Zurie's dungeon this entire time.

She climbed to the center of the dais and *tore* a chunk of flesh from her wrist with her fangs. Blood spilled, and she began to murmur words in an unfamiliar language. The runes crisscrossing the circular stone platform upon which she stood glowed with an otherworldly light.

But how? She was wearing a fucking palladium collar.

In that same moment, her eyes, alight with satisfaction, lifted to mine. "There is no power in this world that can stifle the magic of words or the magic in your blood."

The ground beneath our feet began to tremble and Zurie's gaze snapped back to mine as she shouted to be heard, her eyes bright with dark excitement. "He might kill me, you know."

When my eyes lifted from the runes to hers, her grin grew broader. "Only you have the strength to stop him from killing me if I'm wearing this palladium collar."

She seemed entirely content in laying her fate in the threadbare net of my compassion.

"What if I could bring Mareina back to you?"

Her fangs somehow glinted in the shadow as her smile grew impossibly wide. *Fucking manipulative wench.*

"Is it possible that you've been so surrounded by asshole-sucking sycophants that you've lost your talent for manipulation?"

Zurie cackled as the ground beneath our feet splintered before it stilled, and we held our breath for several moments.

"And I'm certain the only person who hates you more than I do, is her. You'll have to forgive me if I don't have faith in your capabilities to perform such a feat."

From the grin on Zurie's face you'd have thought I'd said something charming. "Of her own accord, my darling. What if I could get her to come back to you? To give you a real chance... And *eliminate* the competition."

Disgust and something darker suffused me. "The one thing I place above my own well-being is hers. And as much as I resent him, if there's anyone else who will protect her in this world, it's him. I will not take that from her, even if it's at my own expense."

Zurie's expression was lined with disappointment. "You really are your father's son."

CHAPTER

FIVE

NAKOA

Not that the temptation wasn't there, but I wouldn't take the only person she trusted from her. This was on top of the fact that my numerous and irrepressible visions had shown me exactly what would happen if I tried to steal Mareina away from him. She would hate me, and it would earn me no fate that I desired for either of us.

Dominating her, forcing her hand as I had was one thing, but taking away the one person in this world she loved....

My cock ached with need as images of Mareina so beautifully bared, bound, and gagged beneath me rose to memory. My mind even went as far as to conjure the taste of her upon my tongue as I'd devoured her. Even my tail coiled around my leg, squeezing tight with desperation.

Somehow, as many hours as I'd spent around Malekai, I'd been able to discern very little about him. My Knowingness had only further enflamed my insecurities and reminded me of all my short-comings. *And his strengths.*

Just when I began to doubt Zurie's spell, the stone around us shuddered as though it was about to cave in on us. A corner of Zurie's mouth slowly tilted up, and blood began to trickle from her nose and into her mouth as a grin split her face. Despite how crazed she looked, I could see a fraction of our resemblance, even if it was only by the crazed gleam and determination in her eyes.

The center of the stone dais cracked and splintered before a *boom* of impact caused an explosion of stone and soil that sent me reeling backwards. Dust clouded the air and when I right myself, it was to find a hulking winged, horned, and tailed male hunched over Zurie's form. Her neck bent at an unnatural angle, and if it weren't for the way her fingers dug into his back, I'd think she was dead.

My heart stalled in my chest. *This is my father.*

As if I'd spoken the words aloud, his head lifted from Zurie's bloody, shredded throat and turned his head to meet my gaze. It was almost like looking in a mirror, though he looked like a wild beast released from its cage. He even *appeared* to be my age. Black eyes roved over me, and for a moment, the rage contorting his features softened before he looked back down at Zurie. Her eyes glistened as she stared into the rictus of his fury. "There wasn't a day that passed where I didn't long for you."

With a snarl, my father dropped her as if she were a venomous snake and turned to face me. Blood dripped down his bare neck and chest, century-old anguish contorting his features. His accented voice sounded like gravel scraping stone from its disuse. "Did she harm you?"

"I... No."

Not directly.

He tugged at the palladium collar around his throat in futility, and I promptly willed it away. He dipped his head in gratitude as long, blade-like claws curled into fists, blood trickling into pools on either side of him. *"I need to feed. I'll be back."*

He hesitated for a moment, stepping closer toward me; his gaze scanned me with an intensity that made my muscles tense.

Too fucking surreal.

For all my years of wishing I'd had a father, the sudden need to escape this bizarre reunion was overwhelming.

Without another word and a powerful beat of his wings, he launched himself out of the dungeon through the skylight and disappeared.

SIX

MAREINA

Lathrimos had proven to be a man prone to emotional outbursts. It was both endearing and, personally, a little unsettling. The two of us had been in flight for only an hour as he gave me a partial tour of my father's realm, and already he'd been driven to tears. *Twice.* Not that I could blame him. If something happened to Malekai, I certainly wouldn't be able to hold a conversation. Lathrimos promised he'd find someone to teach me how to *fold* but insisted that I strengthen and get used to my wings.

Easy for him to say when he only had two of them to lug around, where as I had four.

"Stop trying to fly *against* the current. You have to let it carry you."

My heart gave a painful squeeze as Nakoa's words returned to me.

"I've got you. I can carry us both - I only need you to let me."

You are such a hypocrite, I hissed at myself internally.

Emotion burned my eyes, and no matter how I tried to blame it on our tether, deep down in the darkest parts of my soul that I never allowed to see the light of day, I knew my longing for him was so much more. Nakoa had basically taken a cleaver to my chest and inspected each dark and twisted part of me with a fucking magnifying glass. The parts of myself that I had always hidden from Malekai. Or at least tried to.

As if to punctuate these thoughts, another air current slammed into us, sweeping us 30 feet higher before it abruptly disappeared, and I suddenly found myself plummeting towards sickle-sharp, icy mountain peaks intent on skewering me. Tumbling through the air, I flailed, screaming as I begged my wings to catch on to the constantly shifting currents of air.

Akash almighty, why aren't we on a fucking warm beach?!

A stone wall crashed into me, forcing a *whoosh* of air from my lungs, as Lathrimos clutched me in arms the size of tree trunks.

At the same moment, darkness drew over us like a hood before being shirked, and we were suddenly unceremoniously flung onto wet sand.

"Fucking hells," Lathrimos panted.

My hands trembled as I gradually tried to retract fingernails that I'd dug into the flesh of his biceps. *"Please...* Don't make me do that again."

My gaze leapt around our dreamy, tropical surroundings. "I thought you said you couldn't *fold?"*

"I can't. That was all you."

"I've never folded before."

Lathrimos shrugged like it was nothing out of the ordinary. "Your power will increase exponentially here. This is your home. It boggles my mind you lived your entire life on only a minor percentage of it... How'd you know about this place, anyway?"

My adrenaline was still spiked from flying over those blasted mountains. Before we'd folded, my desire to be on a nice, warm beach had fisted my heart and produced an image in my mind. An image identical to the shore upon which we now stood.

"I don't. I saw it in my minds eye when I was desperate to get out of the sky."

Lathrimos frowned, taking in the secluded Kailuma beach surrounding us with palpable longing. "This was—*is* your father's favorite place in all of Avernus."

Another irksome burning sensation took residence in my eyes that I promptly shoved away. "I wish I'd gotten more time to get to know him."

Lathirmos' voice rose barely above a gruff whisper as he stared out at the sea which I noticed had several sets of eyes, some dark, some luminous, peeking above its surface. All monochrome in color. One of which was a fathomless black.

Like Nakoa's.

My heart gave another painful lurch.

"He'll be back... At least that's what I keep telling myself."

I had to remind myself Lathrimos spoke of my father.

Guilt twisted inside me at the sensation. Malekai and I had just claimed one another. *We were betrothed.* I *loathed* this bond to Nakoa. And no matter how I tried to resist, deny, and ignore it... I fucking *missed* him. I ached and yearned for him. There was a gaping hole in my heart that even Malekai couldn't fill, even if he permeated every other part of me.

Lathrimos *willed* away his boots and took several steps forward, gentle waves sloshing around his bare feet and calves, enormous grey-ish wing tips carving the shallow waves. He was dressed solely in leather armor and some strange type of skirt made of wide strips of the same textile. I'd only seen illustrations of this impractical battle attire in books from Terrenea.

Unable to resist the water for a second more, I *willed* away my clothing and crashed through the waves, squealing my delight before diving into the water a few feet away from him. When I surfaced, it was to find a smile had taken over his formerly mournful expression. "Just like your father."

Emotion pinched tight in my chest, and Lathrimos' smile dimmed slightly. "He *will* be back. Don't worry."

I could tell the words were spoken aloud as much for himself as they were for me, and I was suddenly desperate to change the topic.

And for some reason, imposter syndrome was the first thing that popped out of my mouth.

"I'm terrified I won't be able to take care of Avernus the way it deserves. I've fallen head over heels in love with this place in a matter of days, but I have no idea how to rule a realm and all I've ever been good at is killing. I *hate* it."

Lathrimos was frowning again.

Fuck.

Treading water, I tried to return my attention to the magnificent sea surrounding us.

Lathrimos swam beside me, having liberated himself from his strange warrior attire. "Well, lucky for you, pretty much everyone here is already dead."

I blinked at him, taken by surprise that he'd made an actual joke before my head tipped back with laughter. Lathrimos chuckled, looking a little relieved that I'd been humored. When our laughter died down, he grew serious again. "Ruling a kingdom in the living world is nothing like it is here. I think you're under the very *human* assumption that ruling this place will have the same tribulations and obligations that those in the living world have."

"It doesn't?"

"Not even remotely. Let me remind you that this place is eternal. There is no poverty. There is no death in the way that you think of it. It is a place of rest for the soul between reincarnations and returning to *Akash's* Source. Whatever a soul wishes they can grant themselves. Those who remain without or are in suffering, it is self-inflicted— from karmic debts and their misdeeds sewn in the living world— until they heal and grow from within. And that is something that your innate power helps sustain."

Outside of the soft whisper of the gentle waves kissing the shore, silence hung between us as my chest constricted and the sensation of unworthiness deepened.

"Outside of death, I know nothing of my power, Lathrimos."

Lathrimos' brow pinched with concern, shaking his head as he searched my face in disbelief. "Death is only the beginning of your power, Mareina."

CHAPTER

SEVEN

ZURIE

"My, my, how the tides have turned..." Truly, the sound of Azrael's voice was the smuggest in all the realms, despite its otherworldly resonance. Still, hope fluttered in my chest.

"Aetra."

The sound of his sigh had my despair returning as swiftly as it'd left. "We both know that's not a good idea, Zurie."

Despite my desperation, I was unable to muster any feeling other than *pain*, lying in a puddle of my own sweat and vomit as the withdrawals from aetra overtook me. I couldn't even manage to turn around and face him. When I didn't move, outside of my shivering, the sound of Azrael's boots crunching the tiny pebbles on the cold hard ground that was my new bed felt like fucking blades upon my eardrums.

"Be nice, Az," a rich, feminine voice murmured from the doorway.

Thalia. Scheming cunt.

One would think that the betrayals and manipulations of my

entire family throughout the course of my life would have been enough of a lesson to last me a life time.

Alas, hearts are made to forgive. Even hearts as withered as mine.

There had only been two people in my life I'd ever truly trusted. The first had been my handmaiden, Beatrice, when I was a young female. Though now, I wasn't naive enough to truly believe that she wouldn't have betrayed me as well the moment she was given the opportunity.

One of my sisters had her killed when she realized how close we'd become.

Too close.

When one of my sisters discovered us in bed together, she immediately told my mother and father. She'd lied and said Beatrice had compelled me with her sanguinati magic and venom. *She hadn't.* If anything, *I* had been the one to compel her.

My parents had Beatrice executed in front of me. This was followed by a ruthless beating before leaving me to rot in the dungeon for months, with no one but the *rats* to keep me company.

It was why now I always kept the dungeons almost always empty and rodent-free. A small mercy to whomever met my ire or my *Irae.*

The last person I'd trusted had been Rumiel. Nakoa's father. He had been the one person with whom I thought my heart might be safe. He was a Nephilim, after all. They were *made* to trust and protect. To rely on. To be dutiful and *good.*

When I'd realized he'd only wormed his way into my life, *my heart,* simply to open one of the portals to Azrael's realms, just so that he could *leave* me... It had nearly killed me.

I'd wanted to be everything for him. I *loved* him. Truly loved. At that time, I would have given my life to protect him.

Hence, I wasn't much for this world. They were the only two people who lent joy to my life. Euphoria, even.

And look how it had ended.

When I'd discovered Rumiel's manipulation, I'd sworn that he would *never* be able to leave me, and I put him in a tomb beneath the dungeons. I found out I was pregnant a few weeks later.

How wildly serendipitous that as soon as I release Rumiel, the only other person who could return him to his home, the very guardian of his soul, would return to my home for the first time since he'd brought him here.

I whimpered through the grinding of my teeth, curling in on myself as Azrael squatted beside me. To my surprise, he didn't comment on the stench nor my refuse. He simply stared down at me with pity. The cursed male was just as wretchedly handsome as he was the last time I'd seen him a few hundred years ago. His features weren't classically handsome, but instead something striking and entirely their own: Pale skin, perfectly coiffed raven black hair, and eyes so amber they were gold set amidst features that were somehow both sharp and sultry. And just as it had been centuries ago, the suit he wore was tailored to some other realm's strange, fitted fashion.

"*What?*" I croaked.

"I was *hoping* we could help each other."

Typical.

That was all he ever wanted. More favors. Take, take, take, just like everyone else.

Light footsteps approached from behind until Thalia stood beside him. Or who I'd thought was Thalia. The female shifted to reveal Mors' sister, the Goddess of Violence. I'd never met her before, but I'd seen her effigy and illustrations in textbooks. I might have been surprised if betrayal, lies, and manipulation hadn't been the cornerstone of my entire fucking life.

Again, I could only manage one word.

"*Aetra.*"

Azrael and Keres exchanged a pitying look.

"I won't be making the same mistake twice, darling," Azrael replied coolly, "but if you're amenable, perhaps I can procure something to help momentarily ease the pain."

The compassion on Keres' face almost seemed genuine as she

caressed my filthy cheek with the back of a finger, gliding down to my throat. "How about we take off this pretty little collar, hm?"

EIGHT

NAKOA

My patience wore as thin as the stone of the bedroom balcony I was pacing a hole into. The gnawing agony of the tether bonding me to Mareina had faded to a dull throb, and instead of being relieved, it had heightened my anxiety.

You're losing her.

My anxiety had drowned out my Knowingness, and now I couldn't even tell the difference between it and my paranoia.

A moonless night had fallen and everyone, as far as I knew, was sound asleep. There'd still been no sign of my father returning which had only served to enhance the tension winding through me.

In all my years, I never thought I'd ever be so desperate for Miroslav's presence. I projected my thoughts and my intent into the aether, *hoping* that I might be heard.

Miroslav...

Silence.

Miroslav. Miroslav. Miroslav. Miroslav. Miroslav. Miroslav.

More silence.

"He's ignoring you."

I froze midstep at the sound of the gravelly voice and swept my gaze up the side of the palace wall. Above the balcony, I found my father perched on the balcony above like a gargoyle. Sinewy wingtips and horns pointed like spires above him. He looked more animal than fae. Or whatever he was. A question that had been chiselling away at my fraying sanity because I had never seen a fae who bared my physical traits nor my magical ones.

Dropping 20 feet from above, he lifted his wings at the last second to lighten his descent, sending a gust of air that blew my hair back. My father landed in front of me with the stealth of a feline. His scent, one that reminded me of burning wood and something faintly sweet like amber, was muddled with numerous others, punctuated by the metallic tang of blood. Lots of blood.

My eyes dipped to the black, blade-like claws, tipping his fingers.

They needed trimming.

Fae didn't need blood to survive, and I certainly hadn't either, but perhaps that was in *thanks* to Zurie.

"You're able to read thoughts?"

He shook his head, making the long, overgrown sheet of his hair sway, catching a glint of moonlight that revealed a streak of white. "Emotion. Intent. Desire. Needs."

"How did you know who I was directing my thoughts to?"

"You were deliberately projecting your thoughts. Loudly. My mind is already open to yours. Connected because we are of the same blood and ilk."

My heart leapt in my throat as the question finally reached my lips.

"What are... *we?*"

"Your mother didn't tell you?"

"I only met her yesterday."

"I mean Leilani. She never told you who I was?"

"No."

My father's features tightened, lit only vaguely by the fae light touching the balcony. "Perhaps it was for the best. It would have made things too obvious if you had ever told anyone. We are Nephilim."

The word settled on me like an affirmation, as though this was something I already distantly knew but had never deigned to acknowledge because I didn't have the resources to piece the puzzle together. I had only ever seen them illustrated in historical tomes.

The fact I'd always believed him to be fae based solely on my mother's word made me wonder if I even knew his real name.

"My mother told me your name was Tavian."

The male's brows pinched in disbelief before his head tipped back with laughter that sounded like tumbling boulders.

"Tavian?"

It was a relief to hear and *feel* my father's laughter. It even had a smile blooming on my face for the first time in too many days since we had all been at Val's chasing pixies. Mareina's absence made the memory feel like a vice around my heart.

"Do you know a Tavian or something?"

My father's claw-tipped hand clutches his broad chest as it continues to rumble with laughter. "Yes. Though I imagine the male is dead by now. He was Zurie's Irae and a simpering fool. Miroslav and I had an ongoing game that involved him trying to woo Zurie with everything she hated. Leilani knew the male got under my skin."

Zurie's Irae.

The surprise that he was apparently close with my *adoptive* mother and Miroslav was stifled by the burning of mine and Mareina's tether. My father winced as if it caused *him* pain. Thankfully, he doesn't ask about it because the last thing I feel like explaining to him is the absolutely *fucked* state of mine and Mareina's relationship. Or the fact that she left me for another male.

The moment the thought passed, his expression turned pained, and it really made me wonder if he also had a Knowingness.

"My name is Rumiel. Miroslav told me a lot about you over the years... I even chose your name."

"My name? You knew about me? This whole time?"

He nodded, some unreadable emotion glittering in the twin black pools of his.

"But... If Miroslav knew you were down there, why couldn't he have freed you?"

A corner of Rumiel's mouth tilted up gently in a sad smile. "Do you mean other than face Zurie's wrath and thus certain death because he vowed in blood not to harm her?"

At my silence, he continued.

"Zurie was the only one capable of opening my tomb. She made certain of that."

I shook my head in disbelief. "But surely, there was some way to bargain with her... *Something.* You just spent 120 years in a fucking tomb! This whole time, you were right here! I could have had—

Emotion clawed its way up my throat and I had to draw in a deep breath to ease it away. My father's eyes began to glisten, and he reached out to grip my shoulder.

"You and your *soulbound* are destined to save Bellorum. In order for you both to become the only two people in this realm capable of doing so, there were certain things that needed to occur so that you could become who you are today... Just as a sculptor hammers and chisels away at slabs of marble to create their divinely inspired works, so are we all sculpted by fate..."

Indignance and anger were a buried blade in my chest.

Surely, not all *of that fucking suffering was necessary.*

"... Even if Miroslav *had* been able to free me, Zurie would have killed the both of us, and he would never have been there to save you when you were born, or in the future. And there *will* come a time when you need him to."

"... He took me from her when I was born?"

Rumiel's expression darkened. "Zurie ordered your death when he told her that you were destined to usurp her throne. And your fate, left in her hands, had you grown up with her..." Rumiel's throat dipped as his features tightened further. "It would have destroyed you."

My lips parted in shock... But I'm all too familiar with pain and betrayal. No matter how terrible. Hardening my heart to it is second nature. Something glittered in Rumiel's gaze as he observed.

"I realize that technically she is your birth mother, but... perhaps you wouldn't be too troubled if some heinous accident befell her? Unless you... would like to get to know her, of course."

Laughter bubbles out of me, and the two of us share a dark grin.

Nothing like a little murder and vengeance for some father-son bonding.

My laughter died as realization washed over me.

"Did you know that this would happen? Did Miroslav know?"

A corner of Rumiel's mouth faintly tipped up at one corner. "I have lived for millennia, Nakoa. And I will live for many millennia more. What is a hundred and twenty years in that span of time if it means that I get to share the rest of my life with my son?"

Ohhhhh fuck.

Hardening my heart to pain and betrayal was one thing...

But love?

Fuck, fuck, fuck, fuck.

My jaw clenched furiously as I *willed* my tear ducts to stop producing saline. It seemed they were the one organ unsusceptible to my magic. *Akash damn it.*

Of all the revelations Rumiel had spoken, the most powerful was the fact that this male had *willingly* lived in a tomb for the last 120 years so that I could become who I am today.

Unable to stifle my emotion, I turned away from him to face the mountains looming in the distance. I squeezed my eyes shut, drawing in a deep breath.

Akash, please, please, please.

What I wanted even more than his comforting embrace was for him not to give it to me because if he did, I wouldn't be able to wrestle back the sob desperate to escape me. The fact I could also *feel* his desire to hold me, to make me feel his *love,* only made it that much worse.

He sidled next to me to share the view and a great sigh of relief is punched out of me when he changed the subject, bless him.

"I'm from a realm called Ouranissa. Are you familiar with it?"

I'd only read about it in historical texts where it mentioned primals, gods, titans, archestratim, and nephilim resided to rule over the divine realms and guard the hell realms.

My voice was a croak of barely quelled emotion. *"Vaguely."*

"In addition to protecting Ouranissa, the divine realm where I'm from, I served Azrael, the Vassileon realm's God of Death, as courtier, or liaison, of sorts. Vassileo consists of one living divine realm and multiple 'living' and 'after death' hell realms. I originally came to Bellorum to bargain on Azrael's behalf because the hell realms had grown restless and discontent. Both the dead and the living in Vassileo longed for freedom from hell. They had begun to revolt. And Bellorum and Avernus lie just on the other side of the barrier, diving into our own living and after-death realms. I was sent here to pave the way for their exile, essentially... Which is how I came to meet Zurie."

My brain felt like it was clinging to a rickety rowboat amidst a turbulent sea in the middle of a thunderstorm, considering all the revelations Rumiel continued to flood me with. To imagine that if a realm hadn't begun a revolt, Azrael would have never sent my father here, and I would never have been born, along with all the other infinite things that had to occur leading up to that... The fact that I had been the leader of the Uprising, a revolt against Zurie, made this all seem too bizarrely orchestrated to be a mere coincidence.

"There was only one ruler in Bellorum receptive towards Azrael's *advances."*

Oh, let me guess.

Rumiel gave me a mirthless smile. "Surprisingly, Zurie refused."

Oh.

"It wasn't until King Hadriel attempted to exterminate them that Zurie opened Atratus to them."

That sounds inconceivably benevolent of her.

My tears had stopped flowing so I was finally able to meet my father's gaze. "King Hadriel? The old sanguinati king who started the drakonati genocide?"

Rumiel frowned at this, gaze pointing in the direction of Hades, the continent beyond the mountains we were now looking at. "The one and only... He allowed only Azrael's drakonati to seek exile."

I failed to recall what I'd only read in history books as to what had transpired so many years before I was born, but even my Knowingness remained silent. I waited for Rumiel to explain, but instead, he took me by surprise a*gain.*

"Where is Mareina?"

The sound of her name alone is like a fiery welding iron to my heart. "I'm not sure."

It's not actually a lie. I have no idea where Malekai lives *if that's where they even are.*

Rumiel's brows knit tightly together as his gaze returned to the distant mountain peaks. His words were gentle. Or at least as gentle as his scarred vocal cords could produce.

"She left?"

The gruffness of my voice belied just how much pain I was burying. "Something like that."

"Perhaps she's with her father?"

I huffed a sardonic laugh. The last place she would seek refuge is with her father at the house of nightmares that is Erosyan Temple.

"You couldn't *pay* Mareina to go back to the Erosyan Temple."

The disbelief in Rumiel's expression twisted my stomach in knots.

"Mors is staying at the Erosyan Temple?"

I reared back. "Who said anything about—

Memories flood me all threading themselves together to form a

tapestry and yet another realization washes over me as my Knowingness deigns to speak with me.

Her father is the God of Death.

NINE

NAKOA

I closed my eyes against the cool wind as we soared high above Atratus, allowing myself to drink in this fleeting moment of peace. Flying beside my father filled my chest with a sensation I'd never realized even existed on the emotional spectrum, and I couldn't quite put my finger on what it was.

It was beyond unity because that would refer to a collective coming together for a common purpose. I'd been blessed with experiencing unity for not all, but at least a significant portion of my life: fighting and living beside my *olana kah'hei*, going to war beside my fellow Kahlohani's, the connection I had with the woman who'd raised me...

But my peaceful euphoria was short-lived. Anxiety—fear—clutched my heart in its clawed hands. Life had taught me too many times over that this beautiful feeling I'd never dared to fathom experiencing would never last.

The male was far too in tune with my mind and emotions because, as we cut across the sky like twin blades, he turned his head to shout over the wind.

"When you're this close, I can feel your emotions as if they were my own, Nakoa. Your mind is like a sail without a mast on the wind. Do not allow fear to govern you or steal your happiness as Zurie has."

His words, despite their wisdom, further enflamed my fears.

Out of the corner of my eye, I could see that he was watching me as we flew. After several moments, I finally met his gaze.

"But *how?*"

A corner of Rumiel's lips tipped up in one corner of his mouth to reveal that slight smile I was coming to know.

"There is but one mast that will not bow or break beneath the ever-changing winds of your emotion, and you must allow all other emotion to pass over you like the current upon your wings."

I held my breath as his smile stretched until it split and revealed the fangs framing a radiant smile.

"Love."

The rest of our journey was silent as the seed of my father's words took root in my soul and turned my already toppling world on its head. I had lived my entire life ruled by my emotions. It destroyed my relationship with my *soulbound* because of it, and I could feel it in my soul that something had shifted.

Whatever surprise I would have felt by our arrival to the God of Death's temple was greatly dampened by my Knowingness's words.

They shall never be twain. Your fate is bound to his as much it is to hers now.

Instead of rage, I felt only grief and remorse. My mind briefly flickered back to the Sigil of Mors that had appeared on her arm when we had attempted to swear our *soulbound* vows. To the vision I'd had of Mareina standing in front of the River Oblivion. The *Pharalaki* that had always seemed to follow her wherever she went. It all seemed so obvious now.

Recalling my father's wisdom, I tried to release the fear and tension squirming in my gut at facing Mareina for the first time since we'd nearly killed one another.

Before I could dwell any further on it, my father clapped a heavy hand over my shoulder and bestowed me with a compassionate look just before one of the enormous bronze doors bearing Mors' effigy shifted ajar. Every hair on my body rose as a *Pharalaki* appeared. It briefly seemed to examine us before turning to lead us through the cavernous torch-lit foyer and down a hallway. The shadows seemed to have eyes, making my hackles rise.

"Cecil! Lovely to see you again after all these years."

My father and the *Pharalaki* seemed to have some silent exchange that ended with my father tipping his long-haired head back on a laugh as though *Cecil* had said something wildly clever.

Cecil turned, disappearing in the unsettling and otherworldly darkness of Mors' Temple.

"Mors is a lovely fellow. Much nicer than Azrael. *Mostly.*"

Before I could reply to Rumiel, the *Pharalaki* came to an abrupt stop in front of us and opened a hidden doorway that revealed a set of descending, spiral stone stairs. It stepped aside to let us pass, and the moment we did, it drifted back down the hallway.

"How do you do that?"

Rumiel gave me a funny look. "Speak to them?" He shrugged thoughtfully. "You just have to break free from the prison of your thoughts, I suppose. If you're only listening to what's going on inside your head," he explained with a gentle tap on my head before gesturing vaguely to the world around us, "You can't hear what's going on outside of it..."

My father turned and left me standing on the top of the stairs as he wound down the dark, spiralling steps. A breeze drifted over me, smelling of floral fields, just as a more distant scent caused a painful throb to echo through me. *Night-blooming roses.*

That's all it took to spur me into action. I rushed down the stairs, jaw-dropping when they opened up to a field of flowers and tall grasses undulating in a gentle breeze. A distant mountain range surrounded it and to my right flowed the River Oblivion glowing an ethereal blue. My heart leapt and stuttered at the sight of the quaint home only a hundred meters away. Already *knowing* Mareina was behind those walls.

I didn't give a fuck if Malekai was there with her.

My wings spread wide, giving a heavy flap and launching me into the air with my father shortly behind me. Flying towards Mareina felt like swimming up from the depths of the sea, rushing towards to the surface to take a breath of life-giving air.

As if a meteor had recently crashed, a large crater blackened the ground where I landed. Even more strange, there was no front door. Just the absence of one. My eyes caught on the wooden splinters peppering the ground, sending an icy spear of fear through my veins until a moment later, Mareina, somehow looking even more beautiful than I'd last seen her, appeared in the doorway. Laying my eyes on her cut off my breath like a fist squeezing my throat.

Tension knit her brows as her eyes leapt between me and Rumiel.

"I don't have the desire, nor the energy, to fight with you, Nakoa."

"I didn't come here to fight. I came to make sure you were ok. Miroslav told me you were… unwell." *And because I'm sorry. I'm so fucking sorry.*

The words were on the tip of my tongue, but her gaze was fixed on my father, surely recognizing who he was based on our likeness alone.

"You found your father…"

Rumiel stepped forward, bowing. "Your Majesty."

Mareina looked mildly unsettled by the title, and she didn't bother faking a smile. "I'm relieved to see you two have been reunited. It's an honor to meet you."

"The honor is mine, Goddess of Death."

Mareina frowned, giving a subtle shake of her head. "I know very little of my power, but I certainly hope that it lies with something more than death."

Rumiel's brows pinched. "Living in Bellorum has given you such a human perception. You forget that death does not signify merely an end but new beginnings. Reincarnation. Birth. Respite for the weary. The cleansing of karmic debts. Liberation for the soul… Without these things, the realms would descend into chaos. It is because of death that we are saved. Death brings peace. Healing. Transformation."

Mareina's expression gradually tensed as she took in my father's words. "And what of the suffering? I have wrought more death than any single being should ever be allowed and witnessed firsthand the pain that death can bring."

"Violence and death are mutually exclusive, and one needn't precede the other, My Queen. If you speak of grief, there is much to be learned from it, as there is with all suffering. It is a necessary part of growth within the physical realms."

Mareina's gaze softened even if it appeared as though the weight of the world sat upon her shoulders. Her deep green eyes shifted to mine, making my breath catch all over again.

"What of Zurie?"

"Alive… For now."

Mareina's features tightened as she nodded. "I'm sorry, Nakoa… I'm so sorry I never told you the truth. I—

My chest tightened with guilt. Though I still felt some modicum of betrayal, I understood her reasoning. I also recognized I'd not given her a reason to trust or be loyal to me. And having her stand here in front of, I suddenly didn't give a fuck about any of it.

I just wanted *her*. I wanted my *soulbound*. My queen. The woman destined to be *wife*, I prayed.

"Don't be. Words are not sufficient in expressing the remorse and shame I feel for my past actions."

Mareina cleared her throat, gradually nodding. My mind reached for words that wouldn't come, and thankfully, my father broke the brief silence.

"Where is your father?"

Mareina's expression tightened almost imperceptibly. "Visiting another realm."

I glanced at my father. I couldn't help but wonder just how much he could detect beneath Mareina's words. The tightening of distrust and wariness through mine and Mareina's tether told me she was hiding something. If Rumiel sensed it, he said nothing and merely nodded in acceptance.

Mareina took a deep breath as she held my gaze, something like guilt shuddering through her expression. "There's something I need to tell you."

TEN

ZURIE

"My son will not be pleased to discover you're allowing me such luxuries," I murmured as I stared longingly at my bathing pool. Azrael hummed. "What's he gonna do? *Kill me?*"

My eyes flicked up to his just as he turned to leave. Something wet began leaking from my eyes when I found myself staring down at my bathing pool, as it filled with steaming, fragrant water. I'd already scrubbed my teeth clean and washed off the layer of grime coating me when I was in the shower, and now I wanted a proper bath. Swiping away at the wasted water spilling down my cheeks I gave Keres my back, lest the wretched female witness it. Wisely, Keres and Azrael had refused to let me bathe in peace, though the latter had resigned himself to hunting down Miroslav. Why they thought that I would have any inkling of his whereabouts was beyond me. The male had been plotting against me since before we'd even met.

Both Azrael and Keres were searching for the Goddess of Life, Persephone. I wasn't surprised when they'd chosen *not* to disclose why.

Kere's eyes on my nude form felt like the scrape of a blade as I stepped into the bath. Every hair on my body rose from the delicious heat, and I didn't bother to stifle my groan.

Azrael had kept his promise and procured something to help with the pain. It was a little clay-colored tablet that he said would help block the pain receptors in my brain. Apparently, it was a drug from the largely human realm, Terrenea. The effects felt like putting a tiny bandage over a gaping stab wound, *but* it had reduced my fever and dimmed the splitting pain in my head enough to stand.

Sinking beneath the hot water of the pool was better than any orgasm that any male, outside of Rumiel, had ever given me. My eyes slipped shut as I leaned back and thought I might even be able to have a nap like this. With any luck, maybe I'd drown, and I wouldn't have to deal with any of this anymore. Less so from the withdrawals or the time I'd spent in the dungeon and more so due to the treacherous lovelessness of this world.

You've done nothing to deserve love, the thready, barely-there voice of my conscience whispered. Clearly, I had no argument. The chasm in my chest widened.

"There's something else I'd like to speak with you about."

My annoyance flared. "Oh? Is it to apologize for your deception in leading me to believe you were someone else?"

"I didn't think you would entertain me otherwise."

The sound of bare feet padding against the tiles had my eyes peeking open. My breath caught at the site of her nudity. While I had seen Thalia's nude form, thanks to the glamor, this was the first time I was seeing Keres' bared body. Lithe muscle, the petite palmful of her pert, pink-tipped breasts. Her long, lean, muscular legs. And the hairless visage of her pretty little cunt.

My voice contained far less venom than I'd intended. *"What are you doing?"*

I found myself jealous of the waist-high water licking across her body as she silently strode over, holding my gaze with dark, silvery eyes. Her eyes dropped to my breasts and then *lower,* all visible beneath the clear water. A coy smile tilted her lips when she caught me staring at the tightening peaks of her breasts.

"If you must know, *I'm proposing.*"

CHAPTER

ELEVEN

KERES

For some reason, I was nervous. I didn't even know this female. Gods knew why my heart was fluttering like a bird caught in the winds of a storm. Zurie's lips parted in shock as I neared her. She sat staring up at me with big, beautiful, blue, doe eyes.

"Proposing?"

"Soon, I will take Ishra's throne, and I would love to make you a Queen."

Zurie's mouth snapped shut, gaze shifting to some distant spot on the wall behind me. "I have no desire to be a queen."

Fuck.

What the fuck bargaining chip did I hold if she wanted nothing I had to offer? What more do I have to offer other than... Power?

"I am tired of being manipulated. Tired of wearing masks. Of dealing with people who wish to do nothing but exploit me. And while I may not deserve it, all I want now is peace."

My heart clenched as her eyes lifted to mine, glistening and pregnant with tears. "Take me from this place. Give me freedom and comfort to do as I please, and I will advise you to the best of my abilities. That is all I have to offer."

Three objectives led me to Atratus. The first, I already accomplished by killing my former *soulbound* so that she would reincarnate and forget all about my bother, Mors, who stole her from me.

The second was to ally with Zurie once I took Ishra's throne when Thalia's father passed away. However, when my niece and her *soulbound* suddenly overthrew Zurie I was forced to rethink my plan.

Initially, I thought I'd considered ingratiating myself with Nakoa, the soon-to-be King, but I'd never been particularly partial to males, *and* he seemed irreversibly obsessed by my niece. Not to mention, the idea of stealing away someone's *soulbound* was something I was having a hard time stomaching, considering I knew just how horrific it was. I was a monster in many ways but there were at least *some* things that even my conscience couldn't bear.

And then I realized Zurie would be perfect to rule beside me. I didn't know the first thing about ruling a kingdom. She could advise me. Granted, I would take her advice with a grain of salt because I wanted to be loved and adored by a kingdom—not hated—like her.

My final and third objective in coming here was to find Miroslav so that he could tell me where Persephone, the Goddess of Life, was hiding in exile so that she could tell me where and when Soteira, my *former soulbound,* would reincarnate. Perhaps even convince her to expedite the process if such a thing were possible. However, I would still be forced to wait at least thirty or so years for her to grow into a relatively mature female who would be mentally and emotionally compatible with me.

And now, this wicked female in front of me was tugging at my heartstrings.

Messy. This is going to get very, very messy, Keres, a distant voice in my head murmured, in a bored tone if I'd interpreted it correctly.

Emotions were such fickle things, and I was already so prone to impulsivity. So what if we shared a dalliance? It might last a day or a decade. There was little good in worrying what the future would bring when it came to such matters. I had been betrayed too many times by the people I'd loved most in all the realms. If we shared a deep connection and mutual pleasure could be had, I would take my joy where I could find it.

In my hesitation to reply, something like exhaustion and disappointment settled on Zurie's face as her eyes drifted towards some distant point on the wall behind me. I dared a step closer, between her parted thighs. With the back of my finger, I swiped up a tear caught in her lengthy, pale lashes and brought it to my tongue. The faint scent of Zurie's sweet arousal curling through the air made my heart riot in its cage.

"I will provide you with everything you could ever possibly need and want so long as you remain *loyal* to me. Loyalty, above all else, is what I value."

Zurie's eyes lifted to mine, widening with some unreadable emotion.

"Why is it that you wish to be a Queen?"

My heart gave another stutter as the truth slipped past my lips before I could stop them. "I wish to be loved."

Zurie's expression hardened, making my stomach lurch with the need to gain her approval. "I want to do good in the world and be appreciated for it..."

I held my breath as Zurie openly studied me for several moments. "Ruling a Kingdom is a thankless job. Even when I tried to rule with a gentle hand, I was met with hatred and opposition."

Zurie's hand lifted to twine her fingers with mine beneath the water and tugged me gently into her lap. My heart leapt into my throat as I straddled her, and something painfully familiar tightened in my chest as if trying to close the distance between us. With each breath, my breasts grazed hers, stoking our arousal further as leaden butterflies swirled in my belly.

"And if you wish to be loved by a Kingdom, I am the worst of all to advise you. I fear I have nothing to truly offer you other than companionship, but if you are willing to swear your loyalty to me, I will offer you the same."

Something fierce and possessive rose within me as my hope blossomed. My free hand curled around her throat, and my fangs lengthened in anticipation. With the urge to claim her. Something I hadn't experienced since Soteira, my *soulbound*.

"Where is your *soulbound?*"

Her brows pinched as if I'd ruined our moment, but I couldn't help but ask. "If I have one, I have seen no sign of them. Where is yours?"

Numbness stilted my emotions at the thought of her. Soteira.

"Dead."

Zurie's brows tightened further. "Oh... I'm sorry."

"Don't be. I killed her."

Zurie's breath caught, eyes lifting to mine. I closed the small distance between us, and for the first time in nearly a millennia, my heart soared. Her lips were plush and tender. A sweet respite from the harsh world around us that seemed to fade away all at once. Reality narrowed to only her. The sensation of our hearts beating as one, the sweet glide of our lips and the caress of our tongues, the tingling arousal pulsing between my thighs.

I groaned as I forced myself to break our kiss. There were a number of matters to be taken care of before I would give myself to this female, body, soul, and vow.

"Let us dress. Azrael will return any moment."

The disappointment in her gaze was blatant. I couldn't help but grin and rewarded her by biting her bottom lip hard enough to break the skin. Her blood blossomed on my tongue to bestow a sweetness like raw, dark amber honey. Zurie moaned a sigh of pleasure as I sucked her bottom lip into my mouth to steal a few more drops, releasing it with a loud *pop* and licking my lips. *"Delicious."*

Zurie arched towards me to capture my mouth again, biting viciously into my bottom lip. Surprise was swiftly replaced with desire as blood spilled freely down our chests. My grip on her throat tightened as my other hand reached between her thighs and possessively cupped her pussy.

"Clean it up," I purred in her ear. I pulled back to take in her reaction and found a grin that matched mine. She leaned forward, licking thick stripes up my chest, throat and mouth. When her tongue reached the stiff peaks of my breasts, she held my gaze as she continued to lick up our blood.

Oh my fuck.

I rewarded her obedience by steadily circling her clit and dipping two fingers into her clenching pussy. She whimpered against my throat as her hips thrust against my hand in time with my strokes. It took nothing more than a single whispered word for me to realize I would kill for this female.

"Keres."

Her tongue flicked against the peak of my breast before sucking it into her warm, wet mouth. Her fingers reached the throbbing center of me in a soft, teasing caress that made me desperate for more. Dutifully, she continued licking up the remainder of my blood. "I want more," she murmured against my throat. My heart pinched.

"Sorry to interrupt but you do realize I've been waiting for over an hour."

Azrael.

Neither of us faltered in our ministrations of one another, though I couldn't help but hum my pleasure as Zurie growled. *"Leave us."*

"Well, that's one way to talk to people," Azrael remarked in a bored tone. I turned my head to glare at him standing beside the bathing pool. "I need to find your niece."

"How would I know where she is? I've barely met her."

Azrael's gaze settled on Zurie. "And would you happen to know the whereabouts of your daughter-in-law?"

Zurie pursed her lips, eyes narrowing. "Don't tell me your people are still revolting."

Heaving a sigh, Azrael slipped his hands into the pockets of his strangely fashioned black trousers. "Well, if you ever learn to take away someone's free will, you let me know."

Zurie's lips tipped up in a smile that looked nothing short of villainous. "Sounds to me like you require a rather large favor then, doesn't it?"

Azrael's expression hardened. "As was liberating you from likely spending the rest of your life rotting in a dungeon *and* giving you relief from your withdrawals."

Zurie hummed thoughtfully to herself before returning to her task of suckling at my breasts and teasing my clit. I'd never be able to cum if Azrael didn't leave. He'd told me something of his situation, though I didn't know the details or the severity. Still, he had been kind to me when few others had. I stilled Zurie's motions by tilting her chin up with a curled forefinger. "Tell us where she is, my darling."

The vulnerability that passed over Zurie's expression made my heart squeeze. Her throat worked on a swallow, hesitating. I leaned in to whisper my reassurances against her cheek. "Remember what I said? So long as you're loyal to me, I'll give you everything you need. You don't need to wear a mask or manipulate anyone to get what you need or want." I punctuated my promise by pressing a lingering kiss to the corner of her lips.

Zurie studied my gaze for a moment as if having some internal debate before finally speaking. "I have no way of tracking her, but I'm certain that if you find my former general, Malekai Theikos, she won't be far behind."

As she provided Azrael with directions to General Theikos' home, my heart swelled with affection for taking this leap of faith. *In me.*

I internally vowed to prove to her that it was not misplaced.

"He's one of yours anyway, " she added.

Azrael's eyebrows leapt in surprise. "Oh?"

"His parents moved here from Hades... I believe you'll recognize him too."

Azrael's lips parted as if in realization. My gaze danced between the two of them in silent question and Zuried answered. "The last time Azrael was here, he bargained with me that I allow a few of his people from Vassileo seek exile here. In order to protect their identities, we had all their documentation state they were originally from Hades... And in return, he gave me *aetra.*"

Azrael huffed. "You thought I'd given you a weed."

Zurie frowned. Azrael set a bottle of something down on the floor beside the pool. "Do try to ration it, or it won't last you through the rest of your withdrawals."

At that, Azrael *folded* away, leaving Zurie and I to ourselves. Her gaze lingered on the bottle beside the pool. I traced the tip of my nose against the column of her throat.

"Come to Ishra with me."

CHAPTER

TWELVE

MALEKAI

"*This is not what we agreed upon.*" Leather creaked as I gripped Ceres' tack so tight the leather creaked at the unexpected sound of Miroslav's voice.

Fuck.

I already had enough guilt winding through me at having claimed Mareina without trying to speak to Nakoa first. Not that he would have been even remotely receptive. Our discussion likely would have ended in bloodshed, but at least I would have *tried.*

If for no other reason than ensuring her well-being because I knew no matter how much she loved me, I would never be able to replace her soul *bond* with Nakoa.

Miroslav rounded me to block Ceres' stable door. My anger flared at his admonishing tone but diminished as quickly as it came. And while I was filled with more joy than I'd ever known, it was tainted by guilt and shame.

That being said, Miroslav was a meddling male, trying my fucking patience.

"We *agreed* upon *nothing.*"

Miroslav's expression sharpened his already severe features.

"You have no idea what dangers, what *entities,* await us just on the other side of the metaphorical veil that separates our world from theirs! I can fucking *feel* it weakening! She *needs* her *soulbound* to reach her greatest power! For all our sakes! Have you no moral compass? Who are you to interfere?"

I'd never, in the many decades I'd known him, heard him raise his voice outside of rousing the crowds in Zurie's ampitheater. Which made his message all the more worrisome and had my guilt twisting inside me like a fucking blade.

"The only moral compass I have unfailingly points me in the direction of what is in Mareina's best interest. If you truly cared about her, you would be a little more hesitant to force her into the hands of a male who attempted to *murder* her in a fit of rage."

The words tasted like ash upon my tongue because while what I said was true, I knew that Miroslav was right, and I was fucking ashamed and terrified to admit it. Even if the only reason Nakoa wasn't dead was the fact that he was Mareina's *soulbound,* and despite my own selfish wishes, I had no desire to cause her any unnecessary suffering.

Miroslav's voice came out little more than hiss as his power pressed down on me. I halted in my steps, hackles rising. The beast within me tossed its head and snarled. My fangs lengthened, and the tips of my fingers throbbed with the need to release my talons. Trying to breathe in some modicum of calm, I slowly turned to face him as a broad grin stretched my face.

"You have grown *far* too confident wielding your power over weaker beings, *orisha.* You know what I am. Where is your moral compass that you tempt my beast into wreaking death and destruc-tion upon everyone in the vicinity of this palace?"

Miroslav's magic pulled back, but it was his look of disappoint-ment that made my anger falter. "Your parents were *soulbound.* I wonder what they would have to say."

Miroslav folded away before I could muster a response to that passive-aggressive little dig. I growled, turning back towards Ceres' stable. Watching me with dark, wide, *nonjudgemental* eyes, she huffed as I caressed her cheek and draped her tack over the stable door. "Ready to get outta here, sweet girl?"

I willed an apple into my hand, and Ceres' soft muzzle greedily gobbled it from my palm. Not even a full second passed before the thud of a hoof against a stall door sounded behind me. A grin twisted my lips, easing my tension, as I turned to find Chihiro tossing his black mane indignantly in the stall across from Ceres. "Don't worry. I brought snacks for you, too, 'Hiro."

My heart flapped jubilant wings at the musical sound of clinking teeth as I shook the sculpted bronze box. For nearly a century, I'd hidden my little treasure trove of fangs, molars, and incisors that had previously belonged to the males who had violated Mareina. *Before,* she'd grown into the fearsome warrior she was now. It felt surreal that the time to gift it to her had finally arrived.

I finished collecting a few of my things and the tools required to create the wedding ring that I had always dreamed of making for her —one forged by my beast.

My heart pounded alongside Ceres' racing hoofbeats as joy like I'd never known filled my chest to bursting.

And how bizarre that joy could be stolen from me in a few mere heartbeats.

So consumed by my euphoria, I only vaguely noticed that the normally busy street of my home was oddly empty. A golden aura appeared in the distance, steadily growing in size as an unfamiliar power cascaded over me like a pounding waterfall.

My joy cut off like a guillotine on its victim's head as a broad frame with golden eyes manifested. The male's mouth was a sinister flash of grinning white. "My, my... Your resemblance to him is stunning. How old are you?"

What?

My beast growled low as drakonati fire licked up the palms of my hands. Before I could even wield it, a sting like that of a wasp hit the back of my neck. I drew my hand to the small wound, and my fingers grazed against a metal dart. My vision was already tunnelling by the time I yanked it free.

My body went cold and numb as it slackened and sagged before sliding off the side of Ceres. I couldn't even brace myself for impact before I hit the ground. The sound of bone cracked loud in my ears upon impact. Struggling to maintain consciousness, the only thread of thought keeping me awake was that of Mareina. Relief suffused me as I remembered that she was safe in her realm, Avernus.

I willed my eyes to stay open as the male in front of me fully took form and strode towards me, dressed entirely in black. He knelt inches away from my face and brushed his fingers against Mareina's claiming marks on my neck. The touch radiated so much power, the hairs on my body rose and stretched towards him as if called forth to someone or *something* familiar.

"Now, all we have to do is wait."

THIRTEEN

MAREINA

Based on the look on Nakoa's face, you'd think that I'd informed him that he'd lost a piece of cutlery, and not his *soulbound*—despite the bond between us burning so badly I was surprised I wasn't spitting bile. Guilt knotted my stomach, and my heart broke further at our reality. While I fucking loved Malekai more than life itself, the soul-deep need for Nakoa was undeniable.

"I will still rule beside you in Atratus, but I have responsibilities here as well that require my presence."

Nakoa's black gaze gave nothing away as it remained locked on mine. "Congratulations, Mareina."

The restrained pain in his words was enough to crush my chest.

"Thank you," I managed weakly.

"When can I anticipate you joining me in Atratus?"

"When do you need me?"

Nakoa's hands fisted at his sides. "As soon as possible. I am only waiting to have you beside me to have Zurie pronounce me King so that we may schedule a dual coronation as soon as possible. The longer we wait, the longer my people remain enslaved. I would also request that your consort accompany you. He is my general, after all, and I have every intention of keeping him in my employ. I do hope he hasn't planned on abandoning his duties."

My wariness returned, eyes narrowing. "If you think to manipulate me through him, I can promise you I will not hesitate to give you many more reasons to loathe me."

A corner of Nakoa's mouth tilted up in a joyless grin. "That's the last thing I want, Mareina."

Tension coiled tight between our silence. Unable to bear it, my eyes landed upon Rumiel. Outside of his long black hair boasting a single streak of white, the greatest difference in their appearance lay mostly in Nakoa's more rugged and scarred appearance. Outside of the mass of muscle that I couldn't help but notice, what with him being fucking shirtless and all, he appeared to not have a single scar or blemish.

Rumiel's powerful yet quiet and inquisitive magic explored mine as if he were searching for something. Just as I opened my mouth to speak, I felt the visceral touch of someone brushing their fingers against the new claiming mark on my neck. A powerful shudder ran through my entire body as panic so intense swelled in my chest that I found it hard to breathe.

"Something's wrong."

Without any further thought, I found myself barrelling past them and out of the house. The moment I was past the threshold, my wings spread wide, giving powerful beats before launching me towards the entrance to my father's temple.

Fuck, how did I fold before?

"Mareina, let me help you."

I turned my head to find Nakoa and Rumiel flying hard beside me.

"Take my hands," I shouted over the wind to both of them.

Before they had a chance to ask why, I tucked my wings in tight and reached out with my arms. In the breathless moment that I began to plummet, Nakoa and his father lashed out to grip my arms.

I focused on Malekai's spirit, his presence, as I silently chanted his name.

Space, and the absence of light, swallowed us whole. A moment later, a hole in the fabric of the universe unfurled, and we stood in Malekai's living room.

Malekai's name tore from my throat at the sight of his enormous, prone form laying on the floor like a felled tree. I sank to my knees, gripping his blessedly warm flesh with my hands and shaking him to wake.

"I have to say, I'm rather impressed with your timing."

The sound of an unfamiliar male's deep, lilting voice had my magic spilling out of me in writhing red tendrils as I turned to face him.

Before I could speak Rumiel stepped forward, and I didn't miss the foreboding undercurrent in the rasp of his gravelly, broken voice. *"Azrael."*

"Rumiel," Azrael grinned, eyes sliding to Nakoa and studying him in a way that made my hackles raise, "I see you've produced off-spring during your time off the leash."

"If Malekai has been harmed in away—

"He'll wake soon enough, don't worry... I apologise for employing such a brutish method, but I had to find some way of drawing you out of Avernus and away from the prying eyes of Zurie's palace, ." Azrael's gaze drifted back to Nakoa and Rumiel briefly. "Though I see that was an exercise in futility."

My voice dropped to a growl. *"Tell me why you're here."*

For a moment, Azrael hesitated as something like nervousness shuddered his expression.

"I have two favours I implore you to grant me: I need you to open your realms, Avernus and Bellorum, to some of my denizens that have grown restless within the confines of my realms... *And* I need you to help me find someone."

I shook my head in disbelief. "Why would I do any of this?"

"I'm afraid you don't have a choice in the matter, *but* if you decide to be amenable, you'll be gaining a powerful ally."

Nakoa, Rumiel, and I all replied at the same time.

"No."

Azrael frowned. *"It's an inevitability."*

"Then so is your death."

Azrael gave a sardonic huff. "As much as I wish the solution were as simple as that, it's not. My power is the only thing securing my realms from yours. So as tempting as death may be, it would only further enflame the situation."

"Well then, if that's the case, what difference does it make?"

"When the citizens of my hell realms arrive, you *will* want me as an ally. And I can assure you, I am not easy to kill. *Believe me, I've tried."*

My *arcanum*, as Malekai had called it, *burned* as my magic writhed beneath the surface, desperate to be unleashed. While I may have been powerful compared to some, against someone like Azrael, it would be sheer delusion to think I could overcome him. He had been strengthening and wielding his power for time immemorial. I was a mere 120 years old, and I'd only developed a fragment of my power.

"I think you'll have a better understanding of things if I simply *show* you. If you like, I'll swear it in blood that I will return you."

If it was a choice between going with Azrael and potentially saving my soulbound, and the entire realm, from a slow and bloody death, or not going and being forced to allow Azrael to rip a hole between our worlds... Then, there was no decision to be made.

Nakoa stepped between us. "Mareina isn't going anywhere with you."

Touching Nakoa for the first time since he'd rescued me sent a flood of emotion through me as I laid my hand on his chest.

"It's ok. This is one of our many obligations as rulers, visiting other neighboring and distant kingdoms and realms. If what he says is true, this problem is just as much ours as it is his."

Nakoa's expression became stricken as he shook his head vehemently. "Then I will go in your stead."

I shook my head as Azrael spoke up. "I'm afraid that's not an option, *Your Majesty.*"

Azrael extended a long, elegant hand that coaxed Nakoa's growl. *"Touch her, and you'll be missing a fucking hand."*

That little, malnourished blossom of love Nakoa had planted in the depths of my heart flourished under his protectiveness.

He would never grant me permission, and I wouldn't allow him to come to harm so long as I was alive to prevent it. My gaze flicked to Azrael, who held my gaze knowingly as he spoke to Nakoa. "Do tell your friend that I *folded* his horse to Zurie's stableboy."

Azrael's eyes turned the color of flames roaring to life as I *folded* in front of him and took his hand. Nakoa's roar echoed in my mind as darkness coupled with gravity so powerful it knocked the air from my lungs and drove the contents of my stomach towards my oesophagus. In the next moment, my feet hit a marble floor so hard the impact reverberated through my bones and into my teeth. Azrael gripped me by my shoulders to steady me as guilt sank to the pit of my stomach.

Swallowing back bile, I shifted to take in my surroundings. My lips parted as my neck craned upwards to reach the height of the towering buildings whose spires and peaks were hidden by clouds high above. Ships and other... *things*... flew through the air in front of us. My breath caught on a gasp as the unmistakable form of an enormous *drakonati* soared above us, blotting out the sun and casting us in its shadow. Its body was at least the length of a dozen men, with a wingspan of more than double that.

"I sometimes forget what a beautiful and inspiring place Ouranissa is until I get to witness a newcomer's expression."

I gaped in awe as I watched its red, cream, and gold scales, all in varying shades, glitter and shine beneath the sun as if made of metal, though it undulated across currents of air like fluid defying gravity.

"They're still alive..."

"Oh yes, we have many of them. Though it's probably best you avoid getting near them."

My eyes finally slid back to his as the drakonati disappeared around one of the towering spires. "Why is that?"

Azrael's brows pinched as though I'd just ask a question with a very obvious answer until something like realization settled on his face, and he endowed me with a smug grin. "They can be rather... possessive."

He turned on his heel and disappeared through a set of peculiar, glass balcony doors that slid open parallel to the exterior wall. "Come... Let me show you Ouranissa."

FOURTEEN

MALEKAI

The sound of distorted voices drew me from a sleep so deep not even dreams could enter. My body felt like an anchor sinking to the deepest trench of the sea. And it felt... *good*. Peaceful. In this darkness, without thought, only being, there was nothing to fear or fight. *Finally*.

Distant, angry voices trickled into my consciousness, further stirring my wakefulness. At the rough growl of Nakoa's voice, memories returned, and reality settled in, giving way to some deep inner knowing that something had gone horribly wrong.

"Where is she?" I growled.

The silence I was met with had icy fear further spiking my veins. I turned to find Nakoa standing beside who I could only assume was his father. The male's magic was inquisitive and gentle as it introduced itself to mine. It reminded me of the way of my kind. Introductions were made not merely with brief, verbal greetings but with scents and magical touches. His eyes held mine with a certain knowing that told me he knew what I was.

Nakoa's words were a clipped growl as he explained to me what occurred during my lapse in consciousness. The male looked like he was barely restraining himself from tearing my head off. Not that I could blame him. I'd want to murder me too if I were in his shoes.

Though at the moment, we both recognized everything outside of getting Mareina back, had to take a back seat.

"She went willingly? With... *Azrael?*"

Nakoa's features tighten with what I can only assume his guilt and shame. I huffed a mirthless laugh, shaking my head as I gave him my most disgusted look.

"I will never understand how you treat her so carelessly. Constantly throwing her in harm's way. You have no idea what she's been through. She needs to be... *Protected* for once in her fucking life."

Nakoa looked as though he wished to tear my head off, and my anger burned so brightly that I fucking *wished* he would try. Instead, his guilt was belied by the slight hunching of his shoulders.

"I accept accountability for the error of my ways."

His admission deflated much of my anger. My fingers found their way to Mareina's gift, the little box of teeth in the interior pocket of my jacket as if it would soothe me. Relieved to find it still there, I *willed* it safely away.

"So, how do we get to Vassileo?"

Nakoa's father's expression, somehow, managed to turn even more grim. "There were once portals. A handful of them are located across Bellorum, but only one person can open them other than Azrael."

I wasn't surprised to hear Zurie's name spill from Nakoa's father's lips. Dread sank low in my gut, like an anvil sinking to the bottom of a turbulent sea.

"*Zurie?* Why the fuck would Azrael—Nevermind. There has to be another way. Where's Miroslav?"

"Probably with my mother."

I flick my gaze to Rumiel. "Can you fold?"

"Only the gods and demiurges themselves, and their descendants, have that power."

Gods and demiurges blood?

I'd never heard of or read such a thing... I had seen Zurie *fold* countless times.

Not that it fucking mattered now.

My magic began to seep out of me as my control slipped. Flames licked up my feet, legs, and hands, charring the rug beneath my feet as I chanted the orisha's name.

"Miroslav... Miroslav. Miroslav. Miroslav. Miroslav. Miroslav. Miroslav. Miroslav."

Thick, heavy silence weighed down on us as we waited, hearts pounding, for Miroslav to appear. *Anything* could be happening to Mareina right now. The idea had me ready to burst from my skin with panic. With ever-increasing volume and ferocity, my voice became an otherworldly roar.

"Miroslav. Miroslav. MIROSLAV. MIROSLAAAAV! MIRO-FUCK-ING-SLAV! ANSWER ME YOU CONNIVING, DUPLICITOUS FUCKING CUNT!"

Chest heaving, a wave of power washed over me like a tidal wave.

"I told you this timeline you have chosen wouldn't end well."

I spun to face the stoic, imperturbable bastard I'd beckoned with both anger and relief.

"Can you get us to Vassileo? Do you know how to open the portals?"

An almost imperceptible frown tilted his lips, something like resignation making his voice soft. My panic rose to new, throat-closing, chest-crushing heights.

"Zurie is your only hope."

CHAPTER

FIFTEEN

NAKOA

"*Zurie is your only hope.*" Of all the heinous words uttered in the history of time, that had to be among the worst of them. As soon as Mareina had left with Azrael, I could feel it deep in my bones that he wouldn't bring her back. My Knowingness was only confirmation. Fear and determination fisted my heart as Miroslav *folded* us to my mother's home instead of to the palace. To Zurie. "Why are we here?"

"Because Zurie is gone."

My hands shook as the priceless relics around us began to tremble, along with the mountain housing the cave. To keep my magic leashed stole every ounce of my energy. And if the flames igniting and guttering around Malekai were anything to go by, he was feeling very much the same.

"What do you mean *gone?*"

Wearing a blank expression, Miroslav *willed* a roll of parchment into his hand and passed it to me. Without entirely meaning to, I snatched it away.

82

Nakoa,

I realize I haven't earned the right to call you my son, and I wouldn't blame you if you never allow me to. While I don't deserve such an opportunity to be given freely, I do hope you'll understand why I must take things into my own hands. That, and I found a favorable alternative to living in a dungeon. Perhaps even a kindred spirit to share life with.

Despite my previous actions, I only want the best for you.

That being said, I've taken the liberty of notifying your military and palace staff. In addition, I've sent the couriers to all the Lords and Ladies of Atratus to notify them of your birthright and ascension to the throne. Your coronation and inauguration shall be held four days henceforth, as per the invitations already sent. The staff have already begun preparing.

This was done in both of our best interests. It brings me no small amount of joy that the two align.

Your ally,
Z

P.S. Someone tried to assassinate me at my inauguration. I would be supremely grateful if you didn't die. To ensure you remain unharmed, I will be there to gleefully murder anyone suffering from fatal idiocy.

... For several long moments, I stared in blatant shock at the parchment. Where does one even begin to decipher that message and what had taken place in order for any of it to be possible?

Finally, I lifted my gaze from the paper as Rumiel and Malekai's gaze weighed on me, expectant and increasingly impatient. I attempted to harden my heart to wrought iron steel, but if ever I had a love language, it was violence being wielded in defence and honor of a loved one.

Swallowing back my emotion, I rolled the parchment up with more care than it deserved, telling myself it was only in case I needed to return to it to search further for clues as to where this wretched female had gone.

I passed it to Rumiel, who unrolled it, and Malekai came to stand over his shoulder, both murmuring curses.

Azrael no doubt had something to do with it. Was it he who had offered her exile? *They'd make a fine pair.*

My Knowingness whispered a name I was only vaguely familiar with.

Keres.

"Who is Keres?"

Miroslav didn't often look bewildered. In fact, in the short time I'd known him, I couldn't fathom him being confused about anything.

"The Goddess of Violence?"

My Knowingness filled me with certainty in response.

Now I was doubly confused. *Fuck me.*

Keres is Mors' sister, my Knowingness supplied.

"What in *Akash's* name would she want with Zurie?"

Miroslav gave me a weary look. "I don't know." I didn't miss the way Malekai's brows lifted in surprise. "I have found that the gods tend to prohibit anyone snooping around in their timelines, lives, whereabouts, and affairs. It's not a gift many possess, but the most powerful and well-trained of them, like Mors and his sister, are among them. I've already tried peering in on Zurie and am only able to see her timelines prior to Keres showing up. Apparently, the goddess has extended her protection to her.

"As for your timeline, my visions have shown me few options. The least detrimental of which is that you take the crown. I am certain that The Well will reveal this to you. It has been your destiny since before you were born."

I could only *pray* The Well would actually show me how to bring Mareina back.

My previous visions of my coronation as King suddenly made painful sense. *This was why she hadn't been in them.*

Perhaps The Well wouldn't even reveal how to retrieve Mareina or fix the portals.

I'd grown up sneaking into this ancient cave that my *adoptive* mother had carved into the side of this mountain to hide dangerous relics and artefacts that would be catastrophic to have in the hands of someone with mal-intent.

I took a seat on the cushion in front of The Well, not bothering to wait for the three males behind me. The moment my eyes focused on the surface of eerily still, black water before me, the world around me shifted into one of sleek, white marble. I found myself standing in a foyer with ornate, flowing gold and bronze archways and staircases.

Naturalistic sculptures, all of the same female in various states of undress, held glowing lanterns, wielded vines and water in motion. The space was both stunningly beautiful and entirely foreign, as though from a different age, dimension, and realm... I turned slowly, lips parting in awe as I craned my neck to gaze up at the astoundingly beautiful painted, cavernous ceiling featuring depictions of the same female.

My mouth snapped shut as the enormous front double doors *slid* open. Azrael stepped inside, shortly followed by Mareina. Looking exactly as they had only minutes ago before he'd *folded* her away. My breath caught at the realization that this was the present. Her name was a hushed whisper on my lips as my heart leapt into my throat.

"I have never witnessed such peace and prosperity in a place where *everyone* is thriving...," Mareina murmured thoughtfully.

"All of this, along with Avernus and Bellorum, will be destroyed if the beings of Vassileo break through its barrier." Azrael's gaze shifted from the beauty of his city to hers. "So you see why I must protect it."

"The beings I speak of are in the eleven hell realms I rule, only two of which are reserved solely for the dead."

Azrael gave a subtle wave of his hand and black vapours spilled out of thin air, growing in size until an opaque black portal formed in front of us. Mareina hesitated before Azrael held open his hand to Mareina like a father would his child. Mareina didn't accept his hand, instead stepping beyond the portal ahead of him. My eyes narrowed as I watched Azrael give a small, appreciative smile at her backside.

The world shifted, replacing Ouranissa with bleak stone buildings and icy mountains surrounded by cumulonimbus clouds so dark they were nearly black. Five *red* suns, all of varying size and local, peppered the sky as they kissed the horizon in their lazy descent. In seconds, the sweltering, oppressive heat had sweat seeping from my pores.

The sound of thundering beats had Mareina and I bolting around, whereas Azrael took his time. A black, wolf-like creature of gargantuan size with three heads ran straight for us. Each of its fangs were the length of my forearm and its eyes glowed the color of lava.

"You have nothing to fear, Mareina. Cerebus' will is my own."

Mareina's four wings stretched wide as if in anticipation of taking flight. The beast skidded to a halt in front of Azrael, dousing him in slobber and kisses as she whined and lamented his absence, making my heart clench for Peanut and Bellona.

Azrael stroked and affectionately gripped the creature's fur as he cooed to her. "I missed you too, my sweet baby. Look how gorgeous you are. Such a good girl. You wanna give her a tour of Malovada city, hm? I brought some *tiramissu* just for you, sweet girl."

Cerebus yelped excitedly before laying down, pressing her neck flat against the ground, and Azrael slipped over her shoulders before looking over at Mareina who hesitated. "Unless you'd prefer to fly? But I can't promise you'd be the only one in the sky..."

Cerebus titled her head as Mareina approached, sniffing her in rapid breaths that sent a gust of wind through the thick black sheet of her hair as she extended her hand for Cerebus to sniff. The creature's tongue lapped, covering Mareina's arm in drool. A grin spilt Mareina's face and Azrael's expression lit up as he gave her thickly muscled neck a heavy pat.

"Cerebus is the only true light in this place. Aren't you, baby girl? She's my *arcanum.*"

Mareina stilled for a moment as if surprised by the news. I had no idea what an *arcanum* was, but I would be sure to find out. Azrael extended a hand to help Mareina settle herself in front of him between his thighs. A flare of jealousy seared my veins, but Azrael's hands didn't wander in the slightest. He curved his broad chest over her in an attempt to give her a respectable amount of distance between her back and his front as his fingers sank into Cerebus' fur.

Without any other visible direction. Cerebus rose to standing, causing Mareina to give a little yelp of surprise just before it took off at a galloping pace.

I half-expected The Well itself to take me with them, but I only found myself standing in the wake of their dust. My wings heaved, launching me into the air to fly beside them.

As we rode through the small city, depravity that I'd only witnessed on occasion proved to be common place. Every manner of violence and indulgence unfolded around us. Murder. Brawls. Theft. Sex of debatable consent. And no one batted an eye outside of Mareina, whose face was set in a grim line.

"My father's after realm is nothing like this. There is anguish and all manner of suffering but only in the way of the soul's grieving at its wrongdoings in their former life that they purge until their karma is cleared from it...."

The familiar mask of guilt lined Azrael's features. "First and foremost, this is one of the *living* hell realms. I won't burden you with visiting the hell realms of the dead. I wish they were as peaceful as your father's, but unfortunately, my hell realms are exactly that: *hell.* I cannot fathom how your father created a world that heals instead of destroys. In Avernus they have hope. Here we are bereft of it. And it because of that, for many centuries, my people have been restless and determined to break free."

Mareina's scowl deepened as she takes everything in, both our surroundings and Azrael's words. "You make it sound as if you are losing control."

Cerebus kept at a trotting pace, weaving around the pedestrians in the street who maintained their distance. Though it was impossible to miss the sinister glares of many of them as they watched Azrael and Mareina pass. My hackles rose and my anger burned brightly like wielding iron in my chest. I wanted to eliminate all of them.

Azrael took a deep breath, gaze fleeing Mareina's to pass over his people, each of them watching with expressions ranging from wariness to fear to outright glaring.

He heaved a sigh as if his next words cost him to speak aloud.

"That's because I am. I do not know how much longer my power, already being stretched so thin between eleven hell realms and one divine realm, can hold them back. When I threatened you saying that you do not have a choice in the matter, it was because I don't have a choice either. Such an event is *inevitable* if we do not appease them. If we do not give them *hope."*

Mareina shook her head as despair began to seep in. "So *give* them hope... I cannot allow you to destroy Avernus and Bellorum—

Before Mareina could reply, a deep voice echoed from the skies just as a shadow crept over us."What a pretty consort. I cannot fathom why you would bring her here."

Tipping my head towards the orange and red sky revealed a dark-scaled drakonati soaring over us before diving down. Just before it crashed into the ground, it shifted into the form of a male.

"Unfortunately, this is not my consort. She is your chance at freedom, if you have any, and you will pay her the respect of one, Erius."

Erius approached Cerebus with a fearlessness that could only come from a larger predator. Still, she gave a low growl in warning. Erius raised his hands as if to appease her, and he gave a dramatic bow. The male was dressed in tattered fighting leathers. His black hair was shorn close to his scalp, and his skin, littered with even more scars than my own, was nearly as dark as the black scales of his drakonati. His eyes devoured Mareina in a way that made my hackles rise. "Is that so? Do you plan to liberate us? Or oppress us? My guess would be the latter... Did he tell you what happened the last time we were promised freedom?"

Realization hit me like a hammer. *The drakonati genocide.*

Azrael frowned. "It was an unfortunate event."

That earned them Erius' cackle; a dark, raspy sound. The crowd surrounding us—including every being from demon to human and orc to fae—began creeping in on us.

Azrael paid them little attention, and panic for Mareina rose swiftly in my chest.

"Is that what you call the genocide of thousands of drakonati? An *unfortunate event?*"

Both mine and Mareina's jaws dropped in realization.

"And I mounted his fucking head on a pike," Azrael seethed.

Erius smirked. "Far too little, too late."

My desperation threatened to turn into panic yet somehow Mareina's face remained impassive as she held Erius' gaze, drawing a smirk from him. "I'd be careful with this one, young goddess. Duplicitous is the last of this male's—

"You forget your place, drakonati," Azrael roared. Infused with his magic, his voice wove through the air in a way that crept upon your skin and seeped into your mind. *"It is by my will alone that you maintain this form. Perhaps the time has come for your soul to return to the chasm?"*

Erius smirked. "And start a war with the drakonati? You and I both know that Ataraxus wouldn't take my death lightly."

"I could just as easily return *all* of you to the chasm," Azrael snapped.

Erius' head tipped back with laughter. "Hmmm, yes. Send us *all* back to the chasm only for your own soul to join us. Have you forgotten *your* place? That your fate is equal to our own."

Realization hit me like a tidal wave. *That's why he needs her. If he kills them, he kills himself. And he hoped another god or Goddess of Death would be the solution.*

Azrael stared down from Cerebus's back. "It would be a better fate than having to tolerate the sound of your voice."

Erius merely chuckled and gave another dramatic bow. "My lady. Your majesty." The male turned and strode away, abruptly shifting back into his drakonati form and nonchalantly crushing nearby buildings, along with anyone in them, before he shot into the skies.

The crowd in the streets had gathered, staring at Azrael and Mareina with nothing short of malevolence. A voice in the crowd cried out, followed by another, and another.

"Mortatum ad' Azrael!"

"Mortatum ad' Azrael!"

"Mortatum ad' Azrael!"

The crowd beneath us— filled with demons to humans to orcs and fae—heaved as what I could only describe as black vaporous archestratum appeared to push them back as they cried out to chant in unison, *"Mortatum ad' Azrael."*

Death to Azrael.

Azrael did nothing as the crowd closed in on them.

"Why don't you stop them?" Mareina shouted to him to be heard over the chanting.

"Because the more of them that die, the more of my power dies with them. And they know it."

Without warning, the world shifted before me as Azrael folded with Mareina and Cerebus in tow to stand in a barren alien world.

Steaming pools of black, murky water bubbled in a patchwork array of salt-crusted pools that blanketed the land as far as I could see.

And only a few feet way, a torn hole in the fabric of this realm hovered in mid air. Instead of the opaque black of the portal Azrael had previously opened, we could see straight through this, directly into another world. A crystalline sea of green and endless fields of *aetra* lay just beyond a few hundred foot drop as if a window had opened in the sky. Whorls of black curled away from the small three foot opening.

Electricity bolted through me in shock.

The Kahlohani Islands.

Mareina's features went slack with shock. "You're sure no one has found it?"

Azrael shook his head. "I honestly can't say. I wouldn't *feel* if one or two people left. It would take a mass of them to leave before I noticed the loss."

"What happens when you try to close it?"

Azrael lifted his hands. Dark and gold magic poured out of him, weaving together like a blanket until the hole disappeared.

"Another one opens."

Azrael turned in a circle, searching, before laying a hand on Mareina's shoulder, transporting us to a desert.

Fuck me.

The hole is slightly bigger now, and instead of peeking out on the Kahlohani Isalnds, I see a sandy desert.

Azrael heaves a sigh. "There are more like this peppered throughout Vassileo. It's a blessing they've only shown up in remote locations... Perhaps because it's where there's less magic in the vicinity, but eventually, when they grow big enough, someone will feel the pull of magic."

CHAPTER

SIXTEEN

NAKOA

Leaving Cerebus behind, Azrael *folded* with Mareina back to his palace in Ouranissa. Mareina and Azrael stared at one other as the reality of the situation settled upon her.

"So you see *our* predicament."

Mareina shook her head, no doubt in horrified awe. Azrael's expression tightened with guilt and shame. "It wasn't always this way."

"What happens if they kill each other? It still weakens you?"

Azrael nods. "It takes a part of my soul to the chasm with them."

Mareina studied him for several moments. "And why don't you help them? Try to give them whatever it is they need to be..."

Mareina's words drifted already recognizing their futility.

Azrael huffed a sad laugh. "I may have the power to take life, but I do not have the power to change it. The beings in my hell realms are too many for anyone else to fathom and, with a few exceptions, they are the most wretched and corrupt souls I have ever come across. And while I would not wish their wrath upon nearly anyone, it has become beyond my control to prevent it. If things continue as they are, in a matter of months, those in the barriers between our realms will fray wide open."

My heart pounded a furious beat, knowing that whatever response Mareina would give, it wouldn't be one I wanted to hear. What solution could their possibly—

"What if... Somehow, I could lend these realms my power."

Icy dread trickled into my veins. Azrael grew still.

"You are not made of the aether of my realms. There may be some hope that your power might be enough to strengthen my side of the barrier that separates my hell realms reserved for the dead from Avernus, but in order for your power to strengthen the barriers that divide my living hell realms from Bellorum... We would have to create a syphon to *drain* your power. And you would have to stay in Vassileo. It is not a fate I would wish upon a soul such as yours."

My heart stalled in my chest as it cracked and shattered. My unheard words were breathless and frantic as I reached out and attempted to grip her by the shoulders, but my hands merely passed through her. *"Mareina, no. No, no, no, lohane thili. Please, don't do this."*

The look on her face told me everything I feared to hear. Deaf to my pleas, Mareina merely huffed a heartbroken laugh. "You have no idea the horror I have inflicted on others. It is a fate I have earned."

Azrael shook his head as he studied her. "Because you are not one of the souls in my dominion, I do not know much of your history, but my power still allows me to feel and intuit the merit of every soul in existence. And I can assure you, you do not belong in any hell."

Something like numb resignation settled on her face. "I deserve worse."

No... No. This couldn't be happening.

I had to stop this. There had to be another way. Surely, Moirai— the many-faced Goddess of Fate—had not intended this. An echo of Miroslav's words filled my mind.

'If you do not cherish the soulbound Akash has gifted you, you shouldn't be surprised when she is stolen from you.'

My lips parted in horror in realization. Malekai wasn't the one to steal her from me. It was Azrael. Fate. The universe itself. Mareina's guilt, which I had only ever enflamed. My forcing Mareina into a position of power and obligation.

Azrael seemed to be deliberating something before he spoke. "Shall I take you to back to your... mates. To say goodbye? I would trust your word that you will willingly return with me should you give it."

Raging tears streamed down my cheeks as I desperately tried to grasp Mareina and roared my protest.

Mareina sucked in a deep breath, her heartbreakingly beautiful green eyes swelling with liquid despair as she turned away from Azrael to hide them.

"That would be a promise that I am not certain I have the strength to keep. And even if I did, I know at least one of them would fight to their death to keep me from you."

At least one of them.

Anguish devoured the scant remains of my obliterated heart.

I had done this.

Another roar left my throat, broken and pleading as regret, shame, and desperation spilled down my cheeks. Her eyes lifted to mine, as though some part of her had heard it and a shuddering breath left me.

She stared up into my eyes as if she were looking directly at me. Perhaps she realized that at least one of us, whether it was me, Miroslav, or my mother would see this moment in time.

"*Lohane thili,* please *don't do this. Come back to me. Let me make this right. Let us fix this* together."

Her words were so soft they were almost imperceptible. "*If you see this, know that I am sorry for all that I have done against you. And despite our differences, I cherish our time together. I cherish you... To protect our realms, you will need to find my father.*"

SEVENTEEN

MALEKAI

The vision the well had shown, while deeply unsettling and not entirely clear, wasn't anything I hadn't anticipated. Miroslav had already foretold my fate, even if this was somewhat different than what he had described.

What I hadn't anticipated was witnessing the soon-to-be crowned King shaking with both fury and despair as watery emotion cut through his anguish, and he turned to Miroslav.

"Take me to Zurie," Nakoa growled in a voice that made the hairs on the back of my neck stand on end. Miroslav gave him a pitying look. "They're in Ishra. No one gets into Ishra unless they're invited."

A snarl ripped from my throat. "*Fold* me near their border."

A blanket of violent, madness-inducing fog encompassed their borders and their shores, preventing anyone from entering uninvited. Shrouded in mystery, it was supposedly the most peaceful continent in all of Bellorum.

Compassion tugged at Miroslav's frown. "You know that isn't possible. You won't make it 100 feet past it once the madness seeps in, then how will you get Mareina back?"

A vein in Nakoa's forehead bulged. "Then I need you to bring me to Mors."

Miroslav frowned, eyes narrowing with confusion for the first time in the near century I've known him. *"Mors?"*

If we weren't in such dire circumstances, I might have laughed.

"Mors is her father."

Miroslav's lips parted as several emotions passed over his face: shock, realization and understanding, *embarrassment.*

"Well, as I've told you before, it is no simple feat to locate a god without their permission. Especially one as powerful as Mors."

Judging by the look on Nakoa's face, he wanted to tear Miroslav limb from limb. Before he could attempt to do so, Miroslav heaved a sigh.

"... But I shall continue to try my best."

My eyes burned, swelling with rebellious tears—a mirror to Nakoa's own—as I watched him unravel.

"I cannot fathom waiting a moment longer."

Miroslav gave his head a grim shake. "You have no other choice."

CHAPTER

EIGHTEEN

MAREINA

Nearly three months had passed already, and I'd only managed to fall further into depression. I still hadn't managed to figure out a way to discern how much time would have passed in Bellorum. My days consisted of crawling out of bed to meet my body's needs and feeding at the increasing number of riots. Thankfully, my presence here had managed to seal up the holes in the barriers containing Azrael's hell realms. Under Azrael's request, I was advised only to restrain and detain his hell-dwelling citizens lest it further weaken him. Naturally, this only further enraged his people and inspired more killing. I hadn't seen many children in this realm, but I had to imagine there was an unforgivable number of orphans out there somewhere. He reassured me that his nephilim and archestratim brought them to an orphanage in Ouranissa.

A knock on the door drew me from my thoughts. My senses told me it was one of the palace staff. I *willed* the door open, and as per usual, someone in a shapeless cowl drifted through the room carrying a tray of food, setting it on the petite dining table before leaving the room as silently as they came.

Time, if there is such a thing, passed at a pace so slow it didn't seem to pass at all. If it weren't for the five red suns yearning to kiss the dark horizon beyond my balcony, I'd have no concept of time at all.

Eventually, there was another knock on the door, and my heart lept with relief when I felt Asterion's powerful magic on the other side of the door. "Come in!"

Every bone in my body ached as I forced myself to sit up, head spinning, and then thought better of it. The *rhyton,* a bronze horned-animal-shaped receptacle that had been magically embedded into the center of my fucking sternum to continuously feed it a trickle of my blood and magic hummed through me as it drew upon more of my *life force.* My need to feed had become nothing short of insatiable since it had been placed, and no matter how many of Vassileo's citizens I fed from, it never seemed to be enough.

Asterion strode to my bedside looking dour as ever. The male had become my personal bodyguard and was rapidly becoming a dear friend—my only friend in this place. After pouring my heart out to him about Nakoa and Malekai, and their history, I'd discovered that Asterion had actually known Rumiel before he left for Bellorum hundreds of years ago. *Thousands* in Vassileon time.

Asterion's expression tensed as he stared down at me, shaking his head. His normally stoic demeanor rarely belied his emotions, so to see worry written all over his face made my stomach churn. "That bad, huh?"

Wordlessly, he offered me his bared wrist. I weakly shook my head. "I'll wait for another riot." It was merely a matter of time. Azrael would be thoroughly displeased, but during the riots, many of his citizens would kill each other anyway. I did my best to detain them, as per his request, and leave them to rot in the already packed dungeon cells deep beneath his palace. No matter their depravity, I couldn't help the nausea that caging another being gave me. Personally, I'd prefer death than to be locked away for the rest of my life. I shoved away the fact that this palace, this realm, was exactly that.

"Stubborn, female. Look at you. You'd be useless at a riot right now. You can barely get out of bed."

He wasn't wrong, but I already knew what happened when my venom was involved. And despite the fact I'd probably never see my *soulbound* again, I couldn't fathom giving myself to another male. As if reading my mind, he scowled. "And if your only reason for hesitation is that you fear giving into the venom, then I'm officially insulted. Do you honestly think I would ever betray your trust in such a way?"

I heaved a sigh, trying to swallow back my guilt as I finally held his golden gaze. Unlike the rest of the Nephilim, whose eyes are a solid black sclera, Asterion's are dark bronze. Nearly gold, but not. He was a remarkably beautiful male, as large as Nakoa, with similarly bronze skin. However, the similarities end in their height, muscular build, and skin tone. Asterion's features were cut from granite, each curve and angle sharp and hard in a way that painted a brutal, masculine picture that complemented the terrifying, haunted beauty in Asterion's eyes. I couldn't begin to fathom what he'd survived living here his entire life.

I also had yet to see his true form—the one that included the horns, tail, and armored plating I'd come to adore on Nakoa. My heart clenched at the very thought of him.

At my lack of response, Asterion let out an animalistic growl and bit into the flesh of his wrist a little too viciously. Blood spurt from around his mouth and trailed across the floor between us as he forced his wrist to my mouth quicker than I could overcome my shock and resist him.

Rich and smooth, his blood possessed a hint of something that reminded me of cardamom. I was powerless to resist the scent alone, much less the taste. There was also something so very *other* about his blood. I'd feasted on Nakoa's nephilim blood and on countless other beings here in Vassileo. *Nothing* tasted or smelled quite like Asterion's blood.

The moment it touched my lips, I was surrounded by radiant

light. All sense of time and space disappeared as my fangs instantly sank into the delicate flesh, tendons, and cartilage of his wrist. Somewhere in my distant mind, I felt a pang of guilt because I knew it was a far from pleasant sensation, but I was far too consumed by my hunger to stop.

Asterion made no sound of discomfort or protest, and gradually, the near-blinding light dimmed, and I could see his ever-present scowl. The cinnamon taste of my venom blossomed on my tongue, and a moment later, my pussy throbbed with need. My eyes darted to the impressive length that remained trapped against his thigh in the leg of his fighting leathers. The sight only intensified my longing for Malekai and Nakoa. I yearned to burst from my skin. Fury rose in my chest at where fate had led me.

Asterion gave a grunt of pain, yanking me out of my downward spiral. I released him at once, finally managing to sit up for the first time that day. Apologies and remorse poured out of me as I took in the torn and jagged wound, visible to the bone.

"Oh, fuck. Asterion," I whispered in horror.

He shook his head. "Fuck the wound... Your emotion. All Nephilim are empaths to some degree. It is a particularly strong gift of mine."

I shook my head in disbelief that I'd hurt the one person who'd treated me like a friend and protected me in this *Akash*-forsaken place. All of the pain and heartbreak of the last few weeks and perhaps even life, in general, began to crack the tomb in which I'd buried them.

Asterion's throat worked on a visible swallow, further increasing my guilt because I knew that he could feel these emotions as if they were his own. *"Gods...* Forgive me, Asterion. I'll ask Azrael to relieve you of your obligation—

Before I could finish my sentence, Asterion yanked me against his chest. Arms like iron bars wrapped around me.

His voice, normally stoic and gravelly, was gentle. "Hush, Mareina. You will do no such thing."

His giant hand, large enough to curl around the entire width of the back of my head, began to gently stroke my hair as he heaved a sigh against me, surely feeling my emotions shift from horror, guilt, and shame to relief, overwhelming gratitude, and even platonic love.

Like the swelling pressure of a geyser, a catharsis of all my pent-up emotions rose, threatening to burst free.

Asterion pressed a kiss to the top of my head. *"Shhhh. It's ok. I'll be here so long as you need me, Mareina."*

A choked sob broke free as I buried my face in the stone wall of his broad chest. Asterion bent to sweep me bodily into his arms and strode over to a setee on the balcony.

I wept in his arms and when he heard me sniffling the fluid that insisted on liberating itself of me via my nose, he *willed* a handkerchief into his hands.

And *Akash* almighty, the way it renewed my sorrow and sobbing must have been baffling, if not comical.

The last time I'd had a handkerchief, it had been Malekai's. The memory of him licking my snot off it just to make me smile was enough to break me.

The moons had reached their zenith by the time I woke up, the left side of my body numb and stiff from being pressed against the safe haven of Asterion's hard, thickly muscled body.

I peeked up from his chest to find him sound asleep. His face was slack, head tilted to the side, and lips parted. It felt like a priviledge to see this powerful mountain of a male in such a vulnerable state. To see the perpetual stoic harshness of his expression erased by sleep.

My heart swelled with affection for him. Not only for all that he had done to earn my loyalty as a friend but even simply for the fact that a male as noble as him existed. I sent a silent prayer to *Akash* that one day, some way, somehow, he would find his *soulbound.* If anyone deserved it, it was him. It was heartbreaking to think that so long as he was stuck here in Vassileo, it was highly unlikely that he would ever meet her. The nephilim I'd met here all steered clear of him; males, females, and *aequili* alike.

I laid my head back down on his chest, savoring his warmth and security, thanking *Akash* for him before praying that one day sooner, rather than later, he would find his *soulbound*.

CHAPTER

NINETEEN

ASTERION

I'd been born amongst my kind, yet I'd always been isolated. Mareina was my first *true* friend. Watching her suffer like this, feeling her suffering as if it were my own, was enough to drive me to madness. Which was perhaps why I'd resorted to summoning Azrael. Many years ago, I'd thought him a friend, but he'd taught me otherwise.

As usual, Azrael's office door in the palace was locked but unguarded. No one in the palace was foolish enough to attempt a break-in. Except for me. But I was willing to risk his wrath if it meant there was even a slight chance of convincing him to let Mareina go home. Even if it meant I would still be stuck here.

Alone.

Again.

I stood in front of Azrael's office's towering, bloodwood double doors and gave another scan of the vicinity. Not because I was afraid of getting caught but because I was afraid of accidentally killing someone.

To call my magic *volatile* was an understatement, and if anyone were nearby when I unleashed it, there would be unnecessary casualties.

After confirming I was alone, I allowed my tightly sealed emotions to slip out and, with it, my magic. In moments, I could feel the very fabric of reality beginning to fray, and thus, the wards locking Azrael's office door.

It's a dizzying and deeply unsettling sensation to feel the world as you know it begin to unravel. Even doing it for a fraction of a second allows me a glimpse into all the manifolds of time and existence, and it always feels far too much for my singular brain to comprehend.

Despite the discomfort, I was already getting lost. My consciousness and perception of my 'self' disappeared, slipping through my fingers like the nonexistent sands of time. The sound of creaking and shattering wood, metal, and stone became a distant and faint background noise. Everything in my vicinity was drawn into my void and reduced to a whisper of its former existence, like ash on the wind.

"What the fuck are you doing?"

Azrael growling his fury within my mind snapped me back to *this* reality. Azrael's office had been reduced to rubble. The doors and part of the marble and stone walls surrounding them were gone; not even a splinter remained.

I cast a guilty glance at the destruction before turning my gaze to his. As if it wasn't enough to palpably feel them, I could practically *see* the flames of his rage burning inside him. "I need to speak with you about Mareina."

Azrael's jaw clenched, and I had to consciously put a wall up against his anger and frustration to keep it from bleeding into me.

"What about her?"

"She's miserable. And I think she's dying."

Azrael's body visibly relaxed as he scrubbed a hand down his face. Dark circles lined his eyes, stubble lined his normally clean-shaved jaw, and a general malaise clouded his aura.

"Sounds vaguely familiar," he mumbled, more to himself, it seemed, than to me.

I had to steel myself against his pain. "This is not a sustainable solution, Azrael."

His gaze lifted to mine, indignant that I refused to call him any of the *reverent* forms of address. A tense moment passed between us before he wisely decided to let the matter go and turned to hike through the rubble that led to his, surprisingly, still intact desk and chairs.

"Yes, that was becoming glaringly obvious," he says, gesturing vaguely at his appearance. "If I didn't know any better, I'd think the fates had sent her to *hasten* my death... You haven't spoken to her, have you?"

I rear back slightly. "You're asking *me* if I've spoken to Moirai?"

Azrael shakes his head, heaving a great sigh as if realizing what a ridiculous question it was.

Tension radiated throughout my entire body, trying to restrain my magic as I reluctantly sat in the chair opposite him. "Something must be done."

Azrael gave me a rueful smirk. "Should have known you'd take your job too seriously."

Oh dear fuck. Never in all my years had I ever met someone I'd wanted to punch in the face so desperately. *Or so frequently.*

"She's my friend."

Something I didn't dare mistake for compassion flashed across his face before sighing heavily and kicking his feet up on his dust and rubble-strewn desk. His gaze drifted to the shattered window overlooking the barren wasteland that his world had become as a stifling hot breeze rippled the curtains.

"I'll take care of it."

My brows pinched with concern. That had been... *too* easy.

"You'll take care of *it*?"

Azrael waved a dismissive through the air. "*It* as in the problem. I'll resolve it."

"How?"

Azrael jolted upright, removing his feet from his desk to prop up his elbows and bury his face in his hands, muffling his voice. "Does it matter? So long as she's happy?"

"Of course, it matters."

"Gods, you're fussy."

"Azrael."

Azrael rose abruptly, his erratic energy reaching a snapping point, and I got a another glimpse of the god. His voice boomed inside and outside my mind.

"Do not think for a second that just because you have such a rare and formidable power that it means you can challenge me. It would take nothing more than my mere *will* to reduce you to nothing more than photons of light, *boy."*

Instead of fear or reverence, it was pity that suffused me. His ensuing anguish washed over me like acidic sludge. Azrael and I had beaten the shit out of each other on more occasions than I could keep track, but we'd always left our magic out of it, and it had *usually* been during *relatively* friendly sparring sessions. If it came down to our magic... Maybe he was right. There was no way to be sure without unleashing our powers, and I didn't actually want him to die.

Despite my resentment towards him, I still cared deeply for him. He meant well in most cases but was just fucked up and wounded beyond recognition.

My eyes drifted to the half-broken statue of his *soulbound,* Persephone. Her effigy was peppered throughout the entire palace. And yet, she was nowhere to be found. From what I'd gathered, she was living in hiding somewhere without him actually admitting anything. Where, exactly, no one knew, but the longer she was gone, the worse off Azrael and his realms became.

No longer able to tolerate his presence or the misery and fear consuming him, I stood to leave. Pausing in the blown-out doorway, I cast him one last glance, not bothering to mask my concern.

"Just... treat her as you would Persephone, please."

Pain radiated from him directly into my chest as he gave a sardonic laugh. "I can assure you, that's the last thing you would want for your friend."

Anxiety wound through me. *Fuck. I should never have sought him.*

"Can you promise me her happiness? Her safety?"

The in my chest, mirroring Azrael's, dissipated slightly. "Asterion, if anything, she'll be the happiest and *safest* she's ever been."

How the fuck was that possible?

I turned towards him fully, now even more concerned than before, but he'd already *folded* away.

CHAPTER

TWENTY

NAKOA

In the excruciating 4 days it took for the day of my coronation and inauguration, I'd been both dreading and eager to get it over with. Never would I have fathomed that a day would come when I would be *dying* to see Zurie, but I'd long discovered how fate had a way of surprising you.

As for the mother who'd raised me, the distance between us had begun to wear thin. My *olana kah'hei* had been the only buffer to the loneliness creeping in on me. Surprisingly, Malekai had been... *helpful*. A begrudging respect had begun to develop between us, and I'd even come to appreciate his presence.

However, I still couldn't help the bitterness at the fact Mareina was desperately in love with him. As much as I fucking hated it, I'd begun to see how.

There was a private dressing room sequestered high above the throne room where the ceremony was being held. Bernard, Zurie's tailor, had spent the last three days trying to convince me to wear something other than my fighting leathers. My answer still hadn't changed, even as he stared up at me with pleading eyes, holding a bedazzled black and gold suit aloft.

"No."

Pomona, Roderick, and Lokus snickered, drawing both mine and Bernard's glare. Pomona stepped forward, taking in the black and gold monstrosity. The damned thing had woven gold metal and ruby-adorned epaulettes. Billowy black frills even trimmed the cuffs.

First and foremost... *Why?*

"Have I done something to warrant your wrath?"

The question was entirely sincere.

Bernard's face slackened with shock briefly before contorting to restrain the glistening of his eyes.

Oh, fuck.

Pomona administered a reprimanding smack to my arm. *"Nakoa."* She gently took the garment from Bernard. "Ignore him, darling. He's nothing but a curmudgeon, though he means well. I think the suit is a stunning work of art. Pomona threw me another withering glare. "Even if he makes it hard to tell sometimes."

Bernard sniffled, tugging nervously at the fishnet-like train of his pale lilac-colored garment that looked like a cross between a suit and a ballgown. "Thank you, my lady."

Pomona turned and pressed the hideous thing against my chest so firmly it nearly shoved me back an inch. Wordlessly, her gaze held mine as her expression hardened enough to crack. *"If you don't put it on, I'll put it on you."*

Accepting my fate, I sighed in resignation. Pomona gave me a forced smile before turning back towards Bernard. "Thank you *so* much, Bernard. I'd be absolutely honored if you could design something for me as well, though I know it's short notice."

Bernard's face lit up, swiftly wiping at his eyes with a frilly periwinkle sleeve. "Yes, my lady! It would be the work of a moment for me to tailor a gown to fit you." Bundles of fabric began sailing through the air into his arms.

I took that as my opportunity to leave. One of Zurie's servants, Ellora, remained waiting by the door. For what I wasn't sure. I still hadn't adjusted to being waited on hand and foot. "Do you prefer to change in your rooms then, Your Highness? We are running short on time…"

A growl escaped me and Ellora's fair skin paled further, eyes widening in fear. Habit urged me to glamor away my nephilim features to make myself look more fae, but I suppressed it.

No longer would I hide.

I *willed* the frilly suit to replace my fighting leathers and caught a glimpse of myself in the mirror. Val came and stood beside me, both of us staring at my reflection. The suit somehow became even gaudier simply by being worn, even if it was tailored to perfection.

"I look ridiculous."

Val gave a noncommittal grunt. "You look extravagant."

Despite all the wealth my *olana kah'hei* and I had stolen over the years, I hadn't saved all that much for myself or been big on material pleasures outside of striving to make my home the coziest place in all of Bellorum. I'd rarely worn more than simple linen shirts and trousers or fighting leathers.

"I feel like an asshole."

Val smirked. "Aye. That you are."

"Mareina would laugh if she saw me dressed like this."

Val chuckled. "Maybe, but I think it'd endear you to her. She would appreciate you doing something to spare someone's feelin's bein' hurt, and she'd love you all the more for it."

All the emotion I'd been so desperately trying to keep at bay suddenly clogged my throat. At my silence, Val turned to look directly at me, no doubt seeing the ticking of my jaw and my glistening eyes.

"Awe fuck…" Val tugged me into his burly arms and squeezed me against his chest. Just when a fraction of the emotion began to loosen, a knock at the door sounded. Murmuring thanks to Val, I stepped out of his embrace, nodding to Ellora to open the door.

Malekai stood on the other side, dressed in dark brown fighting leathers with simple but beautiful gold embellishments. It made me feel slightly less self-conscious about my own outfit.

Several days of golden-blonde scruff covered his face. His usually unnaturally bright turquoise and gold eyes were now dark and dull, as though some inner light had been snuffed out since Mareina had left with Azrael. He offered me a stiff smile that gentled as he took in my emotional appearance, and understanding passed between us.

His eyes roamed over my gaudy outfit before darting to Bernard, already halfway done with Pomona's gown. When his gaze returned to mine, he gave me a knowing, compassionate grin. "You look great."

Val stepped forward before I could reply, tugging Malekai in a bear hug. "Good ta see ya, mate... Been a minute."

I hadn't told anyone about Malekai's claiming of Mareina. No one, other than myself and probably Miroslav, knew about it. My gaze flicked to Rumiel, frowning at the interaction as his eyes danced between me and Malekai.

Malekai's grin was warm and unrestrained as his arms wrapped firmly around Val, and his relief at the small gesture was palpable. Truly, Val gave hugs worthy of world renown. When they separated, Malekai strode towards me, nervous tension lining his features as he *willed* a small gift into his hands. It even had a bow.

For the first time in too many days, a vision washed over me.

The chamber filled with my loved ones fell away to be replaced by barren land and dead corpses as far as the eye can see—many of them dressed in Atratusian armor—all rotting beneath the heat of five suns, causing sweat to trickle down my back. The sound of flies was a deafening roar.

The vision lifted, and I was left blinking into the faces of Malekai and Val, both wearing furrowed brows.

"Yew ok, lad?"

I nodded, trying to shove away the anxiety of impending doom.

Malekai hesitated for a moment, still holding out the gift.

"Would it be ok if we spoke in private?"

The prospect of clearing the air between us was both a relief and a welcome distraction. I'd come to terms with the fact that Mareina would always love this male, and if I wanted to have any hope of having her in my life, I would need to learn to accept that. Even more so, if I were to have any *joy* in my life, I recognized I needed to form a friendship with this male.

Drawing in a deep breath to cool the anger and jealousy that flared at the mere sight of him, I nodded and even managed to offer him a strained smile.

TWENTY-ONE

MALEKAI

Fuck me, I hadn't been this nervous since the first time I'd had to kill someone.

I could only assume Nakoa knew what had happened between Mareina and I if by no other tell than her scent alone. My guilt had weighed upon me like an anvil on my chest. For him *and* for her.

He was her *soulbound.* Her happiness came above all else. And I had selfishly claimed her as my own without even trying to bring harmony between the three of us.

For the first time since I'd met him, respect for this male blossomed as something resembling a smile tipped up the corners of his mouth as he nodded in ascent, accepting my gift. I imagined it took no small amount of forgiveness not to tear my head from my neck.

Nakoa's brows leapt as he took it in hand, no doubt feeling the power radiating from it.

"I got you a coronation gift," I added, awkwardly speaking the obvious.

"Thank you. That's incredibly generous of you."

You're a better male than me, a small voice inside me whispered silently to him.

He twisted, tossing a glance around the room. "The only private place nearby is the bathroom..."

I nodded, already knowing where it was. The last time I'd been here had been when Mareina had ascended to Zurie's Irae. My gut clenched at the memory as Nakoa led us into the bathroom, drawing everyone's eyes to us.

I quietly shut the door behind us, sealing us off in the small space. Silence wound tight between us, making the room feel more even more cramped than it already was with our large bodies.

We both spoke at the same time, heightening the awkwardness.

"I'd like to—

"I'd like to—

Nakoa gestured for me to continue.

"Look, I... I'm assuming that you're aware of what occurred between Mareina and me recently?"

Nakoa features tightened. "How could I not?"

I nodded, failing to swallow back my guilt. The words burst from me, all at once alleviating a portion of the last several days' worth of anxiety. *"I'm sorry."*

Nakoa remained silent, his expression unreadable.

"I should have come to you first."

Nakoa gradually nodded. "I understand why you didn't... I recognized, far too late, that I allowed prejudice to influence me toward my own *soulbound.* I failed as a mate. I failed to treat her with the reverence and love she deserves, and that's no one's fault but my own. And considering how things ended here when we overcame Zurie..."

Nakoa shook his head, gaze dipping to the floor as his eyes began to glisten. "I'm not sure I'll ever be able to forgive myself."

Nakoa's shame was palpable as his hands fisted at his sides as if to stifle the saline swelling in his eyes. I stepped forward, laying a cautious hand on his shoulder.

"It takes strength and resilience to forgive, and Mareina is the strongest and most resilient person I've ever known. I have no doubt that her love for you won't be burdened by resentment. All we need to do is get her back."

Nakoa's watery gaze held mine, jaw flexing. "You're right. On all counts."

My hand lingered on his shoulder, squeezing, as a tugging in my chest took residence as if I were being pulled toward him with the compulsion to *hug* him.

Nakoa exhaled a deep breath, rubbing his eyes with thumb and forefinger. "Do you prefer I open your gift now, or later?"

My hand released him as the momentary window to embrace him closed. "Now, if you like."

Nakoa tugged the bow loose, unfurling the linen wrapping to reveal my gift. His jaw dropped. I couldn't help but feel a slight swell of pride at his reaction. My beast huffed. Being so possessive over Mareina, he hadn't been entirely on board with my idea.

Nakoa studied me with keen eyes as if somehow seeing *through* me. I could see the question forming on his lips just as someone knocked on the bathroom door, followed by the sound Lokus' voice.

"Are we fucking or fighting because either way, I want in."

Mine and Nakoa's eyes met as we shared a huffed laugh.

A grin split Nakoa's face as he called out his reply. "Sorry, mate. We've run out of lube already."

Oh my gods...

My eyes scanned the floor for my jaw because... *did he just make a joke?*

Surprise had me frozen in place as Nakoa turned his grin on me, softened by sincerity. "Thank you, Malekai. I needed that."

He clapped me on the back as he squeezed past me and opened the door. My eyes flicked to his *olana kah'hei*, all of whom were openly staring. Pomona gave me an excited little wave from where she was perched on the pedestal as Bernard finished her dress. She blushed slightly when I grinned back. Famei huffed a laugh, tilting his head toward me in acknowledgement.

Though I had grown no small amount of affection towards his *olana kah'hei,* I hadn't yet earned their loyalty. Nor Nakoa's, for that matter. The realization that I *wanted* to felt like a slap to the face. The good kind.

Nakoa turned back towards me, holding up my gift. "Would you mind?"

Some strange emotion clogged my throat, forcing me to clear it. "Sure..."

"It's for protection."

Rumiel appeared at the doorway, silent, as per usual, peering down at the gift. His lips parted in surprise before his gaze snapped to mine, and the gratitude lighting them was unmistakable.

I tied the gift around Nakoa's wrist, causing my fingers to brush against his skin, and I swore I felt a current of electricity pass between us that I think we both tried to pretend not to notice.

When Nakoa and his *olana kah'hei* had been ushered on the dais of the throne room, I hadn't anticipated being invited to stand among them. Val and Roderick stood on either side of me, enfolding me into their little group. Rayne, Vesper, and Rumiel stood beside Roderick, and Lokus, Famei, and Pomona stood on the other side of Val. I couldn't help but feel a tendril of imposter syndrome standing here. It had only been a little over two weeks ago that I'd cut part of Nakoa's tail off. Wished him dead. Had taken his *soulbound* as my own.

If I were in his shoes, would I have killed me by now?

For all his gruffness, Nakoa seemed to have a moral compass and self-control that I, undeniably, lacked. He'd given nearly all the riches he'd stolen from those cunt-faced Lords to their servants. I didn't have to wonder if I would have been as magnanimous.

I wouldn't have.

I would have stolen Mareina away to live out our solitude together in peace, and allowed everyone else to get fucked. I tried to console myself with the excuse that those same servants probably would have tried to have me killed if they knew what I really was but no amount of reasoning would alleviate the fact that, unless Mareina was involved, I was an unforgivably selfish male.

Shame settled somewhere in my chest at the realization. For all his faults, *Nakoa was a good male.*

I scanned the mass of people and their magic gathered to witness Nakoa's coronation to check for any treachery among us, as Zurie had warned. I shouldn't have been surprised at all that the *minoris* outnumbered the Lords and Ladies, who all appeared thoroughly unsettled by having to share space with them.

I didn't miss the way some of them sneered at Nakoa in his true form, towering over the old cleric—the same one that had crowned Zurie, apparently. To the cleric's credit, he didn't bat an eye at Nakoa's black twisting horns, his gigantic membranous wings, or the powerful tail swishing restlessly behind him.

The cleric had begun his speech but it all became background noise when my eyes landed on Zurie and Thalia. Her new lover, presumably, that had liberated Zurie of her collar and dungeon cell. I couldn't help but think it peculiar, considering Thalia had initially seemed keen on allying with Nakoa. To go behind his back was an interesting move. Especially now that Zurie had nothing. There seemed very little for Thalia to gain from stealing Zurie away outside of Nakoa's wrath.

As if by nothing more than the weight of my gaze, Zurie's eyes lifted to mine, her pouty lips pursing. I gave her a bored look. When her eyes returned to Nakoa, I continued scanning the crowd. My soldiers lined the walls, standing guard in their finest military uniforms. I made a mental note to speak with them about my faith in our new king.While the announcement of Nakoa's coronation had been so sudden, I had no doubt many of them were relieved by the change. There had always been an undercurrent of resentment towards Zurie.

An all-too-familiar magic radiated from behind the audience, snapping my gaze to a male dressed in the darkest blue silk suit with a fancy sash around his waist. Miroslav's icy gaze flicked to mine, expressionless, as per usual. Admittedly, I was mildly surprised to see him here, hand-in-hand with a female wearing a silky, dark blue hooded cowl.

The sudden roaring applause of the crowd drew my attention as Nakoa bent at the waist and the elderly cleric placed an elaborately wielded gold crown adorned in rubies that matched the epaulettes on his suit. I'd never seen the former King's crown. It looked... *heavy.*

Nakoa murmured something to the cleric, whose face lit up with unmistakable joy before shifting aside as our new King stepped forward.

The hairs on the back of my neck rose as Nakoa's voice rang out like the tolling base of a bell. The crowd hushed, and something crackled in the air. It took me a moment to realize it wasn't even Nakoa's magic. It was simply his commanding presence. I couldn't help but observe him in awe. For a moment, time seemed to slow as I realized that I had been blessed with witnessing some momentous and fortuitous event in history that would change all of our lives.

The harkening of fate.

Of change.

Fuck, if only Mareina were here to witness this.

Longing and worry for her tightened in my chest to the point of pain.

"I am immensely grateful that you all have gathered here to support my ascension of the throne. I vow to spend every day working towards bringing justice and prosperity to each and every one of you.

No longer, will you live in poverty, slaving away under the thumbs of the majori who glut themselves on stolen power. On aetra.

No longer will you live in fear and exile because you have gifts that strike terror into the hearts of those who would seek to either exploit you or kill you."

A great *boom* sounded as Nakoa released his magic into the room and his wings flared wide, spanning over twenty feet across the dais.

Vesper stepped forward, wiping a rogue tear from her eye. Rayne, shortly behind her, stepped forward with writhing shadows that formed into dark, monstrous avatars. The cracking of bone and sinew sounded as Val and Roderick shifted beside me and stepped forward in their gigantic Lykos forms. Rumiel, even taller than his son, boasting his wings, tail, and lethal horns stepped forward. Lokus, Pomona and Famei joined him, looking no less formidable despite not having beastly forms remained shrouded in mystery because no one would be able to discern their gifts.

The beast within me roared in ascent. My bones ached and my skin itched with the need to shift. My heart pounded furiously.

Fuck me, I had so much more in common with Nakoa and his *olana kah'hei* than I'd ever realized.

How had I never realized?

It seemed a sin that we had been at each other's throats, each of us bearing the same burden in more ways than one.

My beast writhed within me to break free, and again, time seemed to slow as a fleeting window of opportunity presented itself.

Nakoa turned his head to lock eyes with me. Though his features remained hard and unreadable, his message was clear: He was waiting for me. Fear chased up my spine. *Never* had I revealed my beast. It had been beaten into me as a child to remain hidden.

To blend in.

I'd been hiding in plain sight my entire fucking life. *As had Nakoa.*

Nakoa's brow tensed as if urging me on, and I didn't miss the disappointment that flashed across his face. As his head began to turn back towards the crowd, my heart cracked and my beast threw itself against the wall I'd built up around him as we watched my window of opportunity begin to close.

No.

Every cell in my body lit up with my magic and that fleeting, searing pain of the shift as I allowed my drakonati to take over. Shouts and cries rang out as my drakonati's head rose high above the crowd. I had to crouch down low so as not to break through the ceiling of the throne room. Lords and Ladies screamed, chairs screeching and toppling as they tried to flee.

Nakoa and his *olana kah'hei* craned their heads to look up at me. With the exception of Nakoa and Rumiel, everyone's jaws dropped.

Nakoa swiftly tucked his wings in close to reveal his monstrous and formidable *olana kah'hei* standing closely behind him. The Lords and Ladies among the crowd began to angrily shout their dissent as my soldiers roared their approval.

Clearly infused with magic, Nakoa's voice boomed throughout the throne room. *"Silence."*

The room grew so quiet you'd have heard a coin drop.

"I welcome those of you who deem me unfit to rule to challenge me."

Nakoa raised a black-clawed hand. *"I'll even do you a favor and glamor away my nephilim form to bolster your courage,"* he called out as his features turned fae, *"but I implore you to ask yourself one question: are you ready to greet Mors?"*

CHAPTER

TWENTY-TWO

NAKOA

I'd chosen to forgo the ritual of hosting a feast after the coronation. It felt *wrong* to celebrate anything without Mareina here. Without her, there was no reason to celebrate, and it had become increasingly obvious to me that I would fail to even become half the king I'd always dreamed of without her at my side.

For the first time since I was a faeling, I woke up in a puddle of my own cum after a dream of Mareina—and sharing her with Malekai—filtered through my still-waking mind. Something within me was still powerfully resistant to the idea, but I also couldn't ignore that something about the idea had begun to feel *right*.

I cleaned myself up, taking a quick shower after opting to pull my own soiled sheets off the bed to spare one of the palace staff the task. As I dressed, my eyes caught on the crown now sitting in an elegantly carved, velvet-lined wooden box. *Waiting.*

Embrace the King you are destined to be, my Knowingness whispered.

Though my guilt had greatly lessened since my conversation with Malekai, a shadow of shame seeped into my veins as my logical

121

mind reminds me of the fact that I disrespected and dishonoured my own *soulbound. Wounded* her on every level. Took advantage of her. And now, because I had endlessly abused her trust, she was gone just as Miroslav had warned.

Desperate to escape the weight settling on my chest, I left the crown in its box as that voice in my head whispered my unworthiness. Perhaps that was why my visions had become so infrequent lately.

I sigh in relief when I hear a knock on the door, a welcome distraction from the glaring reminder of my misdeeds.

Having wanted to avoid guards listening in on me at all hours of the night and day, I opened the door myself to come face to face with Malekai. There was a slight tension between us and I couldn't help but wonder if he'd had the same dream as I did.

Did Mareina share the dream?

"Zurie requested one of the guards fetch you, but I'd heard you'd dismissed them... So I thought it might be better if I came to get you."

His eyes wandered to the bedroom behind me, nostrils flaring before a knowing smirk tipped up a corner of his mouth. The exceedingly unfamiliar sensation of embarrassment had blood rushing to my cheeks. He graciously pretended not to notice and merely clapped me on the shoulder before walking away. "Me too, buddy."

"Hello, Zurie." Zurie's features tensed, mouth curling in a barely-there frown. "Nakoa."

My eyes lifted to Thalia, who gave me a guilt-less smirk that made my hackles rise. "As unseasoned as I may be at this court posturing bullshit, I can't imagine stealing a prisoner is the best way to go about gaining allies."

Thalia's bored look shifted to an entirely different person that took me several moments to recognize.

Keres.

Malekai, who stood beside me, huffed an unimpressed laugh. Rumiel's expression gave nothing away to belie the anger I felt pouring off him in waves. Whether it was towards Keres and Zurie, or just Zurie, I had no idea.

I could only manage a sigh, exhausted beyond caring at this point. All I wanted was Mareina back. "I need you to open the portal to Azrael's realm. To Vassileo."

Zurie's face scrunched up in disbelief. "What in *Akash's* name for? It's a chain of hell realms."

I reached out with my Knowingness to see whether there was any note of deception or if Zurie was merely pretending to be unaware that Azrael had taken Mareina to Vassileo. To my utter surprise, I found none.

Malekai and I exchanged a look before I spoke, giving him the chance to stop me from speaking the truth.

"Because Mareina went there with Azrael. "

Zurie's lips parted, eyes rounding slightly as she opened her mouth to speak, but Keres laid a hand on her forearm to give her pause.

"Willingly?"

"Yes."

Keres and Zurie exchange a look that tells me they're already aware of Azrael's problem.

Shaking her head in disbelief, Keres frowns up at me. "Even *if* Zurie opened one of the portals, how in the fuck do you actually expect to convince Azrael to let her go. He'll kill you. He's one of the most powerful gods ever to exist. His power rivals that of a Primal. He basically *is* a primal."

By allowing his godsforsaken denizens into our realm. It went against everything I'd ever believed in. Everything I'd thrown in Mareina's face and led her to believe.

But it felt careless to give Zurie the *entire* truth. My expression hardened at the lie forming on the tip of my tongue, but before it could breach my lips, Zurie's face paled in realization.

"You plan to let his people in..."

Keres snorted a derisive laugh. "*Akash almighty*. You've been King for a day and you're already putting your own needs over the needs of your citizens? How very typical. I'd actually had high hopes for my niece's *soulbound*."

Malekai's growl was utterly inhuman, a mirror to my own anger. It twined with guilt that welled up inside of me at just how right she was.

Keres rolled her eyes. "*Down drakonati*. I didn't say *no*. I just want to ensure you know how it will look to your people. There'll be a revolt. You'll be hated. There'll be assassination attempts... By saving her, you're dooming yourself."

Her words only further steeled my resolution. "If I don't save her, I'm already doomed."

Zurie looked ill. Perhaps her withdrawals were returning. It couldn't possibly be empathy eating her alive as she stared at some distant corner. When her eyes lifted to mine, the determination in them was unmistakable.

"Blame it on me."

Shock suffused me, and I scoured her for signs of deception. How could this possibly be of benefit to her... The female was a snake in the grass. A duplicitous, deceitful, highborn wench of the highest order. She reached out to grab my forearm but then stopped herself.

"They already hate me. Even my allies hate me. It makes no difference, but *you* have a chance. The people love you already. You saw them out there. Don't throw it away. Tell them Azrael paid me or something; it doesn't matter. And then when Azrael's citizens arrive, you can save them. Again. As you are destined to."

Emotion swelled in my chest.

You will not cry. You will not cry. You will not *cry.*

I cleared my throat, scrubbing a hand down my face. Gratitude washed over me as Malekai clapped a hand on my shoulder. "Sounds good to me. He agrees, don't you, *your majesty?*"

Relief and gratitude washed over me for the male and his

attempt to draw their attention. If I'd had to speak, all that would have come out was a choked sob on the word *mommy*.

I cleared my throat, managing a nod, as my eyes darted away.

"You'll have to come with us... In case we can't find Azrael. To open the portal again," Malekai added.

Zurie nodded in affirmation despite being sheet white.

"For whatever solution he's discovered in bringing her there, he won't let her go. You know that right?"

I buried my rising panic. The words feel lame even to my own hears. "His original request was that we allow his people in... It was Mareina's suggestion that she stay there with him to bolster the barriers between our realms. To spare us from the havoc his people would cause."

Zurie's gaze wavered, likely recognizing that she'd never sacrificed herself for her people as Mareina had. Her words came out softer than I thought her capable.

"He's a dying god with a dying realm, Nakoa. If Azrael agreed to her staying there, it's because it's of greater benefit to him. The only hope you have of getting her back is either by stealth or force."

Azrael's words echoed in my mind.

'... *We would have to create a syphon to drain your power...*'

"So be it."

Keres sighed heavily, speaking to no one in particular. "*Fuck me, this is gonna be terrible. You do realize that, don't you?*"

TWENTY-THREE

KERES

Much to our surprise, Nakoa had invited Zurie and I to stay in her old rooms. He'd chosen to remain in the palace's North Wing where his *olana kah'hei* had taken residence. Zurie seemed a little shaken up by the time we returned to her old rooms. My brow knitted as I watched her distant eyes scan her room, which had remained basically untouched. I rounded her, slipping a comforting hand over her shoulder. "You ok?"

Zurie's face grew flushed, trembling with emotion. *"I'm scared."*

That violent and vengeful thing in me awakened, promising death to any who threatened her. I was still reeling from the fact that this female, the first in over a thousand years—since Soteira—had somehow managed to steal my heart. And in such a short period of time, no less.

My reply was ridiculously gentle. I hardly recognized my own voice.

"Of what, darling?"

Zurie bit a pouty lip as if it could hold back the sob I could see was intent on being set free. "Have you been to Vassileo?"

A tear streaked down her cheek, punctuating the question, and I couldn't resist the opportunity to snatch it up for myself. I pulled her against me, relishing the way her body instantly relaxed, and I leaned in to kiss it away.

"No, but I have visited other hells. I can't imagine they're much different."

"I've been such a lazy, selfish, terrified fool all these years, and now I feel as though it's all catching up with me. The last time I even stepped foot out of this palace was at least a hundred years ago. More, probably. Much more. I can't even fucking remember it. And do you know why?"

Her gaze held so much remorse and shame as she stared up at me. "Because I'm a coward. My entire life, my family plotted against one another. Against me. Against everyone. I'd always innately assumed that it would be the same with *everyone*. On the rare occasion the loneliness had become too much to bear, and I'd throw the occasional feast or ball, there was always an attempt on my life... And now, after all this—a lifetime of *fear*—I'm going to die in Vassileo. I know it."

I tucked away a stray piece of Zurie's ash-blonde hair behind her ear. "Remind me, my love, what happened to them?"

Zurie's brow pinched, and she looked so fucking beautiful *and* adorable I could scarcely breathe. "They died?"

I chuckled softly, grazing my nose across her rosy cheeks to take in her scent before pressing a kiss to each one. *"You killed them.* Not your guards or anyone else. *You did.* Every last one of them."

Even outside of what Zurie had told me over the last few weeks, I'd heard numerous stories about her and her ruthlessness over the years. Admittedly, the female had always piqued my interest, but I'd been so focused on Soteira that the thought of actually connecting with her had never even crossed my mind.

Zurie's eyes frantically searched mine.

"You're a survivor, my love. And if anyone dares to judge you for the way in which you've done so, I will gladly mete out judgement upon them with..."

I leaned in again, grazing my lips across hers as I punctuated each of my words with a tender kiss to her lips and jaw.

"My bare..."

Kiss.

"Fucking..."

Kiss.

"Hands..."

Kiss.

"As I tear their throats out."

I drew back to see Zurie's reaction. Her tears had stopped, and her pupils were blown wide with desire. I greedily filled my breast with the scent of her arousal as a grin curled my lips.

Zurie's voice was little more than a moan of need. *"Fuck, I love you."*

CHAPTER

TWENTY-FOUR

ZURIE

Never in my life had I felt so seen. So appreciated. So understood. *So loved.* At my words, my mouth crashed down to Keres'. I took her lip between my teeth, biting hard enough to draw blood so I could suck it away. Moaning my pleasure as I sucked it into my mouth and released it with a loud *pop*. She fisted the front of my dress, groaning into our kiss before hastily pulling back. "How much do you like this dress?"

It was perhaps the most beautiful dress Bernard had ever made for me. I grinned against her lips. *"Burn it for all I fucking care."*

Keres chuckled against me as she tore the silk panelling in half. My palm-sized breasts jiggled at the sudden motion.

"So fucking perfect," she whispered reverently as she knelt, tearing the skirting open. Her lips parted in awe as she discovered I'd worn no undergarments. Silk pooled around my feet as Keres' hands skated upwards, and she gently buried her face between my thighs, taking in another lungful of my scent.

"Godsdamnit, where have you been all my life?" she growled.

My heart clenched with an emotion I hadn't felt since Rumiel.

"Hiding," I whispered.

Keres looked up then, wearing more adoration than I'd ever seen directed at me. Adoration I hadn't earned or deserved, but I was too unfathomably selfish and starving to entertain the idea of denying my heart what it wanted.

"You never have to hide from me."

"I'm a monster, Keres."

"Oh, but darling, I wouldn't want you any other way."

Keres stood, picking me up like I weighed nothing and tossed me on the bed before climbing over me. Fisting my hair in her hand to bare my neck. "I want you to be mine, Zurie. Only mine. Tell me you want the same."

My heart swelled with so much love for her that it pressed upon my throat. And it was nothing short of terrifying. Anytime I'd ever give my heart to someone, it had only ever ended up broken beyond repair. My voice wavered, and I failed to stifle the tremble of my bottom lip. I'd never felt as vulnerable as I did in that moment.

"I already am."

Keres searched my eyes as if waiting for a *but* to follow. I had none. Irrevocably, this female had stolen every wretched part of me, and for the first time in all my years, something new and innocent and beautiful began to blossom.

Her lips upon mine felt like glorious nature reclaiming and infusing new life into the dead and decaying.

Keres willed away the flowing dark red, one-piece silk garment that I'd had Bernard make for her. It had been billowy enough to give the illusion of being a dress but actually had pant legs, as was her preference. I'd instructed him to make it backless *and* low-cut because I longed to devour her every moment of every day, even if it was only with my eyes.

Most of our *joinings* had been rough and passionate, but what we shared had turned into something else. Something tender and unspeakably beautiful. Something both of us had always longed for but never had.

Keres' lips and tongue teased my already sore nipples to needy points as she expertly worked my clit with a teasing caress of her fingers. "My greedy heart wants to hear you say it, love…"

My hips writhed as that coiling, tingling energy approached its peak under her ministrations. *"I'm yours, Keres."*

"Such a good girl," she whispered against my throat as her fangs lengthened to sharpened points. "I'm going to mark you now…"

My orgasm felt like the birth of a thousand stars. *"Gods, yes."*

Keres' fangs sank deep into the delicate flesh of my neck, igniting something deep within my soul.

Each gulp of my blood was mirrored in the pulse in my clit as my orgasm continued to work its way through me. She released her bite only when the last of my orgasm passed, and as its haze lifted, the need to claim her in return *burned*.

It felt like nothing short of a privilege to push this goddess on her back, to part her thighs, and gaze down at her pink, *wet* perfection. To witness her vulnerability. To receive her love.

I licked up every drop of delicious arousal dripping from her entrance before gently sucking her clit into my mouth as I slid two fingers inside of her to tease a spot I'd come to know well. I pressed upon the soft area just above her pelvis as I stroked the inner wall parallel to it, and my tongue flicked steadily against her clit.

The soft little cries and moans spilling from Keres' throat, coupled with the wet noises of my fingers working her pussy was enough to have my own core clenching with need again. In under two minutes, her tight channel was spasming. Fluid rushed out of her, and I drank every fucking drop.

My fangs weren't nearly as long as hers, but they were just as sharp. Before her orgasm waned fully, I made my mark against the thick flesh of her inner thigh. Keres whimpered as the fierce clenching of her core renewed. *"I love you."*

TWENTY-FIVE

MAREINA

I'd been less resistant this time when Asterion had urged me to feed. The effects of his blood were unlike anything I'd ever experienced before. I'd been dying to ask, but the male seemed so plagued by whatever was already going on inside his mind that I couldn't bring myself to add to it by potentially stirring up the long-buried emotions tied to his origins.

This time, I'd managed to feed from him without tearing out any chunks of flesh, and we'd both dutifully suppressed the symptoms my venom induced. For the first time since I'd arrived to Vassileo, I felt some modicum of peace.

Asterion and I laid on the couch in one of my rooms, reading together with my head at one end and his head at the other, and our legs comfortably twined together. The comfort, intimacy—however platonic—and familiarity of the position managed to reduce the constant pain in my chest and the tether between me and my mates to a dull, throbbing ache.

The book I'd managed to dig up in Azrael's library was breathtakingly licentious and proved a worthy distraction from my recent celibacy.

The presence of one of Azrael's palace staff had Asterion and I peeking over the tops of our books at one another. At the sound of their knock, I called them in.

A hooded figure appeared, reminding me somewhat of my father's *Pharalaki*. Except, apparently, these ones could speak. And in a surprisingly feminine voice.

"His Majesty requests your presence in his study."

Well, that's a first.

Since I'd arrived, I'd barely seen the male.

My gaze slid back to Asterion, whose brows were now lowered with unmistakable concern, instantly winding the tension in my chest. "I'll come with you."

"I don't think I'll ever get used to these statues…," I remarked, gazing up at the towering stone effigies lining every—single—wall. All of depicting the same female. Asterion gave a noncommital grunt, throwing the statues a cursory glance before his gaze returned to the palace staff member leading us to Azrael's study.

"Do you know who it is? Are they sculptures of someone real or…?"

"They're of his *soulbound.*"

My brows leapt. "Where is she?"

Asterion shrugged a single shoulder, the thing bigger than my actual head. "No idea."

Ouch. I rubbed absently at my chest, just above where the rhyton was buried, as the pain in my chest burned anew at the reminder of my own soulbound.

I shifted my gaze from the creepy effigies to Asterion. The male was, at the best of times, *dour.* But this? The rigidity of his muscles, the tension carving into every feature? Was definitely not the norm.

"Are you ok?"

Asterion's gilded gaze snapped to mine. "Yeah, why?"

"Ever since Azrael sent for me, your scowl's become…. significantly more *scowl-ly*."

A corner of Asterion's mouth quirked, relieving a fraction of the tension in his features. When he held out his hand, I placed mine in his, and he tugged me into his side. "Sorry. I just… anything that involves Azrael puts me on edge. *Azrael* puts me on edge."

Before I could ask him to elaborate, we arrived at a set of open doors, and our escort gestured for us to go in before they turned and left.

Asterion and I entered the study, far cozier than I'd have anticipated, to find the god himself sitting in a chaise longue reading near a crackling hearth. Thanks to his magic, the temperature inside his palace was crisp. A surprisingly delicate ceramic tea set decorated with flowers and vines sat on the low table in front of him. His gaze lifted from the book in his hand, bearing a title I couldn't read. "Oh good, thank you for joining me."

As we sat down on a couch across from him, Asterion promptly tucked me under his arm, and I couldn't help but feel as if he was protecting me from something. From Azrael.

"What's going on?"

Azrael replied with an enigmatic smile, eyes shifting between the two of us. "You two have grown close."

At my wary silence, Azrael continued. "I'm told you've been unwell."

My head turned to Asterion, failing miserably to hide the guilty look on his face. Gradually, my eyes return to Azrael. "I'm fine."

Unconvinced, Azrael studied me for several moments. "Well, that's a relief. I know you've been burdened with a lot since arriving… Tea?"

This is fucking weird.

Azrael gestured at the teapot, already pouring himself a cup. A dark, purple-y, red liquid pours from the spout, boasting tendrils of steam. The scent of ripe, tangy berries filled my nose, and my mouth instantly began to salivate.

"Yes, please."

Azreal quirks a brow. "Asterion?"

Asterion narrowed his eyes for a moment before scrutinizing Azrael, before finally sighing and relaxing a little as he leaned back into the couch. His protective arm slid off my shoulders. "Fine."

Azrael passed both of us our teas before taking another gulp of his.

"How have my people been treating you?"

Why even bother asking? I sighed around a gulp of what was perhaps the best tea I'd ever tasted in my entire life as the flavor of summer berries burst upon my tongue.

"They keep me well fed."

Azrael smiled bitterly, studying me as I took another delicious sip of tea. "You've sent more people to the chasm in the few months you've been here than I have in at least a millennia... There are faster ways to kill me, you know."

Numbness slid through my veins like ice water as dizziness overtook me. Asterion's hand shot out to yank me backwards, preventing me from crashing face-first onto the coffee table. *"Mareina..."*

Asterion's gold eyes glowed brightly before their light began to flicker, and his body swayed forward before Azrael lept up just in time to tilt his body backwards, where he sagged into the couch beside me.

I opened my mouth to ask my friend if he was alright, but his name got lost on the tip of my tongue. My eyes took in our surroundings, landing on the male sitting in front of us sipping tea.

"Truly, I am sorry about this. You've given me no choice."

Anxiety was a crushing weight upon my chest when I tried to sit up and realized I couldn't.

"What's happening?"

"Currently, you and your friend here are experiencing the symptoms of a little cocktail I made just for you two. The first is Mortsbane. Lethal to a human, but only causes a lapse in motor function for a brief period of time and nullifies magic in immortals. Even those as powerful as yourself," he adds, eyes dipping to Asterion, "The second, is the River Oblivion."

River Oblivion, River Oblivion, River Oblivion, River Oblivion.

I chanted the name inside my head like a prayer, hoping it would tell me what it meant.

"Difficult to procure, but highly effective."

"You *poisoned* me?"

Azrael tsked. "Nonsense. If I wanted you dead, you'd be dead. What I want is for you to forget. Not everything, mind you. Hence only giving you a single drop. *I'm not a monster.* I just need you to be less... *volatile.* I want you to be happy. And, as I very well know, that's an awful lot to ask of someone mourning the absence of their *soulbound.*"

Images flashed in my mind of Nakoa and Malekai, their faces and all our memories slipping away like water through a sieve. Tears sprung to my eyes. The word was a tremulous whisper.

"No..."

Azrael frowned. "Mareina, be reasonable. You'll be happier spending eternity here if you don't have them holding you back."

Never in my life had I begged, but I didn't dare hesitate now.

"Please, no..."

Azrael's eyes glistened as he held my gaze and stood, stepping around the table to sit down beside me. "I envy you, Mareina. All the pain and longing that's been weighing you down since you arrived will be gone. You'll be happy now. You're *free.*"

Watery rage streamed down my face as I tried to lift my arms so I could wrap my hands around Azrael's thick fucking neck and watch that burning light fade from his eyes. Instead, I only managed the twitching of my fingers. Azrael's eyes dipped to my hands at the action. "... You'll be right as rain by morning."

Azrael leaned in, sniffing at my neck briefly before sitting back up.

"Fuck. I can still smell that *Akash*-forsaken drakonati on you."

Drakonati? Realization hit me like a sledgehammer, and a new kind of pain pierced my heart. That's what Malekai had been hiding all these years. *Why would he hide it from me?*

Not that it mattered now.

Azrael willed a glowing vial into one of his palms, uncorking it with unseen hands. Pale blue glowing fluid defied gravity, streaming into the air, rippling until each droplet trembled and the light illuminating it began to *separate* from the fluid itself. Azrael murmured in a language I couldn't understand that seemed to guide the light towards me. A scream tore from my throat as it disappeared beneath my skin, burning like white-hot fire before dissipating.

My breaths came in short, quick pants as sweat trickled on my brow. Something felt wrong. *Empty.* And yet, I couldn't place what it was.

A male sitting beside me sniffed my neck, growling his displeasure. "It'll have to do."

I willed my stubborn limbs to move but they remained fixed in place.

His fingers grazed my throat, frowning, and a moment later, I felt the distinct tingling, itching sensation of a glamor setting into place. "Can't have these anymore, now can we?"

My words were a slur, my tongue uncooperative. I had no idea who the male in front of me was, but some innate hatred towards him burned bright. Inherently sensed that this wrongness writhing inside me was because of him.

"One day... I'm going... to... kill... you."

Azrael gave me a sad smile.

"Perhaps, one day, I'll let you."

CHAPTER
TWENTY-SIX
AZRAEL

Inhale for thirteen, exhale for thirteen.
Inhale for eight, exhale for eight.
Inhale for five, exhale for five.
Inhale for three, exhale for three.
Inhale for two, exhale for two.
Inhale for one, exhale for one.

The *vortex breath,* thanks to the Hindu Pujari I'd met on Terrenea, I'd learned the quickest way to reach Somnus, God of Dreams, and pretty much all things regarding the subconscious mind. It was the work of a few moments for my mind to slide deep enough into a meditative state to reach out to him via my subconscious. I guided my mind to linger on the male as my mind slipped further into the unconscious realms.

Somnus was already there waiting for me, starry eyes and all. Though the cosmos whirling in his black eyes did nothing to soften his hardened features.

"Never, in all my years, have I met such a conniving—

Fuck.

I willed myself calm. It was hard to keep mental barriers intact when you were half asleep. And if I let my impatience or anger get the best of me, I'd be swiftly returned to my physical body.

"Before you get all judgy, *brother*—

"*Would-be brother-in-law*—

I rolled my eyes, mentally taking deep breaths to remain calm. "Potato-tomato."

Somnus' eyes narrow. "I believe you mean, *po-tay-tow, po-tah-tow.*"

Deep breath in, deep breath out. Gooz-frah-bah-and-what-not.

"*You know precisely what I fucking mean,*" I snapped.

"What do you want, Azrael? You can't possibly be daft enough to ask for my help when you've just—

"I know where your *soulbound* is."

Somnus' eyes narrowed with suspicion before his features slackened in realization. Something sinister took hold of his expression, and he stepped toward me, holding my gaze and luring me into his realm via the twin portals of his eyes. His magic, carrying both the soothing calm and the *weight* of all the oceans in all the realms, pressed against the barriers of my mind.

"You would dare withhold my soulbound from me?"

Oh fuck. I'd forgotten how powerful he was. The male was calm and otherwise, so benevolent and kind that he could easily be underestimated. And if it weren't for the thick muscular sinew of his tall body, perhaps even mistaken for weak. If I allowed him to continue, he would easily break through the barriers protecting my mind from him and steal my only bargaining tool.

Or discombobulate my psyche into mush. I imagined it would take exceedingly little effort for him to have me drooling on myself and babbling like an infant if he so wished.

Sweat trickled down my back as I gripped hold of the cord binding his soul to his corporeal form and gave it a firm *yank.* He stumbled forward, glaring up at me as he caught himself.

"You would do the same if it meant finding *your* soulbound."

Somnus' jaw feathered. Even he, one of the most morally upright beings I'd ever known, had a dark side that could be easily ensnared when using the right bait.

What wouldn't *we do for those we love?*

"What favor do you ask of me?"

I heaved a sigh of relief. I hadn't been entirely sure he'd be agreeable, being so... righteous and all.

"I need you to alter a few memories."

"You've dosed them with the River Oblivion, I'm not a fucking miracle worker."

"Just a drop! It'll be easy for you to rearrange things and erase a few... *people.*"

Somnus remained silent for several moments, burning a hole through my face with his judgemental gaze that.

"You're a sick fuck, you know that?"

"Mmmm, yes... And you're going to do my bidding so you can unite with your own *soulbound.* What does that make you?"

"Guilty."

I gave him a saccharine smile. "I'm *so* happy we're on the same page, darling."

"You realize the River Oblivion's effects are only temporary for a god, don't you?"

"Which is precisely why I've summoned you. *You're* going to make her forget all about her *soulbound* and that meddling *drakonati* she's chosen as a mate so she can live in fucking peace for once in her *Akash*-forsaken life."

Somnus quirked a bitter brow at me. "Projecting, are we?"

I heaved a sigh, rolling my eyes. The male was infuriatingly astute.

"Projecting, are we?" I parroted in a mocking tone.

Somnus stared at me, unsmiling.

"As you already know, *our* niece is sound asleep, as is Asterion, making them ripe for all your mental tinkering and altering so that I can get back to finding *my* soulbound."

Somnus' glare hardened further.

"You're putting her at risk. It could fracture her mind. There are too many traumatic memories embedded within her subconscious and inextricably *tied* to other people. If she'd been living under a rock, then it might be a simple task—but you're asking me to alter the last hundred years of her history, in addition to major events not only in her life but in the world at large. *Anyone* could come along and reveal the truth. *Like overthrowing Zurie—*

I groaned my frustration, waving a dismissive through the air. This male was one of the most powerful gods in existence.

"Can't you just... remove her from the equation?"

"As in, she wasn't the one who usurped her?"

"No one here even knows anything about Atratusian politics. When she came here, Nakoa hadn't even taken the throne. Wouldn't it make sense to just... erase all of it? Alter her memories so that she reunited with her father after all these years and was finally able to abandon her duties with Zurie, stayed in Avernus with her father and mother after meeting them?"

Somnus scowled. "Keres *killed* her mother, remember?"

"All the better to make it so that it never happened! She no longer has to mourn her!"

"And if she has no mates to protect, why would she even agree to go with you?"

"First of all, *she* suggested it. And it wasn't merely to protect her mates but all of Bellorum and Avernus. She's proven to be quite the martyr."

Somnus shook his head at me, wearing a look of damning disappointment. "Do you honestly intend on keeping her in *hell? Forever?* I *know* you Azrael. Not even *you* are that cruel."

I swallow back the guilt burning in my chest like fucking bile.

"You're gravely mistaken if you think so highly of me because that's exactly what I intend to do. It may have been her idea initially, but her power is *breathtaking*. Even *with* her slaughtering my denizens in droves, I can feel my realm *healing*. The very fabric holding together my realms grows strong by the day. I'm afraid I can't let her leave."

Somnus' expression remained so blank that I couldn't help but wonder if he'd even heard me. If his mind had drifted back off to wherever his physical body was.

"You're making a mistake, Azrael."

"Well, it's not too late for me to pour a cupful of the River Oblivion down her throat and make her forget *everything*. I was trying to do this the *compassionate* way. I could have done what Keres did to your brother and just dump her body on a beach somewhere."

Somnus frowned, finally giving me a reaction. "You're also forgetting the fact that Avernus will fall apart without her or Mors there."

Massaging my temples between thumb and forefinger, I heaved a longsuffering sigh. "*So, find Mors.* You're boring me with this minutiae, Somnus. Congratulations. *I'm fucking bored.* Now, do you want your *soulbound* or not? If I were you, I'd hurry the fuck up because her life may or may not depend on it."

Somnus *growled*. The male was normally so well-mannered and self-restrained that I couldn't recall having ever heard him growl.

"*If you lay a single one of your filthy, degenerate, fucking fingers on her, I swear to Akash that I will turn your mind into fucking soup and burn all your realms to the fucking ground.*"

I laid an affable hand on his shoulder. "You know how much I love soup, darling. Don't tempt me."

Somnus' gaze slid to the offending hand as if I'd flung shit on his shoulder, turning his back on me and striding into the darkness. "Meet me here tonight. By the time you go to sleep, it'll be done. And I expect my *soulbound* to be happy, healthy, and *safe*."

Oh, my dear, sweet, sweet, Somnus. You're much too late for that.

I blew out a helpless breath, recalling his words.

"*I'm not a miracle worker,*" I shouted to his back as his form began to fade. Somnus tossed me one last glance, filled with promised vengeance before he disappeared entirely.

TWENTY-SEVEN

MAREINA

The sensation of a large, muscular body pressing against mine registered in my mind, gently stirring my consciousness. Calloused fingers grazed along the peaks and valleys of my curves. My heart swelled with love and comfort for which I'd always longed. *"Lohane thili,"* a distant but familiar, gravelly, baritone voice whispered against my forehead.

Soulbound.

My breath caught in recognition, and I opened my eyes to find the scarred face of a male my mind couldn't place, but without a doubt, my soul *knew.* My heart swelled to bursting with love for this male whose name I couldn't recall. Not a scrap of fabric separated my body from his as he rolled me on my back and settled himself between my legs. Despite the fact that his remarkably long, thick, and perfectly sculpted cock was nestled firmly against my dripping entrance, regret lined every single of his handsome features. "I never told you I love you, Mareina."

Emotion swelled in my chest, clogging my throat as the male's eyes glistened with a sadness that mirrored my own. *"I'm so fucking sorry."*

Long hands cradled my head as he bowed forward to kiss away my tears. "I have loved you from the moment I laid eyes on you, *maha loha.* And I'm so fucking sorry for everything I've done to make you doubt that."

Without knowing how or why, my reply slipped free and this strange male that my soul knew pressed his forehead to mine. *"I love you in this life and every life to come."*

My eyes slid shut in ecstasy as his fingers carded through my hair, gripping tightly as his body grew tense with restrained emotion. Warm droplets tickled and slid over the curve of my neck where he buried his head. Shifting his hips, his cock stroked through my folds and against my clit, illuminating every molecule in my body.

My hands slid into his hair—now suddenly shorter. The love swelling in my chest doubled as the male holding me against him pulled back slightly, and his hand fisted my hair, baring my throat to him. I opened my eyes to find the male with dark hair and scarred features now replaced by a male with golden-blonde hair and turquoise eyes. His breath punched out of him as he took in my features; he somehow looked more shocked to see me than I was to have this stranger pressed between my thighs. *"Tessari mú."*

My treasure.

The words and their translation filled my mind like a beacon of light as my soul *sang* at the sight of him, chanting over and over, '*I love you,*' wholly unconcerned by the fact that his name eluded me.

Guilt fisted my heart as anger and hurt hardened his features. The deep velvet of his voice was filled with wounded accusation.

"You left us."

My breath caught. Crushing remorse suffused me despite having no idea why. My mind felt like it was trying to wade through an impenetrable wall of fog.

Those glittering turquoise and gold eyes dipped to where his enormous cock laid against my clit. His hips slid forward, making my own give an involuntary twitch. Taking his cock in his hand, a breathy moan left me as he swept the head through my slick folds. The action made my legs part further and my back arch. His eyes lifted back to mine. "Look at the mess you're making, *tessari mú.*"

I propped myself up on my elbows to peer between us just before he *slapped* my clit with the steel-hard length of him. The clear, gooey wetness of my arousal strung between us. "See how desperately you need us?"

His gaze returned to mine. "Or do you need me to remind you?"

My breath caught as I watched his length slide against me, making my needy pussy clench around nothing. "Perhaps I should punish you, hm?"

The male aligned his length with my entrance, slowly pushing in, and I gasped at the tight, stretching invasion. My core spasmed around him, causing him to give a low growl. His hips pulsed in slow, shallow movements that rubbed his thick crown against the shallow pleasure center inside of me. He spat a wad of saliva onto my clit and stroked his thumb through the mess, making my cunt clench tight with need.

His movements stilled, a wicked grin curling a corner of his mouth to reveal a dimple. "Only good girls get to come when they want, Mareina. You know better."

The male's words were like an incantation that summoned liquid heat to trickle from between my legs. Stepping off the side of the four-post bed, he slowly slid out of me, making me whimper at the loss. His gaze was ruthless as he gave me a nod of encouragement.

"On your knees, Kalini."

I bade his command and knelt in front of him, presenting my backside and dripping wet pussy to him. He gave a vicious growl at the sight, swiping a thumb against my entrance. When I glanced back, I found him licking my arousal from his thumb. Halfway through the motion, a feline grin curled his lips as he leaned forward to fist my hair and murmur in my ear.

"Swallow every inch of his dick and show us how pretty you can cry."

His gaze lifted higher to something or *someone* in front of me. I faced forward to find the male with the scarred features standing at the edge of the bed, mere inches away. Black, twisting horns now crowned his head, and gigantic black and brown membranous wings stretched wide. My lips parted in awe as they stared down at me with a look that promised retribution.

Something warm and thick brushed against my throat before caressing my unhinged jaw. My eyes were so fixed to the male's face that I hadn't noticed his tail. Though I did *not* miss the near-forearm-sized length he was stroking.

"If you're a good girl, maybe I'll choke you. Would you like that, *lohane thili?*"

Gods, yes.

The scarred male's tail wrapped around my throat, squeezing lightly, as the blonde male's cock slowly began to push into my entrance. A sighed moan escaped me, and when I failed to heed his demand, the male behind me wrapped his fist in my hair and pulled me flush against his chest as he continued to thrust inside me in firm, steady strokes. His voice was a growl with barely restrained power. "I want you to take both our cocks, Mareina. Show us how fucking sorry you are. I want you to fucking *beg.*"

Sorry for what, my mind couldn't seem to place, but it was then I realized the crushing weight on my chest was *guilt.*

Something inside me burned with the need and desire to do exactly that. I didn't see so much as I felt the two males' eyes meet. "I want her just like that, Malekai."

Malekai... A sense of inner knowing washed over me at the sound of his name. *So why can I not tie a single memory to him?*

The scarred one tucked his wings in tight before stepping on top of the bed, bringing my face nearly parallel with the thick length dripping pre-cum on the sheets. Still fisting my hair, *Malekai* collected my wrists in one hand, pinning them against my lower back as the pace of his thrusts slowed.

Holding the scarred one's gaze, I opened my mouth, extending my tongue in invitation. He took me by surprise when after sucking on his cheeks, he spit a wad of saliva onto the flat of my tongue. The sensation of *rightness* washed over me as I swallowed.

"Good fucking girl," Malekai growled in my ear just as the scarred one bent forward, capturing my throat in one of his large hands, and brought his lips to mine in a bruising kiss. The pace and fervor of his thrusts increased, causing wet slapping noises to fill the air.

The male in front of me cut off our kiss. Black iris-less eyes held mine as he stood upright and aligned his cock with my mouth. What sounded like a cross between a growl and a purr resonated from his chest as he slowly began to thrust in and out of my mouth and my throat.

Garbled moans of pleasure left me as drool seeped from the corners of my mouth. With both of their hands fisting my hair, their thrusts turned brutal, and *overwhelm* began to leak from my eyes as I held the scarred one's gaze.

A large mirror appeared, hovering perpendicular to us and endowing us with a view of our debauchery as Malekai's voice took on a hardened, cruel edge that, for all his inexplicable familiarity, sounded entirely foreign.

"Look at what a beautiful fucking mess you are, Mareina. See how perfectly we ruin you. You belong to us."

I could scarcely breathe, yet my pussy still spasmed with my rapidly approaching orgasm. Malekai's hand released my wrists and came down, smacking my clit *hard.* "Did we say you could fucking cum?"

His fangs sink into the flesh where my shoulder met my neck. White hot pain lit every one of my senses on fire, only ebbing when he started to drink. Malekai groaned around his mouthful.

As if in synchronicity, both of their strokes slowed. I felt his venom seep into me, painful at first, before it dissipated, replaced with desperate arousal. His free hand travelled up my side to my breast, pinching at the hardened, aching peak. My core gripped Malekai's think length again as I cried and whimpered around the cock buried in my throat. The male in front of me withdrew finally, giving me a chance to take gasping breaths. Saliva strung between my mouth and his length, dripping onto my breasts and lubricating exactly where Malekai was teasing my nipples as he drank my blood.

Both males growled their pleasure at my begging.

"Please... Please, please, please, please, please."

The male in front of me brought his tail forward to swipe through my spit and brought it to my clit, bending forward to lick away my tears and murmuring blessed words against my lips. *"Come for us, lohane thili."*

When his tongue sought mine in a sensual caress, I was already cumming so powerfully that if Malekai weren't clutching me against his chest, I'd collapse.

The scarred male broke our kiss and stood upright to return his length to my mouth. With a breathy sigh of pleasure, my lips and tongue travelled the length of his cock. In need of my worship, I murmured my praise before attempting to force him down my throat.

I gagged around him, making my pussy clench hard. Malekai released my throat, and his strokes turned punishing.

Gingerly curling his fingers around the back of my neck, the male in front me increased the pace of his thrusts to match Malekai's. His cock thickened further, again in synchronicity with Malekai, whose hand pushed away the tail to stroke my clit himself. Another orgasm ripped through me as their cocks pulsed inside of me.

Fresh tears bloomed as the male in front of me held my gaze, and the three of us cum in unison, and I knew without a doubt that my heart was fuller than it had ever been.

"Remember that I love you, Mareina."

TWENTY-EIGHT

MAREINA

"You look lovely this morning." I turned away from the mirror to find Azrael standing in the doorway, dressed sharply in the modern-fashioned suits popular amongst humans from Terrenea, as per usual.

And yet, something is off.

I returned my gaze to the mirror, trying to stifle the unease working through my body, fidgeting with the corset. Whilst rather suffocating, it had a remarkable effect on accentuating my curves. I willed my voice into something casual. Pleasant even. Lest Azrael be made aware of the strange, unfounded suspicion that I'd woken up with a week ago.

"Thank you... I can't remember the last time I wore a dress."

Looking at myself in the mirror, dolled up in the best way I could manage, I looked like a different person entirely. My eyes dipped to the scar I discovered on my forearm, bearing the name of the blonde male in my dream, and I tugged my sleeve back over it. Something deep inside me told me I needed to hide it. *Protect it.*

A week ago after having the most delicious erotic dream of my entire life, I'd found it on my forearm when I'd bathed to wash the arousal soaking my thighs. I'd been both thoroughly unsettled and reassured by it.

While I had no recollection of it being *carved* there, there was but *one* way someone would be able to put their name on my body in such a perfect scrolling script—and it required my permission. Even before I'd noticed it, the moment I woke up, I felt a profound, unignorable longing for the males in my dream.

Logic told me that some sort of memory-wiping potion had laced my food or drink. It would also explain why I longed for the males in my dream with such a soul-deep need. Despite having no memories of them, I *knew* them. My longing for them hadn't waned in the least.

Fuckery of the highest order is afoot, and Azrael has something to do with it.

"Are you hungry?" Azrael asked.

Why, yes. I am. For your *blood.*

I feigned a sigh of relief. "Gods, yes. I'm fucking starved."

"Splendid. Join me for lunch?"

Lunch? Since I'd arrived in this realm *months* ago, not once had the male invited me to lunch. My suspicions rose further.

"Sounds *delightful,*" I replied a little too sweetly.

Azrael studied me for a moment as a tight smile crept across his face as he lingered in the doorway.

To smile or not to smile? I turned away from the mirror to look back at him, giving him the most casual look I could manage.

Suspicion narrowed his eyes.

Fuck, I shouldn't have smiled. I don't just give away smiles. Who the hells do you think you are?

My smile faded. Azrael's suspicion eased.

"Right...,' he announced awkwardly before turning on his heel to leave.

Stupid. Stupid. Stupid.

Stringed instruments tickled the air as Azrael rose politely from his seat as I entered the dining area and I barely succeeded in stifling my eye roll.

Gallant are we, you duplicitous cunt?

Azrael's gaze remained fixed on me as I strode towards him and I began to perspire beneath the mask of *nonchalance* I was wearing.

Nonchalance.

Nonchalance.

Nonchalance.

You are the Queen of Nonchalance.

My voice turned airy and high-pitched.

"Thank you for having me…"

Gods, you're a terrible actress.

Azrael's eyes narrowed again, this time with concern.

"Are you feeling ill?"

Fuck me, why am I smiling again?

I cleared my throat as I took my seat across from him and made eye contact with about a dozen fucking effigies of Azrael's *soulbound* that all seemed to have been sculpted to boast the most judgemental expression fathomable. Twelve of them surrounded us in a circle from their columns only feet away from where we sat beneath Vassileo's five *Akash*-forsaken red suns. Despite Azrael keeping his courtyard a balmy 72 degrees thanks to his magic, sweat trickled down my back.

Why am I so nervous?

What if he's done nothing wrong, and I'm just losing my fucking mind?

Awkwardness settled between us. The food, though undoubtedly delicious, held zero appeal to me despite my immense hunger. My fangs ached, and I couldn't help but shift restlessly.

Why are we even here?

"Is there… Something in particular you'd like to discuss with me?"

Azrael gave me a polite but notably forced smile. "I realize that, while your desire in coming here is due to your desire to protect Bellorum and Avernus, but... I feel I owe you a great deal of gratitude..."

Oh...

The tension in my body that had been building for over a week, eased slightly.

Maybe I am just insane.

"... Despite the *astronomical* number of people you've killed here, which bears its own consequences that I won't bore you with, your power is... breathtaking in magnitude. The wards holding the realm together feel stronger than they have in millennia. I've been working closely with the alchemist who created the rhyton, and I'm certain that soon, we'll find a way for you to feed as much as you need while also helping me hold the fabric of this realm together. I'm not afraid to admit, I owe you a great debt, and... I hope that one day, I'll be able to repay you."

I couldn't help but feel a little speechless. *And wildly disarmed.*

No one had ever expressed gratitude so freely to me. Or at least as far as I could remember. Internally, my mind battled with his seemingly sincere kindness and my rapidly dwindling sanity. From beneath the table, my thumb found it's way to the scar on my arm bearing Malekai's name, and it instantly grounded me.

"Thank you... Though, it's not like I had anyone or anything tying me to Bellorum, and my father's been ruling Avernus on his own since time immemorial. If anything, I just wish I'd been able to spend more time with him and my mother before coming here."

Azrael gave me a sad smile. "Perhaps they can come visit sometime."

Right. You're officially insane.

Magic crackled through the air moments before a male with giant wings and golden, iris-less eyes stepped through the garden doors. His mouth opened to speak, but his words were cut short when they landed on me. Both his astounding beauty and a strange familiarity to him that I couldn't place stilled the breath in my lungs.

Azrael's body went rigid at the sight of him. "Asterion. You're supposed to be travelling to Creshmir to meet your new squadron."

"I was, but there's another riot. They've set fire to Malovada city."

TWENTY-NINE

I f it weren't for the oppressive heat of the suns, the flight to Creshmir might have even been enjoyable. Instead, my boob sweat was enough to tempt me into flying naked. Just when I decided in favor of it, the sound of wingbeats behind me snagged my attention. Tendrils of red magic were already pouring out of me as I whirled around, shocked to discover the male who'd blessedly interrupted lunch with Azrael.

"Don't you have a squadron waiting for you?"

A rueful smirk tilted his lips, otherworldly golden eyes glinting in the sunlight. "No one waits in Vassileo. Not even the nephilim. And Azrael might feel comfortable sending someone to quell a fiery riot in Malovada alone, but I don't."

A surprising swell of appreciation burned bright in my heart. I'd always fought alone, even if it was beside a whole company of soldiers. Survived a war alone. Served Zurie alone. Lived alone. My life in Atratus had been utterly bleak at best.

So, for this male to be concerned *for me...*

My throat caught on emotion. "Thank you."

However, since seeing Malekai's name on my arm, my mind had

spun, trying to find memories that weren't there. Still, every time my fingers brushed across that scar, I felt some sense of inner knowing that things weren't quite as they appeared to be. The fact that I could *feel* the love radiating from that mark was a constant source of stability for my unravelling mind.

The question leapt from me without any prior thought.

"Do you trust Azrael?"

The male flying beside me snapped his gaze to mind as if surprised by the question. "Not even with a butter knife."

More of my anxiety lifted as I chuckled as his gaze lingered on me. "My name is Asterion."

Drenched in gore and caked in soot, Asterion and I took in the remains surrounding us. Malovada had been reduced to rubble, and my belly was full to the point of bursting.

"I think I drank too much..." I heaved a sigh, cut off by an abrupt belch. I clapped my hands over my mouth as embarrassment licked up my cheeks and neck like flames. "Oh, gods. I'm so sorry about that. I think it's all the demon blood... Gives me indigestion."

Asterion's mouth twitched for a fleeting moment before splitting into a broad grin, and he *laughed.* Though I hardly knew him, I had a strong feeling it was a rare sight. It transformed his handsome but forbidding features into something *divine.*

And contagious.

My own laughter erupted, easing every muscle in my body and making affection blossom for him in my chest.

When was the last time I'd laughed like this?

Our eyes met through our shared laughter, and I felt a seedling of friendship planted firmly between us. Something inside my soul seemed to say, '*I know this person.*'

Our laughter slowed, and Asterion opened his mouth to say something, but the presence of foreign magic cut it short. Our gazes snapped to the doorway behind me before we shared a knowing look. I had to stifle my groan as I turned to greet our enemy.

I desperately wanted a bath.

A male appeared in the doorway of the decrepit building we'd just raided. The same one I'd seen challenge Azrael in the street when I'd first arrived. *Erius.*

He grinned wide at the sight of me, his smile unnaturally bright against his dark skin. "Hello, *not-consort.*"

Thoroughly exasperated, I patted my belly. "Look. I'm *stuffed.* Gorged, in fact. So unless you feel like spending the rest of your days collared and in a dungeon already packed to the brim with the denizens of this *Akash*-forsaken place, I suggest you preoccupy yourself elsewhere."

Erius burst into laughter. "A collar?" Another burst of dark, raspy laughter. His voice sounded as if the flames of his belly had permanently singed his vocal cords.

The building around us burst apart like an explosion as his form shifted into the epic beast of lore lurking beneath his skin. Staring down at us and grinning with razor-sharp teeth as long as my legs, the baritone of his voice echoed in our minds. "I'd fucking *love* to see you try and put a collar on me."

Asterion growled from beside me, and I couldn't help but be awed by his true form. Glinting, gold, twisted horns rose from his head, making me wonder if they were actually metal. Gold armored plating protruded from his skin. His golden, iris-less eyes, normally dark, began to glow as if lit within by a burning star. However, none of that is what had my jaw plummetting to the floor. A black void began to emanate from him. Broken chunks of plaster, wood, and cement slid across the floor towards him to then be reduced to ash before disappearing entirely.

I stumbled backwards against the gravitational pull tugging me towards him, my long braid streaming in front of me.

I gaped, the drakonati half-forgotten. I'd never witnessed such an astounding gift. I had only ever heard of it existing on one occasion… The primal of light. An entity so old and long forgotten that I couldn't even recall her name.

"Very impressive, Asterion, but is killing me worth killing your only friend?"

Asterion's scowl deepened, and his lack of response had realization washing over me. Erius chuckled, watching as I stumbled backwards again when the force of his gift had my feet sliding against the floor, dragging me towards him.

All at once, as if by the flick of a switch, the void around Asterion left, and his glowing and golden features dimmed.

Asterion gave me a heartbreakingly apologetic look.

"You can't control it…" I breathed as my braid slapped back down against my body.

Asterion's eyes fell to the floor in shame.

Erius hummed. "Such a pity. I *almost* feel guilty."

My eyes snapped up to the drakonati's. My magic writhed, seeping out of my skin in blood-red vapors, condensing into something corporeal. An oddly familiar ice-cold metal slid around my neck, and all at once, the connection to my magic cut off. It felt like losing a limb. The dragon's clawed foot lashed out to curl his talons around me as a female appeared beside him, pressing a hand to the beast's leg.

Asterion's roar was the last thing I heard before the world around me disappeared in a flash of black and returned in the form of icy winds and barren mountaintops. Erius shifted back into his fae form. Something like genuine guilt shuddered his expression as he looked me up and down. The female beside him, with skin the color of the snow surrounding us and hair the color of blood, laid a hand on his shoulder. Something silent was communicated between them before she flashed me an unreadable look and slipped through a tall, narrow crevice in the stone wall of the mountain.

"Did Azrael hire you to kidnap me?"

Erius quirked a brow, grinning innocently. "Who's Azrael?"

I fucking knew it!

"If you plan to kill me, you're welcome to try, but do *not* lock me in a cage."

The male had the audacity to pull off *nonchalance*.

"I plan to do neither."

Erius turned and squeezed through the stone crevice, leaving me standing in the ice-fucking-cold. My heart squeezed painfully as I tugged in futility at the collar on my neck, taking in my surroundings to find that I had, without my wings, zero hope of escape. Sharp cliffs dropped off in every direction except the staggering mountain wall behind me. I stepped towards the edge to see how far the fall would be. Perhaps if I jumped, I could make a run for it after I healed... but that would still leave me wingless, weaponless, and with a magic-suppressing palladium collar around my throat.

Azrael, you wretched, filthy, conniving, slimy—

A shadow blotted out the five red suns, and I twisted to look up and find another dragon with scales of darkest green and black circling high above the peak just before it tucked its wings in tight and plummetted towards me. It shifted at the last minute to reveal a towering fae form. My heart stuttered at the sight of him.

Malekai.

The male from my dreams.

But not.

Unlike Malekai's turquoise and gold, this male's eyes were a green so dark they were nearly black, like his hair. A scar that looked like melted flesh crept up one side of his neck and jaw. And though I had merely dreamed of the male, I recalled with crystal clarity the elegant flow of his perfectly sculpted features.

Up close, I could see the dark-haired doppelganger's features had replaced elegance and warmth with cold brutality. His features may as well have been hewn from the very stone of this mountain.

Even so, he was so similar to the male from my dream that simply staring at him knocked the fucking wind out of me. So stunned, I mindlessly stepped backwards—off the fucking cliff edge. His hand shot out, gripping the front of my fighting leathers, and bodily tugged me away from the edge and into the hard, muscled wall of his chest.

My heart seemed to split wide open and *bleed* at the sound of his voice—one so very similar to the male I'd been pining after in my dream. His dark eyes twinkled with affection and mirth. "Don't try to die on me when I've only just found you."

At my astounded silence, the male craned his neck towards me. My eyes slipped shut, and I remained still as he took in my scent. I swore I could hear an echo of Malekai's voice, again whispering Aurealingan words I shouldn't know the meaning to. *'Katadamna kaza, tessari mú.'*

His magic brushed against me as if attempting to introduce itself.

My eyes stung with that broken feeling in my chest increased to haemorrhaging. My hands gently wrapped around the forearm still gripping my fighting leathers.

Gods, what is this?

Not-Malekai pulled back, eyes widening slightly at the sight of my welling emotion. His brows furrowed, and he leaned to kiss away the liquid leaking from each corner of my eyes, licking his lips that tugged at a smile.

"Mmmm... You're not at all who I was expecting. Truly, the fates must favor us."

While there were *many* arguments I had to offer in reply to that statement, never in my life had I ever been made so speechless. When I gaped like a fish out of water, stuttering my reply, the male brushed his finger across the collar on my throat. Snow crunched as the metal landed heavily at our feet.

And despite the fact the male had just gifted me my freedom, all thoughts of escaping dove straight off the cliff's edge behind me.

"Who are you?"

The male's mouth split into a dazzling grin boasting white teeth, lethal fangs, and a pair of heart-melting dimples. *"Ataraxus."*

CHAPTER

THIRTY

MALEKAI

"I have a favor to ask you." The deep rumble of Nakoa's voice returned me to the present moment, where I was currently sitting, reading up on the hell realms of Vassileo. All *Akash*-forsaken *eleven* of them. Normally, I erred on the side of optimism, but I couldn't help but feel this overwhelming sense of doom.

Eleven.

Fucking.

Realms.

Where would we even begin?

I was relieved for the distraction. Whatever the favor required, it would distract me from our dwindling likelihood of ever finding Mareina. Since Azrael had taken her, I'd been researching his realms relentlessly, oscillating in and out of anger and despair. Wretched, violent sobbing included.

I lifted my gaze from the ancient, yellowed tome of flaking parchment pages to Nakoa. He was dressed in the same well-worn trousers and shirt I'd first met him in, with no crown in sight. I nearly *tsked* aloud. This wouldn't do at all.

"Where is your crown?"

160

Nakoa's brows lowered. "In a box, in my closet."

My frown was genuine. Taking a deep breath, I silently deliberated where to begin and how to put it lightly. I hadn't tiptoed around my words. *Ever.* But perhaps because he and I shared the same excruciating absence of our mate, it inspired my elusive compassion.

"I understand you spent much of your life in hiding, yes?"

I took Nakoa's silence as affirmation.

"And Mareina mentioned you come from... humble beginnings?"

More silence, more brow furrowing.

"Look, I appreciate your desire to remain humble and modest, but your people *want* a king. They want your leadership. They *long* for the future you've promised them. But seeing you dressed like..."

I hesitated, not wanting to offend the male with whom I had such a tenuous truce. A corner of Nakoa's mouth quirked in an almost smile. "A peasant?"

I chuckled with a sigh of relief. "Yes. A peasant."

Nakoa huffed something that sounded almost like a laugh, further dissipating the tension in the room. "Yes... I suppose you're right. I just..."

I quirked a brow. "Imposter syndrome?"

Something vulnerable softened his gaze and his voice grew raspier. "In part, yes. That, and it just feels wrong to wear it without her here."

Nakoa's throat worked roughly, and my heart clenched to the point of pain. Before I could think better of it, I rose from the table and rounded it. I wrapped my arms around his giant body, nearly as giant as mine, and he went rigid against me.

"Don't fight it, fucker. You need this just as bad as I do."

I heard Nakoa gulp, trying to swallow back his emotion. Gradually, his body relaxed. I'd never been good at giving emotional support, but again, because it involved Mareina, I felt his pain as if it were my own.

Nakoa's arms wrapped around my back.

While this whole scenario felt strange—bizarre even—it also felt comfortable. He drew in a shaky breath against my chest, and it inspired a rogue droplet to slip down my cheek and into the beard I'd recently grown. Not for aesthetics, mind you. Every second not spent studying Vassileo further diminished our likelihood of never finding Mareina if we couldn't find Azrael. Which also hinged upon him being agreeable—

"What in the 69 fucks is this?"

Nakoa and I separated from one another like we'd both been burned. With much-synchronized throat-clearing and tear-hiding/wiping.

At the turning of Nakoa's back, I faced Lokus, Rumiel, Pomona, and Val. All four of them gaped.

"What? Males can't hug?"

Lokus' brows leapt further. "Do you wanna know the last time *that* male gave me a hug?"

I smirked, already knowing where this was going. "Let me guess. Was it the last time you *weren't* a dickhead?"

Pomona and Val snorted their laughter, and I even heard Nakoa chuckle behind me as he finally dried his eyes enough to face them.

Lokus narrowed his eyes, lips twitching. "You make a fair point, *drakonati.*"

THIRTY-ONE

NAKOA

I couldn't help but be impressed when Keres successfully *folded* my entire *olana kah'hei*, Rumiel, Zurie, Malekai, *and* a whole boat to the Kahlohani Islands. Zurie wore a tight expression as she stepped up beside me. "Your court will want you killed for this. The Lords and Ladies..."

"*My* court," I remind her, gesturing to my *olana kah'hei*, "would do no such thing. *Your* court is welcome to try, but I doubt they've already forgotten that I was the one killing *them*."

Zurie nodded, some of the tension draining from her body, and stepped back into Keres' arms. My gaze drifted to my *olana kah'hei*, and all of their eyes were already fixed on me and shining with unmistakable pride.

Pomona stepped forward, placing her small yet calloused hand on my chest. *"You did it."*

I curled my fingers around her palm, my chest filling with overwhelming gratitude and love. It eased some of the crushing pain in my chest that Mareina wasn't here with me to witness this. The culmination of all the sacrifice and suffering swelled in Pomona's eyes as she looked up at me, and I felt mine burn in response.

"We did it," I whispered between us.

She gave me a watery smile, causing a tear to descend the apple of her rosy, freckled cheek. I leaned forward and pressed a kiss to the top of her head before giving the rest of my *olana kah'hei* a nod of gratitude. Sending a prayer up to *Akash* in gratitude for them, I also asked that I would one day be able to do for them everything they'd done for me. For our cause.

I turned to find Malekai waiting by the rail of the quarterdeck, staring out at the wasteland that had become the Kahlohani Islands with a dour expression.

Earlier, I'd accompanied him, Rumiel, Keres, and Zurie to lead a group of our soldiers to each of the islands to evacuate and free the remaining slaves. I'd wanted Zurie to see firsthand what she'd done. The poverty, the hunger, the mostly barren and rotting land, the gaunt look in everyone's eyes- including the fae she had running the islands and enforcing her slavery.

Some of them had been happy to pledge their allegiance to me, even if it meant serving out sentences of indentured servitude in mines for as long as three decades, depending on how long and how much they'd aided in enforcing the slavery on my islands. A few of them, however, had taken one look at me and my demon-esque features and vehemently refused.

Mareina's words, spoken not so long ago, echoed in my mind.

"... If you want true *loyalty, you will help them."*

But as I'd looked them in their hate-filled eyes, I also realized that there were some who didn't want to be helped. I dealt them mercifully swift deaths and fed the beasts of the Kahlohani seas with their corpses.

Throughout all of this, I'd anticipated a cool indifference from her. Instead, Rumiel and I had felt remorse and anguish pouring off her in waves.

My pity for her, however, remained rather nonexistent. What else did she expect? What had she thought slavery would look like?

Did she think exploiting the land, overharvesting, and leaching the soil of all of its nutrients wouldn't *kill* the island itself?

Even Keres had worn a torn, but no doubt admonishing look on her face.

This was my first time returning to the islands since the war. I knew things were horrific, but seeing it all first-hand after so many years... Words could not describe the simmering rage burning in my chest. It made me want to kill Zurie all over again.

She's the only one who can open the portal.

I hadn't even asked her yet *how*. And I didn't care so long as she did it.

"Are you ready?" I asked, approaching Malekai from behind. He turned to face me, unmistakable guilt weighing his expression.

"I'm sorry, Nakoa."

I nodded, taking in his pained expression. "I know."

While he hadn't outrightly enforced the slavery here, he'd still served Zurie in nearly every way she'd asked. As had Mareina. Apparently, it was easy for people to ignore what remained unseen. It had worked in Zurie's favor that the islands were far enough away to remain out of sight and out of mind from anyone who might otherwise care where aetra came from.

Malekai stepped towards me. "I have no excuse, and I know there's nothing I can do to make it right, but for what it's worth, for the first time in my life, I have conviction and faith in the King I am serving, and I will do everything within my power to do you and our people justice."

The tension and anger that had taken hold of every taught muscle in my body lessened, even if only a little. Appreciation for this male blossomed further in my chest and I gave him a nod in acceptance.

Malekai turned and stepped onto the railing of the quarterdeck, *willed* away his clothes to give us all an unabashed view of his golden backside before stepping off the railing.

I found myself holding my breath in that slip of a moment when he plummeted through the air and disappeared from view, returning a moment later as a gargantuan beast. The beat of his wings blew my hair back, tangling it in the crown he'd so easily convinced me to wear. Thick, lethal-looking horns and ridges ran in two rows across the top of his head and down his neck. His turquoise and gold scales glittered so fiercely beneath the sun I was forced to squint. My hand absently rubbed at the golden scale he'd set into a bracelet that he'd gifted me for protection.

The sight of his drakonati soaring through the air was nothing short of breathtaking, and for a moment, the world fell away as I stared in awe.

Rumiel stepped up beside me, giving me a nod of affirmation and radiating pride. "You make me proud beyond words."

My breath caught at his words, lancing a sweet, sharp pain straight through my heart. At that, his wings unfurled, and he took to the air.

A moment later, my own wings stretched wide and beat powerfully to lift into the sky. I hovered there for a time, overcome with emotion as I took in the sight of so many of my hopes and dreams culminating before my very eyes.

My affection for the male I'd once hated soared to new heights as I watched Malekai set the world on fire.

CHAPTER

THIRTY-TWO

MAREINA

eads turned, double-taking as *Ataraxus* led me through tunnel after tunnel inside the mountain. Despite the frigid temperatures outside, it was balmy and warm inside. We passed through a cavernous dining hall where hundreds, if not thousands, of drankonati dined.

I craned my head backwards to look up at the ceiling before returning my gaze to Ataraxus. "Why am I here?"

His features tensed with remorse. "I'm not one for dishonesty, and I'd be loathe to begin our relationship on lies, so I'll risk your wrath and be honest: Azrael made a bargain with me."

Relief washed over me that this male actually told me the truth. Ataraxus' expression softened with apology as he continued. "He asked me to keep you distracted and sated."

I quirked an accusatory brow. "And what do you have to gain from this bargain?"

Ataraxus' gaze somehow turned both dark and reverent. "You mean other than *you?*"

My breathing hitched as something pulled tight between us. If it

167

was anyone else, I'd fucking gut them where they stand, but for some reason, I felt powerfully compelled to do the opposite.

"When he initially approached me, I thought to convince you to open a portal for us. To leave this place. Not the whole of Vassileo, just the drakonati, but..."

His words drifted and I was left holding my breath. Ataraxus shook his head as if deciding whatever he was about to say.

"... Anyway, I should clarify: I have no desire to keep you here against your will. Though I do wish more than anything, you allow me to remain by your side. And I would also like to have my healers remove that cursed *rhyton* Azrael buried in your chest. Until then, I would ask that you allow me to persuade you to bring me back to Bellorum with you..."

I opened my mouth as if it would conjure a logical reply, just as my gaze caught on a giant male with a leashed collar around his throat as he walked by. All dressed in fighting leathers, three females trailed behind the leashed male. Gaze drifting across the dining hall, I found several more leashed males peppered throughout—often several males to one female, sometimes the reverse, but only the males were leashed.

Were these slaves? Prisoners? *How strange they're all male.*

"The drakonati keep slaves?"

Sex slaves it would seem.

Ataraxus frowned. *"Slaves?"*

I inclined my head towards the nearest leashed male. Ataraxus followed my gaze, bursting into a hearty laugh. "They're newly mated. We're a matriarchal society. Every newly mated male, as a display of their undying love and devotion to their females, wears a leash and collar. Usually for an entire moon cycle, but sometimes for longer. It depends upon each mated pair."

My brows had taken residence somewhere uncomfortably close to my hairline. Ataraxus' lips twitched with amusement. "I nearly forgot that's not custom to anyone in Bellorum."

"Have you been there?"

"I was born there."

Realization dawned on me. *Hades. The drakonati genocide.*

Ataraxus gave me a sad smile in confirmation that made something in my chest squeeze tight with sorrow.

"How did you survive? And how did you get back here?"

Rationale told me Azrael before he answered.

"You probably know her, actually. I owe her my life..."

Her?

"Queen Zurie."

My jaw hit the stone floor so hard it was a fucking miracle it didn't shatter. *"Zurie?"*

Ataraxus' eyes dipped to where my lips were parted, and I didn't miss how his pupils flared wide. Again, my logical mind admonished me as my body arched ever so slightly towards him as he curled a finger under my chin.

My heart thundered in my chest in anticipation.

Gods, when was the last time I'd been kissed?

Instead of kissing me, the male gently closed my mouth before brushing a thumb over my bottom lip. The action proved to render me equally stunned. *And aroused.*

Ataraxus' nostrils flared, bestowing me with that luminous grin again before he leaned forward and pressed a kiss to my forehead in a way that seemed so familiar it stole my breath. His words were murmured in a low voice against my forehead. *"This is Kismet, Mareina, and you make it all worth it."*

Sometime later, we reached a large set of stone doors, and Ataraxus turned to me, wearing a look that didn't suit him. He gave me a sheepish grin, only one dimple making an appearance, as he opened the doors to reveal a beautifully appointed bed chamber that boasted a thermal bathing pool in a far corner.

My eyes stuttered as they landed on... *a grand piano?*

"The drakonati build pianos in hell?"

Ataraxus chuckled. "Not in this hell, unfortunately."

My brows lifted. "Sooo…"

"So I stole it."

"From who?"

Ataraxus smirked. "Azrael."

My head tipped back in a surprised laugh. "How wildly endearing."

This male bargained with Azrael to kidnap you, my rational mind unhelpfully provided as my intuition batted the thought away.

Ataraxus gave me a feline grin. "You have a choice…," he announced from beside me as I took in the warm setting. A live, crackling hearth illuminated the space, decorated with furs, red and gold artfully woven rugs, and a bed pallet that looked cozy enough to *die* in.

A choice…

As far as I could remember, that was perhaps the first time in my entire fucking life that anyone had ever actually given me *a choice* instead of attempting to force their will upon me. And despite the fact that logic would tell me to kill, something inside my already aching heart blossomed just for him.

He dared a glance at me. "You can either bathe in here, in the privacy of my room, *or* you can choose the far less appealing option of utilizing the communal baths. Admittedly, they are quite stunning and perhaps more elaborate than this, and I understand if you feel safer amongst a crowd."

My brows pinched with something very near disbelief. I'd had countless males attempt to force themselves on me. A handful of which had succeeded when I was hardly more than a youth before I'd gained the skill and knowledge of how to protect myself…

Never had a male so brazenly given me a *choice.*

I trained my features neutral even as my heart swooped like a butterfly against the winds of a storm. "And… if I were to choose to bathe here in your rooms…"

Ataraxus' heated gaze held mine, belying his longing.

My heart pounded violently as I found the courage to finish my sentence. "… and asked you to join me…"

He hesitated for several moments, studying each and every one of my features like they held the answers to life's great mysteries.

"I would deny you nothing, Mareina."

THIRTY-THREE

ZURIE

The fog gathering at our feet seemed to have a sentience of its own. Nissi Tis Pillis had always given me the creeps. It was a jungle island constantly shrouded in fog and a magic that made my skin crawl. You could be standing in an open space, and you'd still get the unsettling sensation of being watched.

It was somewhat reassuring to see the shifty-eyed looks of Nakoa's *olana kah-hei*. It told me I wasn't alone in my fear.

A visible tremor took root as I clutched the dagger in my hand. Keres' hand settled on my lower back, rubbing soothing circles. Her voice lowered so that only I could hear her.

"Are you sure you wanna do this? Tell me you've changed your mind, and I'll fold us back to Ishra, where they can never reach us."

I looked up at her, wearing a tremulous smile. My heart filled with more gratitude and love than I'd ever known. "I've never been more certain of anything in my entire life."

She took a deep breath, gradually nodding. "I'll be right here. No matter what shows up on the other side of the portal."

Gods, this female.

I pushed up onto my toes and pressed a lingering kiss to her lips. "I love you."

Her fingers carded through my hair, holding me against her briefly before I pulled away. Nakoa's eyes felt like a guillotine on my throat. I couldn't blame him. He was probably waiting for me to do something horrible, like stab him in the back.

Admittedly, it was a fucked-up, morally corrupt plan:

Open the portal, let gods know what creatures through, blame it on me, rally ~~our~~ his army, and start a war so my son had a real chance at saving his soulbound.

It might not say much about my character, but the only qualm I had with said plan was that it was dangerous. But this was my one *Akash*-given opportunity at redemption, and I wasn't about to fucking waste it.

In case any of his drakonati had needed to return to his realm, Azrael had given me a blade laced with his magic. It seemed uncanny to me that he had been right in taking such a precaution. The last time I'd used this blade, a drakonati child who had survived King Hadriel and his genocide had flown all the way from Hades, hoping to seek shelter in my distant kingdom.

I hadn't had the heart to kill him… And certainly not so soon after I'd given birth to Nakoa. At that thought, my eyes landed on Malekai. He'd fought as a soldier in my army for decades by the time I'd met him and promoted him to General. He and the child had looked so alike I couldn't help but wonder if they'd been distantly related. If it hadn't been for the drakonati child's burn scars, I might have even thought they were the same person.

Perhaps they'll cross paths now…

Taking a slow, deep breath, I stepped beneath the lone stone archway and drew Azrael's blade across my hand. The blade seemed to have a hunger all its own, as if it encouraged me to press deeper than I'd intended, severing muscle and tendon.

I stifled my whimper, drawing the blade vertically down my hand, wrist, and forearm. The white-hot pain was all but forgotten as I watched in awe. Darkest gold and black shadowy tendrils of magic seeped out of the blade to join the blood spurting from my arm before spilling to the ground.

Keres snatched the dagger from my hands. "*Akash's sake,* female. What the fuck are you doing? It requires blood! Not your *life!*"

Just as it had the first time I'd used it, my vision tripled and swayed, and I felt some of my life force drain from me. I forced myself to murmur the Vassileon words Azrael had taught me.

"Khế hōs kaleídhi kai aíma hōs ragída, to péplo metaksý zoïs kai thanátou zō."

With soul as key and blood to bind, I rend the veil 'twixt life and death entwined.

THIRTY-FOUR

MALEKAI

Zurie swayed and stumbled. No one moved to catch her except Keres as she shouted her name. *Well, that was... unexpected.* Nakoa and I exchanged a look, that said we were both wondering the same thing. *Did she just die?*

Keres hefted Zurie into her arms and glared at us in a way that told us if her hands weren't full right now, she'd likely try to murder us. "If she doesn't wake up, *you're all fucking dead.*"

Nakoa's lip curled at the threat, but I laid a hand on his chest before he could further inflame the situation. "She'll be fine, Keres. It's just a scratch... Look, it's already healing."

It definitely was not.

If anything, she was in desperate need of stitches because she was still bleeding out. Keres opened her mouth to argue but was cut short by the trembling of the ground beneath our feet. Magic crackled through the air as a tangible pressure began to build. Initially negligible, it rapidly turned into something painful.

Dark vapours that condensed and shifted into liquid began to spill out from beneath the stone archway, and we all leapt out of the way as it spilled towards the suddenly tumultuous sea behind us.

Waves crashed against the shore as if trying to spit out the black liquid poisoning it.

As a group, we shared frantic looks. *"I told you this was a horrible fucking idea!"* Keres hissed, still cradling Zurie against her chest. Her words could barely be heard over the raging winds.

Nakoa and I exchanged a knowing look and stepped towards the portal.

"Wait!" Rumiel and Pomona leapt forward, dragging him back as Val gripped my shoulder and Pomona yelled above the building storm. *"Are you insane? You'll die in there! And what good will all of this have been then! All for fucking nothing!"*

Val's eyes bore into mine in earnest. "She's right, lad. Yew, try ta walk through that thing; there's no telling where you'll end up. And it'll likely be nowhere near Mareina. I want her back, too, but this isn't the way."

Before we could deliberate on it any longer, the black vapours and liquid disappeared, the winds and sea calmed, and the crushing pressure in the air was lifted, replaced by silence and calm.

Zurie's head lolled against Kere's chest. *"What happened?"*

Keres' lip trembled as she dropped to her knees. "You nearly *died*, that's what happened."

Zurie's despair was not what I'd expected. Her heartbreak was palpable. The tears in her eyes genuine. *"What?* But last time—That can't be—

"Last time you opened the portal, you were giving something back."

As one, we turned to find Miroslav standing behind us. Zurie's lips parted in realization, clutching her bleeding arm to her chest.

"Now, you want to take something. Someone. Someone who has become vital to the survival of that realm. To Azrael."

Miroslav scowled at the group of us.

Fuck.

My chest heaved in protest. Suddenly, that crushing weight returned, but it had nothing to do with the portal and everything to do with the fact that Mareina was *still* no closer to coming home.

I marched toward the portal where Azrael's gods-forsaken blade lay on the ground, a black and silver abomination, to pick it up. Nakoa launched himself forward, trying to pry the thing from my hands. *"You don't get to leave too, you fucking prick."*

Before Nakoa gained any chance of stealing it from me, the thing disappeared out of thin air. Miroslav's voice was like a thunderclap. "You *will* die."

Nakoa and I shoved away from each other to see the blade in Miroslav's hand. "Is that what Mareina would want? Your Kingdom needs you. *Both* of you, believe it or not. And most of all, *she* needs you."

"What other way is there?" I roared back, "If it comes down to her or me, it will be her *every-fucking-time!* Now give me that *Akash*-forsaken blade or I swear to all the gods in the fucking pantheon that I will let my beast fucking *eat you alive."*

My drakonati roared inside me, eager to burn everything in its path. *Akash knew* we'd wanted to roast Miroslav like a fucking rotis-serie for *decades.*

Nakoa's fist came out of nowhere and hit me square in the nose. After the audible *crunch* of bone breaking, I hit the sand hard enough that it knocked the wind out of me.

"Give me the blade, Miroslav," he growled.

Miroslav rolled his eyes at us as if we were children. Nakoa's *olana kah'hei* watched, tension lining their features.

I wheezed, trying to force air back into my lungs, as I reset my broken nose and crawled to standing. "With all due respect, *Your Royal Highness,* but you've got a kingdom to look after... *and a family."*

I had no one.

Lies, some inner voice hissed at me as I studied Nakoa and some ache built in my chest. Outside of Mareina, I'd never loved or consid-ered anyone outside of my blood relatives, who were all well and dead now, to be family, but this male had changed that.

Nakoa's scowl was powerful enough it should have singed my beard clean off. "If we get Mareina back, that won't matter. And she loves you more than she'll ever love me."

Oh, fuck...

Without even meaning to, my hand clutched at my chest as if I were wearing a string of pearls and needed saving. *Fuck me, that hurt to hear.*

I opened my mouth to pour out my reassurances but was swiftly cut off by Zurie, who stomped through the sand, holding her mangled arm to her chest.

"You're right. And she will always love him more than you unless you give her a reason too—which will be *impossible* if you fucking kill yourself or allow this *beast* to sacrifice his life for her. She will *never* forgive you in either circumstance."

Nakoa's ire seemed to wither away at that. As did mine.

Time seemed to move in slow motion for some reason when I saw Zurie's eyes lift to Miroslav's, and something silent seemed to be spoken between them. Azrael's blade appeared in Zurie's hand in the next moment. Drawing the blade across her throat, she whispered Vassileon words that I shouldn't have been able to understand.

"Khḗ hōs kaleídhi kai aíma hōs ragída, to péplo metaksý zoïs kai thanátou zō."

With soul as key and blood to bind, I rend the veil 'twixt life and death entwined.

Keres' eyes widened in shock as she lunged forward to catch Zurie before she could hit the sand.

When the portal opened this time, the ground didn't tremble, screaming winds didn't roar, and violent waves didn't crash.

Instead, as if Azrael's realm and magic had been appeased with her earnest and selfless offering, a clean, black dot appeared that widened into the mouth of a vaporous black hole.

Keres was screaming something my mind failed to absorb as she knelt and lowered Zurie's motionless body to the ground. To my surprise, Rumiel appeared beside her and pressed his hands to Zurie's body. A radiant golden light radiated from them, so bright it was nearly blinding.

Our plan had been to open the portal, unleash hell, and return to Atratus to gather our army, but Nakoa and I both stepped towards the portal as if that thread tying our souls to Mareina's was reeling us towards her. Perhaps it was also the hungry, dark energy emanating from the portal that seemed to beckon us forward. Nakoa's *olana kah'hei* shouted for us to stop, but their pleas grew distant and barely audible over the deafening whispers of countless souls.

It wasn't until Miroslav stepped in front of us, blocking our path, that the world seemed to return. *"If you want to succeed in bringing her home, you will wait."*

CHAPTER

THIRTY-FIVE

NAKOA

My heart pounded an erratic beat as my gut twisted with anxiety and guilt. I was asking too much. I knew I was. And it will undoubtedly lead to the death of hundreds if not thousands, according to the sole vision I'd had since I'd awoken from my coma. Yet another reason I'd been so eager to leap through that portal without following through with our plan.

It had been merely days since my coronation, and I was already trying to send my army into what would likely turn into a war.

That you may not survive, my logical mind helpfully reminded me as a memory of the vision depicting a sea of rotting corpses returned to my mind.

Hours had passed since we'd opened the portal, and still nothing had come through it, as far as we knew. It was just... *there.* Maybe on Vassileo's side of it, it also appeared to just be a strange, black, vaporous hole in the fabric of reality, and nothing dared to enter it. It didn't exactly look welcoming. Maybe the portal had opened up in some remote cave in the mountains where no one would find it.

And we couldn't ask Zurie about it because she was, as far as we knew, still unconscious. Rumiel, who I hadn't even known possessed healing magic, had been able to close the wounds on her throat and arm, but she'd looked pretty dead when Keres had *folded* away with her, cursing the day I was born. Our only hint that Zurie was still alive was the fact that Keres hadn't shown up to try and kill us all.

And despite all of that, my *olana kah'hei* had imparted all manner of encouraging words to me, but somehow, only what Malekai had to say managed to set me at ease.

The male had watched me pace a crater into the dirt outside the doors to the coliseum that housed the training arena, where our soldiers spent much of their time training, before finally venturing inside. When he noted the rigidity of my body and the tremor in my hands as the weight of a thousand gazes beat upon our faces, he approached my side and *bowed* before requesting a private audience with me.

Amusement flickered on his features as he straightened and met my gaze. That was all it took for my tension to begin bleeding away. His voice took on a dramatic and reverent tone, gesturing me towards an empty hallway.

"Your Majesty."

My *olana kah'hai* did an impressive job of holding back their snickers. I had to bite my cheek until it bled to stifle my chuckle.

"I'm gonna punch you in the dick as soon as we leave here," I murmured in a voice only he could hear. Malekai chuckled as our backs finally turned to the arena. *"No need to threaten me with a good time."*

We rounded the corner and stepped into an empty locker room nearby. Malekai looked me up and down, taking in my crown and the new clothing that Bernard had made for me—w*ithout frills.*

"It suits you, ya know..."

At his words, I finally exhaled the breath I'd been holding. His eyes dipped again to my unsteady hands as I pinched the bridge of my nose.

"I'm asking too much of them. I know it. Why did I ever think I could do this? I'm a fool. I haven't earned their loyalty. Their trust. I can't even—

"—Hey Nakoa..."

I heaved a heavy sigh, eventually looking up from where I'd buried my face in my hand. "Yes?"

"Can I borrow your crown for a minute?"

"*Huh?*"

He nodded at the crown on my head. "Your crown. Pass it to me. There's some fluff in it."

Fluff?

"Oh... Thanks." I removed it from my head, feeling like I'd simultaneously liberated the weight of the world from my shoulders as I handed it to him.

Malekai gifted me another one of his disarmingly charming smiles, as he took the crown and set it down on a nearby bench before he turned to face me again.

"And your... cape-thingy, please."

What the hell is going on?

"My cape-thingy?"

"Yeah, turn around. I think there's a shit stain on it."

I reared back, twisting to try and look down at the offending garment in horror. *"A shit stain?"*

Malekai's mouth trembled with restrained laughter. "Yep, just there."

He unfastened the cape from my shoulders and turned to set the cape down beside my crown.

"What the fuck is going?"

When Malekai turned back towards me, his fist made a beeline for my face, and I was too shocked and stunned to do a damn thing about it. I stumbled backwards, crashing into a set of lockers behind me. I gaped at him in shock, chest heaving. *Was this revenge for yesterday?*

Malekai grinned, widening his stance and beckoned me forward. "One for one. Come on. Don't hold back on me now, fancy pants."

My heart squeezed so fucking tight with love for this male.

He was distracting me.

When I rose from the dented mess of lockers, Malekai's feral grin was a mirror to my own. *"How did you know violence was my language?"*

Malekai's smiling face scrunched up in a wince of anticipation as he watched my fist come sailing towards him. Another loud crash rang through the locker room as Malekai's body collided with the lockers beside him. Blood trickled into his left eye as a bought of hearty laughter rumbled out of him.

"Awe fuck, mate. Again? Already?"

I glanced over my shoulder to find Val, along with the rest of my *olana kah'hei,* pouring into the locker room. I waved them off as Malekai accepted my offered hand and I pulled him to standing. "We're fine."

I felt more than heard Pomona's admonishing scowl. *"You're both bleeding."*

Malekai's laughter slowed enough for him to speak as he gave Pomona a bloody but no less dazzling grin. "Be a lamb and close the door, would you?"

Excitement flooded my veins as I braced myself for Malekai's next punch, sucking on the blood from my split lip just before Malekai's fist connected with my jaw. I stumbled backwards again, falling against the lockers as my head spun and raucous laughter consumed me.

Roderick giggled, and even Rumiel's and Rayne's lips twitched in amusement.

Pomona shook her head, giving us her most maternally admonishing look. "You're both *insane.*"

Lokus' eye's bounced between us, looking thoroughly unimpressed. "This locker room smells worse than an unwashed asshole. If you're gonna trap us in here, the least you could do is make it worth it. None of this *tit-for-tat* nonsense. I want a real fight. Between real males..."

Something silent passed between us when Malekai's eyes met mine as I peeled myself from the lockers.

Our wild grins widened.

"And those can only ever end one way, boys...," Lokus continued.

Malekai and I turned to look at him as he nodded and gave us a stern look. *"With someone's dick in your mouth."*

Silence fell between us for a brief moment before the group of us erupted in laughter. Val smacked Lokus on the back of his head, who had the audacity to look affronted. *"What?* Don't you, *of all people,* try to tell me you wouldn't buy tickets to that show."

THIRTY-SIX

MALEKAI

P ride blossomed in my chest as I watched Nakoa inspire an audience of thousands of soldiers that I had commanded for decades. I had never seen them so impassioned.

Or so unified.

For once, they'd been given a cause worth dying for, all for a King *and Queen* worth fighting for. The fact that that cause was Mareina— a female many of them had fought beside and had *earned* their respect—was more than enough to inspire them. With the added threat of the open portals... the threat of imminent doom... It took very little to inspire them to raise their arms.

The plan was rather genius on Zurie's part. And more benevolent than she'd ever seemed capable of.

Chills rose on my skin as Nakoa's powerful wings beat the air, lifting him high above a sea of soldiers all dressed in dark green and umber fighting leathers. His voice boomed through the coliseum, and I swore I could feel the crackle of electricity.

"Your Queen gave her life to protect this realm! To protect you, her people! But she is alive and suffering at the hands of the demons who have

robbed us of the greatest Queen Atratus would ever know! And they will suffer the wrath of Atratus for daring to take what is ours!"

Our soldiers raised their swords as another impassioned roar rent the air.

If only Mareina could see this. See how much she is loved.

Keres was nowhere to be found, likely glued to Zurie's side. *If she was still alive.* Without Zurie, it was a risk to go through that portal... Though, before we'd left Nissi Tis Pillis, I'd taken Azrael's blade, and somehow, the words she had spoken stuck. They'd repeated over and over again in my mind.

When I was a child, my parents had spoken their native language only when they thought I was too young to understand, or too distracted or far away to hear. On the few occasions I'd tried speaking it, I was admonished for it. They'd never spoken it in public, and at hearing their accents, if anyone asked where we were from, they'd only ever said Hades.

When I asked, they told me we were from Hades. I had been born in Atratus to parents who, as far as we knew, were the only ones who had survived the drakonati genocide. The only time we would shift into our drakonati forms was late at night, and we'd venture out to sea where no one could see us.

And instead of flying, we would swim.

It wasn't until after my mother was killed during the war that I'd flown for the first time. I'd been desperate to share my secret with Mareina, but I'd kept hearing my mother's warning voice.

"Trust no one with your secret, tessari mú. Always remember that it was love that incited the genocide of our people."

It hadn't been. It had been hatred. It had been an old sanguinati king with a young wife who fell in love with a drakonati slave that got her pregnant. The sanguinati king hadn't even realized until the child grew to be an adolescent and had his first shift. The king murdered his wife, and there were rumors as to whether or not he'd succeeded in killing the child.

My parents never told me this. I'd read it in a book, in Zurie's library of all places, many years after my mother had been killed.

THIRTY-SEVEN

MAREINA

I *willed* my blood-crusted clothing away as I strode toward the thermal bathing pool. The heat of Ataraxus' gaze licked up my backside like a flame. Electricity seemed to flood my nerves as I descended the steps of the pool. Even so, *Akash*, something about this felt right.

And wrong.

Images of the males from my dream swam to the forefront of my mind. However, when I turned and caught sight of Ataraxus, peeling away his well-worn fighting leathers to reveal the rippling muscles of his stomach, chest, and arms, I quite literally stopped breathing. Every thought in my mind evaporated.

The burn scar covering part of his jaw and neck ran all the way down the left side of his chest, arm, ribs and abdomen. Not that it took away from the stone-cold masculine beauty that hid the warm personality I had glimpsed beneath.

Familiar, familiar, familiar.

Something about him was so fucking familiar it hurt, and it gnawed away at me that I couldn't figure out *why*.

His sculpted mouth quirked up in a somewhat sheepish grin when his hands reached the waist of his trousers. He had the audacity to hold my gaze as he shoved down and stepped out of his trousers. I failed to restrain the tiny gasp that escaped me at the sight of the long, thick cock that sprung free, decorated with thick veins and a broad crown.

Fuck me, that's going to hurt.

At first.

And then it will feel divine.

My throat nearly closed at the sight of him stepping into the bathing pool.

Oh gods. Was this really happening? I genuinely couldn't remember the last time I'd been remotely intimate with someone.

Ataraxus slowly approached me in the water, stopping far enough away the prevent his cock from poking me in the ribs.

"I'd like to suggest something…"

My gaze lifted to his as something pulled painfully tight in my chest, as if it were trying to *yank* me towards him. As if feeling the same impulse, he stepped forward, curling his hands over my hips and pulling me against him. His cock slid upwards against my abdomen, making me clench with desire.

Akash, it would be a fucking miracle if he didn't hear the way he made my heart leap.

"There are a number of things that need to come to light before… *we proceed.*"

Oh gods… Was he… turning me down?

"Please don't look at me like that, Mareina, or I'm liable to make regrettable, irreversible decisions."

His hands came up to cup my face, guiding my gaze to his.

"Believe me when I say…"

His mouth pressed a kiss to my forehead in that painfully *familiar* gesture.

"Soon there will come a day…"

His hands gripped me tight when a soft moan escaped me in anticipation, and then satisfaction when his lips grazed my jaw, pressing another kiss to the sensitive flesh.

"That I am going to kiss, lick and suck every drop of arousal your pretty little pussy has to give..."

"Oh, gods. Please..." My words came out a whispered whimper, and I felt his mouth spread in a grin against my throat as he pressed another kiss there. His hands gently but firmly fisted my hair to bare my throat to him.

"Fuck every hole and fill you with my cum as I cover you in claiming marks."

Without any thought in doing so, my hands drifted across his back and down towards his—

"But, much to my dismay," he added, collecting my wrists, "that will not be today."

Ataraxus's chest heaved, and I could already feel the precum of his cock against my abdomen, which was otherwise dry, above the water.

"Why?"

Ataraxus' eyes slipped shut, jaw flexing as if he were bearing the weight of some great pain. He dropped his forehead to mine, and I swore to *Akash* I couldn't even fucking pretend I wasn't trying to inhale this male's panted breaths.

After a few moments, he finally straightened and stepped back slightly to leave room for chastity as he drew one of my hands to his mouth and pressed a kiss to the inside of my palm. All the while, his dark eyes peered into mine. When they snagged on Malekai's name, his lips parted in something like awe. Though I saw no hint of jealousy.

"I know this is going to sound weird, but I need you to speak with your uncle."

I rear back. *"My uncle?"*

I've never even—

My words cut off as some memory that feels more like a distant dream flashes through my mind. *"In time, his memories will return..."*

The confusion pummelling me was dizzying. I dropped my forehead into one of my hands, and the next thing I knew, Ataraxus was sweeping me up in his arms and carrying me across the bathing pool. He then set me down in a carved-out seated area beside several bottles of oils and bath salts.

Ataraxus sat in the lounge seat beneath the water and pulled me against him so that I could sit with my back to his front. For the first time in as long as I could remember, I felt safe. My heart squeezed as my body relaxed into him.

"He's coming *here?*"

Ataraxus huffed a laugh behind me as he lathered a fragrant liquid in his hands and began *massaging it. Into. My hair.*

Some strange emotion clogged my throat, and my eyes began to burn. This gentle touch was unlike anything I'd ever known. *This male is taking care of me. Grooming me, for Akash's sake,* instead of fucking me senseless to chase his own pleasure.

"No, he'll bring you to his realm. As soon as you fall asleep."

I was certain most people would still be fretting over the dizziness, confusion, and whatever it was that still needed to come to light. Or having an appointment with the God of Dreams.

But for me, the most unusual thing was this kind male, his gentle touch, and how *safe* I felt in his arms.

Ataraxus must have noticed the wobble in my chin, or the biting of my cheek. His gravelly voice became tinged with sadness. *"Akash,* what you must have been through, Mareina, for something so simple as this to incite the healing of a deeply buried wound."

One of his hands found mine and wove our fingers together.

The emotion welling up in my chest drove me to silence. Ataraxus continued washing me, and arousal soon replaced catharsis. Ataraxus' heavy cock was like an iron rod against my back. The rumble of his voice drew me out of the haze I was slipping into.

"Does your *arcanum* have a name?

My brows leapt as a pang of guilt rung through me

"It hadn't even crossed my mind… I hardly know anything about *arcanum,* actually."

"They're something like a witch's familiar, but for a god. They can enhance your magic, manifest into physical forms other than a serpent for extended periods of time, guard you when you're sleeping… I've even heard something about a few of them being able to influence time itself because their power draws not from your own, but something else. *Somewhere* else. Azrael has one…"

My brows pinched as my mind wandered.

Cerebus.

Azrael's words return to me. '… *Her will is my own.*'

My eyes landed on the sleeping serpent laying in the center of my chest.

"I don't know much about my power either. I've only just recently come into it. Though I'm not entirely sure I *want* to know much about it."

Ataraxus stilled beneath me. "Why?"

"Because all I've known is death. I'm sick of death. I don't want to take life. If anything, I want to *give* life. I want to do something *good.*"

Ataraxus resumes his ministrations, massaging my neck. "Death can also be a gift, Mareina… It paves the way for new life. Reincarnation. Respite for the soul…"

I'd heard all of this before, but I couldn't help but yearn for something more.

Akash, please, anything but death.

"And if you've only just come into your power, are you so certain that it's death over which you preside?"

Something inside me stilled.

"… I don't know, actually."

Ataraxus pressed a kiss to the top of my head.

"After all of this passes, I would be honored to help you connect with your power and your *arcanum*."

My heart squeezed with gratitude.

And fear.

Of all that lies ahead.

"I would love that."

THIRTY-EIGHT

MAREINA

Why am I standing in a field of... Crystals? Despite being utterly fucking *stumped,* I felt *calm.* A single moon hung in the dark, clear sky above me. Forests stretched wide on either side of this clearing boasting rows of *thousands* of slender, jagged crystals sticking out of the ground and rising about eight feet into the air. Varying in color, some were white, pale blue, or pink and purple. What's even more bizarre is the fact I felt called to touch every single one of them.

Just as I approached one of them, I felt a great presence at my back, and a dark, smooth, velvety voice stopped me in my tracks.

"Mareina..."

I turn to face Somnus, and am surprised not by his likeness to my father, or the fact I feel like we've met before, but instead the blood splatter across his face, bare chest, and wings.

He also looked fucking *exhausted.*

"Akash almighty. Are you alright?"

Somnus glanced down at himself when my eyes scanned over his bloody form. He grunts in acknowledgement, *willing* away the blood, replacing it with a fresh set of clothes. "Sorry... My mind is elsewhere..."

I got the impression he meant *literally*.

"... But I created these for you," he continues, gesturing at the crystals. "They contain your memories."

I open my mouth to ask the obvious, but he waves my obvious questions away. "It would probably just confuse you if I tried to explain everything myself, but I will suggest that you start with *that* one..."

I shift to follow his line of vision to find a glowing red and black crystal.

"It's not a perfect method, but it's the best I could do without potentially fracturing your entire psyche."

Which was inarguably the most fragile part of me.

Intuition told me I owe this male a great deal of gratitude, though I couldn't even begin to fathom just how much.

"I'm not sure what to say other than I feel like I need to say thank you?"

My uncle gives me a sad smile. "Not exactly... but you'll see soon enough. I'm sorry to say that I won't be here by the time you finish." He throws a cursory glance at all the towering crystals. It looks like I'll be here interminably. "Don't worry about how long it takes you. Everything you need is here. And most importantly, you're *safe.*"

Safe...

The word triggered something within me, and for a fleeting moment, I was standing in front of Ataraxus, his cold features gifting me a warm smile as his thumb stroked my cheek.

The vision was gone in the blink of an eye. Still standing in this field of crystals, Somnus' mouth tipped up in a soft, knowing smile.

"Who is he?"

"You already know that answer, Mareina... Just remember, when you reach Nakoa and Malekai, make sure that you take Ataraxus back to Bellorum with you."

My lips part as the idea of going back to Avernus with Ataraxus filled me with a glimmer of hope.

"When you wake up, your *soulbound* and their army will likely arrive soon after."

My breath caught as my heart nearly leapt out of my throat. Before I could muster a response, Somnus was gone.

My mind reeled, reaching out with frantic hands to latch onto something that wasn't there.

As if with urgency, the red and black crystal glowed brighter. My heart pounded a frantic rhythm in my chest as I pressed my hand to the crystal. The world around me shifted, and suddenly, I was standing in Azrael's study, watching myself sip tea beside... *Asterion?* I round the lounge chair to see Azrael sitting across from us, wearing a sad smile.

"... There are faster ways to kill me, you know."

THIRTY-NINE

NAKOA

Every night since we'd set the Kahlohani Islands aflame, I'd had a reoccurring nightmare where I returned to watch my home, my land, my dreams be reduced to ash. At first, I would search from the sky, watching it burn while icy terror bled through because I *knew* that Mareina was there somewhere. I just had no idea where and no way of finding her. Still, I would fly into the flames—into my old home where Leilani had raised me—and scream Mareina's name over roaring flames and collapsing wood.

The echo of her cries would lead me on a chase until I burned along with her.

I'd returned to this nightmare again tonight, but something about it felt different. I was standing in my mother's old bedroom, each wall consumed by flames, and yet I was still.

Waiting.

From one moment to the next, I was no longer standing in my old house. I was standing in a palace that looked vaguely familiar. The flames burned higher, and it was only when I noticed the towering statue of a familiar female I'd never met that I realized where I was.

Azrael's palace.

Mareina's—

Before the thought can even finish, a deep, velvety voice calls behind me.

"You won't find her here."

I turned to find who I can only assume is Somnus based on his likeness to Mors; though he is notably fairer, his features less sharp, more... *boyish.* There's something more innocent about him. And a little more... lonely.

When my eyes locked onto his purely black ones, I home in on them, squinting until I realize that his gaze isn't merely black, like mine. A light glimmered in them that wasn't a reflection of the flames engulfing Azrael's palace but the stars. A whirling, glittering, distant cosmos. Instantly drawn into them, the burning heat and fire around me fades.

"Don't."

Somnus' voice is deep and smooth, like a thick velvet blanket.

I reared back slightly, almost dizzied by his strange, enchanting power.

"Where is she?"

"The mountains... With another *soulbound.*"

The words seemed to cut the air off in my throat as I anticipated a blinding stab of jealousy that didn't come. Perhaps it was the dream softening the blow of what should have been devastating news.

"Who?"

"His name is Ataraxus. Another drakonati."

I scanned my Knowingness and my heart, still waiting for jealous rage and betrayal to burn through me like the flames consuming the palace. Instead, I felt *relief.*

She's safe. Surely?

Somnus nods. "He guards her with his life."

I have so many questions, but none are more important than the task at hand.

"Do you think Azrael will let her come home with us?"

Somnus frowns. "Not even remotely."

Talons of fear sank into my heart.

"Will you help us get her back?"

Somnus' frown hardened with regret and anger.

"Ataraxus will. And you need to ensure you take him back to Bellorum with you."

"... That is not what I asked."

Somnus heaved a sigh. "I cannot."

My words came out as harsh as I intended. It was his niece for *Akash's* sake. *"Why?"*

"Because I made a bargain with Azrael. And he will kill *my soulbound* if he discovers my betrayal. Even *this* risks his wrath."

"Are you not powerful enough to kill him?"

"If I were to be cunning about it, certainly, but killing—while sometimes necessary—is not always the answer. Azrael is suffering. And like you, he is not beyond redemption."

The weight of Somnus' gaze somehow grew impossibly heavier as though he was *willing* me to feel the gravitas of his words.

"And... If he were to die, his hell realms would open up to all of Bellorum and, eventually, Avernus. His power would dissipate across the universe in which his realms exist, and the barrier that separates Bellorum from Vassileo would unravel completely. Our worlds would blend. The beings from Vassileo wouldn't merely find their way to Bellorum via some portal— all of Bellorum would become a hell realm. And the divine realm of Ourinessa would be destroyed. There would also be no one to hold dominion over the souls of those in Ourinessa or Vassileo. The dead realms would merge with the living realms. I cannot even begin to fathom the consequences of such a thing because it has never happened. Azrael *must* live."

My gaze returned to the flames, and it felt like I was reliving the nightmare for the first time. My guilt doubled down on me. Not because of how I hurt Mareina, destroyed our relationship, or played such an integral part in Mareina's feelings of obligation to martyr herself, but because I realized then that I was *absolutely* ok with facing those consequences if it meant getting Mareina back.

"If you came here thinking that would be enough of a deterrent to prevent me from killing Azrael—

Somnus' laughter cut me short.

"*Akash*, no. I'd kill every last one of you if it meant saving my *soulbound*."

The nonchalance and honesty of his admission had me seeing him through new eyes and wondering how I'd presumed him *innocent*.

Somnus offered me an easy shrug as if we *weren't* standing in a palace on fire, collapsing around us, and he hadn't just blatantly admitted that he wouldn't hesitate to murder us. "Nothing personal. You'd do the same for yours."

The groan of metal and crashing of stone were stark reminders that time was of the essence. Somnus' features darkened as he looked away to some distant point. I recognized the expression because I had worn it each time a vision overtook me.

My voice became tinged with desperation. *"How do I get her back?"*

It became clear to me that Somnus was no longer listening when his lip curled, eyes locked on something in the distance, growling something that I couldn't make out over the sound of the destruction around us.

Panic leapt through me as the nightmare around me began to collapse. Blood dripped from Somnus' hands a moment before he disappeared. I turned to look for an exit as the feeling of claustrophobia gripped me. One of the statues cracked beneath the weight of a beam. Instead of it bearing the effigy of Azrael's mate, it was Mareina. Just before I was crushed beneath the weight, I was jolted awake.

FORTY

NAKOA

Keres, who was supposed to be the one *folding* my army to the portal still hadn't returned. I could only guess my birth mother wasn't dead because Keres hadn't come to wreak her revenge. *Yet.* Which is why I was now standing in front of Miroslav, asking for his help. *Again.*

The slender, seven-foot-plus male wore a haughty but unreadable expression as he looked down his nose at me. "Under one condition."

I quirked a brow. *"Go on..."*

"Invite your mother to the palace. Your *real* mother. Leilani."

He needn't have specified. There was only one female who had earned that title. And it certainly wasn't the female who had given me to Miroslav to kill. Still, I'd been too much of an emotional wreck after everything that had happened with Mareina to acknowledge *any* of the emotions I had regarding the fact Leilani had lied to me my entire life. Not that it made me love her any less. I missed her terribly. I just couldn't handle anything else right now.

"Agreed... but it has to be after we get Mareina back."

Miroslav's expression softened, gradually nodding. Silence hung awkwardly between us for a moment, and I finally took it as the opportunity I'd been waiting for. The last I'd be given before I potentially led us all to death if my fleeting *vision* held any truth.

"By the way..."

His slender, elegant brow arches as if I've finally said something interesting for the first time.

"I know that I owe you my life... and even though words will never be enough, I just wanted to say thank you. For rescuing me from Zurie, saving my life on so many occasions, protecting my mother and Mareina—for everything that you've done."

Miroslav stared at me for so long that part of me wondered if he'd heard me until I saw the faintest glistening in his eyes. He opened his mouth to speak, hesitating. His gaze fell for a moment as he cleared his throat.

My chest grew tight with emotion, but when his silvery eyes returned to mine, all evidence of his reaction was gone.

The timber of his voice became softer than I'd ever known it could be. "You were destined for greatness, Nakoa. I would not have robbed the world of that. Or your mother."

Don't cry.

Don't cry.

Don't cry.

Don't cry, you fucking fool.

A great breath fled me as Miroslav broke the tension by changing the subject and bestowing me with the best news I'd heard since Mareina left.

"I found Mors."

Hope swelled brightly in my chest. If anyone stood a chance against Azrael, whether we had to kill him or not, it'd be Mors.

"Though, there is a rather... *monumental* obstacle."

For fuck's sake.

I anticipated Miroslav reminding me, like Somnus, that we can't kill Azrael because of *blah, blah, fucking blah morals.*

"He's not quite himself..."

My brows pinched with both frustration.

"Which means...?"

Miroslav heaved a sigh, rubbing his temples between thumb and forefinger. The gesture made me recognize how exhausted he actually looked. The male had always seemed so imperturbable that I'd forgotten the fact that he was, indeed, susceptible to stress. Even if he seemed above it.

"It means that he doesn't know who or *what* he is and has little to no control over his power."

My face scrunched up in confusion.

"I'm sorry... *What?*"

"Keres forced him to drink from the River Oblivion."

CHAPTER

FORTY-ONE

MAREINA

Waking up beside Ataraxus where he'd *spooned* me to sleep—after he'd displayed an astounding level of self-restraint and integrity—felt as surreal as it felt natural. With my face buried in the firm, muscular cushion of his chest, his arms wrapped around me, and our legs woven together like we'd come into this world that way. His chest rose and fell slowly as I peered up at him. My heart began to race as memories of my dream filtered in, and my memories settled.

The suffocating weight of guilt and unworthiness that had shadowed me all my life began to lift, replaced by a quiet spark of purpose. *Inspiration.* Though remorse would always live in my heart, I would no longer allow it to shackle me. At some point, when walking through those memories housed within my uncle's crystals, I recognized in stark clarity just how much all that shame had held me back. *I'd* always ever been the only person holding me back.

Not Zurie, or duty, or circumstance.

Me.

And continuing to carry the burden of guilt and shame did

nothing to serve justice to those I'd wronged. Justice, I realized, laid in devoting myself to the people who needed me. My *Soulbound,* the people of Atratus, and all the precious souls under my care in Avernus.

At the sight of Ataraxus' stark, coldly handsome features softened by sleep, my heart swelled with affection.

But oh, sweet fucks, did I have to pee. I carefully disentangled myself from his limbs to relieve myself in the surprisingly functional and well-appointed bathroom. Because we were in a cave, I'd honestly been expecting a hole in the floor.

When I crawled back into bed, Ataraxus gave a deep sigh of contentment as his hand roamed up my hip before dipping to the opposite side of my waist and pulling me firmly against him, incidentally pressing his hardened length and the warm sac beneath, against my stomach and hip.

"... Just pretend it's not there," he murmured, voice rough with sleep, eyes closed, and a grin curling his lips.

I chuckled, allowing myself the luxury of wrapping my arms around him. "That's no small task."

Ataraxus' eyes opened to slits as he hummed thoughtfully, wearing a lazy grin on his face. I watched as reality settled back in for him, and his grin faded to something somber.

"How're you feeling? You've been asleep for two days."

Is that all? I'd had to touch about a gazillion crystals and relive countless memories.

"Nervous... Somnus told me Nakoa and Malekai would arrive sometime after I woke."

Ataraxus studied me, unsurprised by the information.

"I have to say, I rather admire how well you're taking... *everything.*"

I huffed a mirthless laugh. "Oh, no. I'm going to absolutely murder Azrael... but part of me feels reticent to end this moment.

Where we're all still alive, even if we're separated. And we've only just met..."

Whatever softness Ataraxus' features had been lended from sleep, disappeared as concern filtered through. Desperate to have *just a few more minutes* of peace before we all potentially met our doom, I cleared my throat to preface the changing of the subject.

"Thank you, by the way, for..." My words drifted, trying to find the appropriate description for such a bizarre situation.

Ataraxus quirked a brow.

My cheeks stained rose as I managed to finish my sentence.

"... For not allowing me to seduce you."

A smirk curled his mouth as his hand slowly came up to tuck my hair behind my ear, and his thumb returned to stroking my cheek. "Of course... You're my *soulbound*. How could I ever do something I knew would wound you or betray your trust?"

My initial internal reactions to those words were a variety of words, all along the lines of *you are not worthy.*

And for the first time in my life, I paid them no heed. Yes, I had done horrible things, but I had also done selfless things and possessed a burning determination to *continue* to do selfless things. *To be better. To do something good for the souls of Avernus and my people in Atratus.*

The only way I could do that was by forgiving myself and letting go of my haunted past, which I could now recognize would otherwise hold me back like an anchor mooring a ship.

I had also begun to realize that one's capacity to love was equal to the love they had for themselves. And I wanted to love my *soulbound.*

All three of them.

Tension darkened Ataraxus' features. "What will Nakoa and Malekai say?"

The question alone knocked the wind out of me. *"Fuck..."*

"That bad, huh?"

I shook my head, heaving a large sigh. "I mean... Nakoa is my *soulbound,* so that would make you *soulbound* to him as well, right? And as for Malekai... We've claimed one another and bonded in the drakonati way. I'm not even sure what that means, to be honest, we didn't get a chance to discuss it, but he is my chosen mate. He's as much a part of my soul as Nakoa is..." My eyes flick back up to his nervously, "... and you, I imagine..."

"And how well do they get along?"

Oh gods...

I failed to hide my wince, inspiring a hoarse chuckle from Ataraxus. "Having more than one *soulbound* isn't a common thing where you're from?"

"Unfortunately, no."

He hums thoughtfully. "Malekai is your chosen mate... Have you ever wondered..."

My chest clenched in pain. "All the time..."

Ataraxus heaves a sigh. "And if he were to ever meet them...?"

"There's nothing that could separate us. Of that, I'm sure. I would learn to love that person, if for no other reason than him. Just as the three of you will, I'm sure."

Ataraxus pressed a kiss to my forehead. "Well, if it makes you feel any better, when a drakonati claims and bonds with another, the magic infusing their venom weaves itself into your magic, and thus your soul. It's why it burns so much. It's changing things on a physical and metaphysical level. So, for all intents and purposes, he *is* your *soulbound...* One of them," he adds with a cool wink.

The fact that Malekai hid all of this from me creates a knot in my stomach that I can't seem to bury away. Until the heat radiating from Ataraxus seemed to increase, and I caught a flicker of the beast inside of him.

"... But you should know now that even though there may be two other males with whom you share part of your soul, there will be parts of you that belong only to me."

His eyes darkened in a way that told me there was something more beneath the surface than just the warmth and chivalry he exuded. I couldn't help but feel guilty when arousal wove through me. Ataraxus' nostrils flared as a uniquely smug, masculine grin curled a corner of his mouth. His thumb brushed my lower lip, tugging it down enough to graze my teeth and my fangs.

"There may be a pantheon of gods, but I will be the only one you worship..."

My fang nicked his finger, and he spread the blood across my lips. Without consciously meaning to, my tongue sought out his sustenance as I held his gaze. Arousal and hunger bloomed deep as the space between us pulled tight. Pre-cum leaked from the large, thick length pressing against my bare skin. His pupils blew wide, and it was clear there was something more he wanted to say... *Do.*

But he's an observant male. Guilt fisted my heart, and his eyes tracked my throat dipping, my breath catching.

Ataraxus' dark, sultry expression lifted like a cloud revealing the sun. "Don't worry, Mareina. I will earn their respect. And yours. They'll be eager to share you with me."

I finally exhaled the breath I'd been holding.

"He looks a lot like you, by the way..."

Ataraxus quirks a dark brow. "Oh? Somnus didn't mention it."

I hum in affirmation. "So much so that you could easily be confused for brothers. *Twins,* even, outside of your dark hair and somewhat... colder features."

Ataraxus chuckles at this. "I can assure you I'm anything but cold. At least with you."

I smirk, forcing myself to neglect the urge to lean in and kiss him.

"You don't have any long-lost siblings or anything?"

Ataraxus frowns. "No. Definitely not."

"How can you be so sure, though?"

Ataraxus' throat worked on a rough swallow. "Because I was my mother's only child before her husband murdered her."

FORTY-TWO

MALEKAI

Miroslav was dressed in black trousers and a tunic while the rest of us, *all 2,000 of us*, were dressed in fighting leathers. Though it might make a mockery of the rest of us, it was obvious that his presence bolstered our soldiers' confidence and courage.

Many of us witnessed first-hand the ease with which Miroslav could kill in an instant, with nothing more than his *will*, all without spilling a single drop of blood. He was an Orisha, but unlike Famei, he was one of the few *original* Orishas. Beings so powerful that not even Zurie dared to mess with them lest she incur their wrath. They were also known to be reclusive and rarely left the haven of the Yatól Mountains. Outside of Miroslav and Famei, I'd never seen another of their kind.

But fuck, if it wouldn't make me feel that much better if Mors would show up.

I scrubbed a hand down my jaw, anxiety reaching a crescendo the seemed to be triggering Pomona and Val's maternal instincts.

Fuck me, what I wouldn't give to have Nakoa here to punch me in the face.

"Yew, alright, lad?" Val asked as he clapped me on the back, and Pomona rubbed soothing circles on my shoulder, looking just as tense as I was.

I blew out a breath, needing to expel this energy somehow. "He wouldn't have left without us, right?"

Val huffed a nervous laugh. "What? No... No? No. No, no, no. Mm-mm. No. He wouldn't do that."

That instilled *zero* confidence.

Pomona glared at him. "Maybe if you say *no* again, you'll find that conviction you're looking for."

A hush went out across our army, and a few of them began pointing towards the skies, drawing my gaze.

Oh, thank fuck.

Nakoa, side by side with Rumiel, made a swift, sharp descent before drawing up at the last second in an impressive, near-silent landing.

His *olana kah'hei* rushed him, battering him with questions regarding his whereabouts that he shrugged off. His eyes lifted to mine, an obvious apology in there somewhere when he saw the tension lining my features.

Nakoa made a beeline for me. "Somnus visited me."

Oh, thank fuck.

"Is he coming?"

Nakoa shakes his head. "No, but... he told me she's in the mountains somewhere... Safe."

Despite the fact he used the word *safe,* anxiety and dread fist my heart. I can see the hesitance lining every bulging, rigid muscle of Nakoa's body. *"Safe?"*

Our soldiers' roars rent the air as Nakoa worked them into a frenzy, but I was too busy staring at the gaping portal to pay attention to what he was saying. His father and *olana kah'hei* seemed to be in a similar state. Though their thoughts were surely consumed with the task at hand, mine were consumed by the thought of Mareina in the hands of another male since Nakoa had divulged Somnus' visit to him. And my emotions couldn't decide whether to be relieved or heartbroken that it was with another *soulbound.*

The hairs on the back of my neck rose at the sensation of the dark, heavy magic bleeding from it. My heart pounded in my chest with undeniable fear and impatience to step through the cursed thing so I could hurry up and get Mareina back home safe and sound. It was black and completely opaque so we *still* couldn't see what laid directly on the other side of it.

Lokus gave a derisive snort, scowling at the portal as if it had personally offended him. "Fuck *that.*"

He stomped off toward the jungle, carrying a long, crooked, broken branch and jabbed it through the portal. We all watched with bated breath. *Including Miroslav.* When nothing happened, Lokus wiggled it around before drawing it back out. The stick remained exactly the same, but he appeared unconvinced.

Lokus scratched his beard, leaning on the branch.

"Anyone got a dog and a leash?"

The question earned him a few chuckles and eye rolls. Lokus' mischievous grin illuminated his face as his eyes landed on Roderick, *the lykos wolf shifter.*

Roderick heaved a long-suffering sigh, stifling his own grin. "Fuck off, mate."

"I'd bet my whole fucking ball bag that you've got a leash and collar lyin' around somewhere in that kinky little bedroom of yours."

Roderick gave him a dazzling smile as he tossed him a wink. "I do, actually, but it's not for *me* to wear."

Lokus tossed his head back with laughter, easing some of the nervous tension in the air.

As though not entirely convinced, Lokus jabbed the branch back in, swinging it around halfway down the length. After a moment, the branch was halted mid-swing, and something *yanked* on it. Before we could even react Lokus shrieked as he was pulled through the other side faster than he could let go.

FORTY-THREE

ASTERION

I'd spent the last two sleeps—there were no windows or clocks to tell time—watching the people trapped in this enormous maze of a subterranean dungeon beside me, trying to determine just how many of them were worthy of a life cut short. Because someway, somehow, I would get this fucking palladium collar off me, and raze this *Akash*-forsaken place to the ground. The demons, humans, fae, and other beings inhabiting Azrael's realm were all pretty wretched.

In all fairness, I couldn't imagine there were many decent creatures here outside of the all-female prisoners Azrael had cleverly locked me up with on the off chance I figured out someway to remove the collar. Like by bribing one of my fellow nephillim—and throwing caution to the wind by unleashing my powers, killing everyone in my vicinity so I could escape.

After Mareina had been taken, Azrael appeared an entire breath later and slapped a palladium collar on my throat and a dart in my neck.

I'd woken up to the sight of a gaping, black hole with whisps of black magic pouring into it that had appeared near the farthest wall, only a few feet away. *Outside of our cell,* much to my dismay. It blended in somewhat against a dark backdrop of shelving and other storage items that seemed to have been haphazardly left there.

The females stuck in the cell with me yelped as a long, crooked branch suddenly jabbed through the portal, wiggling around.

What the fuck is that?

I cautiously stepped toward the bars of our cell and attempted to reach through them to grab the wriggling thing. One of the females ran up to stop me—the one who had helped me keep my calm and sanity—especially when I'd first arrived. She had power I'd never come across before. She could influence people's emotions and, thus, their actions.

"Don't. You have no idea what might happen—

I shrugged her off. "If I do what? Grab a stick? It's not like they can pull me through these palladium bars."

She frowned, flicking a glance toward the portal just as the branch disappeared. My heart sank. *Fuck.*

Heaving a sigh of disappointment, I returned to the wall opposite the presumed portal and sat heavily. Praying that something, *anything,* would happen. Hours passed, and I'd just nodded off to sleep when I heard the female's gasps and hushed murmurs. I snapped awake, heart pounding, to see the branch being swung around violently.

I leapt forward, squeezing my arm through the metal bars and reaching as far as I could. The branch incidentally slammed into my palm. A grin split my face as victory purred to life in my chest—what victory, only *Akash* knew—and I yanked on the thing as hard as I could.

A tall, lithely muscled male wearing a fancy pair of fighting leathers, with tousled blonde hair and skin covered in tattoos, bodily slammed into the bars of my cell. His eyes went comically wide at the sight of me as he backed away, taking in the sight of our bleak surroundings.

A harsh look carved his features as if I were the one who'd put the portal here. "Who're you? *And where the hells are we?*"

I narrowed my eyes in disbelief.

"You're in a prison. In *hell.* If anything, I should be the one questioning you."

The male's brows leapt.

"You don't happen to know anyone by the name of Mareina do you?"

Hope ignited in my chest. Even if it was at the chance for someone else to escape this hell. For someone I'd only met once, despite the innate familiarity I'd felt towards her. Something deep inside me knew that the female I'd followed to that riot had a capacity for good. For greatness.

"Are you here to help her?"

I saw that hope mirrored in the blonde's gaze, though I could see the distrust wavering behind it.

"So you do know her?"

"Four wings. Kills in droves. Has a surly temperament."

The male's eyes went round as saucers. *"Oh, fuck…"*

The male leapt backwards as he took one final scan of our surroundings before turning back towards the portal.

"No! Wait!"

Before the words had finished leaving my mouth, the male disappeared. With a roar of frustration, I gripped the cell bars as if I could pull them free.

The female with the strange gift appeared at my side, laying a hand on my shoulder and channelling *peace* into my very being. My heart rate slowed, and I breathed in a calm breath as I peered down at her—she was quite small. Pretty and fae.

"Thank you."

She gave me a sad smile before silently returning back to the group of females against the wall. With a heaved sigh, I laid back down on the ground, staring at the portal with near-unblinking eyes for a mind-numbing period of time.

Not that I'd ever experienced it for myself, but I'd heard that there was a significant difference in the way time passed in other realms. While It could be hours, days, *months*—

Before I could finish the thought, two males stepped through. I gradually sat up at the sight of them, shocked to see a Nephilim who had come from *outside* Vassileo, dressed like some warrior king, no less. A blonde drakonati male stood beside him who had the distinct air of someone who had spent his life in the military. In unison, their eyes met mine before taking in the near-endless rows of individual prison cells.

Several more people appeared behind him, all wearing a look of dismay.

Fearful they'd turn around and leave again, my words came out in a rushed. *"I know Mareina."*

CHAPTER

FORTY-FOUR

NAKOA

"*I know Mareina.*" My heart stilled as I took in the imprisoned nephilim male. I wasn't sure whether to consider him an enemy or ally, but my initial instinct was a protective one. Rumiel stepped forward, his jaw slack. *"Asterion?"*

Both males appeared equally shocked to see the other. Rumiel made quick introductions, skipping the part about being buried alive and *exhumed* 120 years later. After a brief discussion and Asterion's retelling of the recent events regarding Mareina, Malekai wielded his drakonati fire to melt the palladium bars of the cell.

By the time the door to the male's cell swung open, the prisoners in the other cells were all rioting to be freed. Val, Roderick, and Pomona took the liberty of removing Asterion's palladium collar, following those worn by a group of females sharing his cell. They stuck close to his side as he approached me. "Is it safe for them? On the other side of that portal?"

My gaze fell on the females' dirt and blood-crusted faces. Dark circles lined their eyes, their hair was matted and clothes torn.

Still, I saw no rats. At least there was that.

I exchanged a look with Malekai. Creepy as the isles of Nissi Tiss Pillis may be, they weren't dangerous.

"Yes. They'll be safe there so long as they don't try to swim in the sea."

Akash only knew when we'd be back. *If* we'd even make it back. But Nissi Tiss Pillis was a far safer place than any hell. *Even if worse came to worst, none of us survived, and the females were all stranded there.*

"Yes, they'll be safe there... I just can't make any promises about when we'll return."

If we return, the fear in my mind whispered. Much to my dismay, my Knowingness often remained silent when I had adrenaline pumping through my veins.

Asterion gave me a nod of gratitude, ushering the females, who were all staring at the portal with wary, nervous eyes. I couldn't help but stare as he murmured words of reassurance to them. One of them appeared reluctant to leave him, but eventually, all of the females took hold of each other's hands and disappeared through the portal together.

The rioting of the prisoners peaked when they saw the females disappear, all bellowing for their turn to be released. "How long do we have before one of Azrael's guards comes to investigate all the noise?" I asked, shouting to be heard.

Asterion huffed his derision. "They won't be. Even the food is *willed* into their cells, and their refuse is *willed* out. Whoever enters this prison dies in this prison."

"So how do we get out?"

Asterion frowns. "I have a way, but it's not ideal."

Malekai shifts impatiently on his feet. "So long as we survive. I don't care what it is."

Asterion's frown deepens, and he and my father exchange a knowing look, but he eventually nods. As if it were a cue, Rumiel stepped forward. "If the layout of the prison hasn't changed since I was last in Vassileo, the entrance should be some distance in that direction."

Mine and Malekai's brows pinched as my *olana kah'hei* shift nervously beside us. "That still doesn't explain how we're going to escape this prison..."

The foreboding look in Asterion's eyes has unease winding through me.

"There won't *be* a prison after I unleash my magic."

FORTY-FIVE

MAREINA

My eyes scaned the broad, scarred, muscled planes of Ataraxus' body. Outside of the desire his powerful form inspires, it was also a map of his history that I wanted to travel. Something deeply rooted in my soul longed to know more about this male that I'd only just met but was undeniably one of my *soulbound*. And while I was filled with gratitude that against all the bizarre and gut-wrenching odds, we'd *miraculously* been united— there was also an unshakable sense of dread.

Somnus told me Nakoa and Malekai were coming for me. I should have been ecstatic. Instead, my gut was churning, and a tremor took over my hands. Ataraxus stole concerned glances as he tugged his trousers on, tucking away his long, thick, half-mast erection.

My breathing stilled as he stalked over to me topless, momentarily easing my anxiety. He tugged me against him before taking my head in his hands and guiding my gaze to his. "I won't allow anything to happen to you, Mareina. Neither will Nakoa and Malekai."

The fear in my chest pierced deep enough to draw tears.

"It's not me that I'm worried about."

Ataraxus leaned in to capture my watery emotion with his lips.

"It doesn't end this way, Mareina. If I've learned anything in my life, it's that *Akash* is conspiring *for* us. Not against us. She didn't bring us together just to tear us apart. No matter what happens, have faith in this."

I wasn't sure I could muster that kind of faith. While meeting Ataraxus had been nothing short of an absolute fucking miracle, I had also experienced and witnessed too much senseless suffering to have such an unwavering ideology.

Before I could reply, there was an abrupt knock on Ataraxus' bedroom doors. Ataraxus hesitated a moment, holding my gaze. "We *all* leave here together. Understood?"

I managed a weak nod. Ataraxus pressed a kiss to my forehead before calling out. *"Enter."*

Erius and the pale female, whose name I still hadn't learned, stood beside him. I'd tried asking her shortly after I'd arrived, and she'd only given me a blank stare before giving me her back and walking away.

Both were fully dressed in fighting leathers and wearing tense expressions. Erius's breath came in quick pants. All of which painted a scene that spurred my anxiety.

"A portal's been opened."

Apparently, either the drakonati weren't fond of permitting riders, or they didn't socialize with anyone outside of their own kind because they had zero harnesses. And despite having four wings, there was no way I'd be able to keep up with their gargantuan 70-plus-foot wings.

Which is why I was currently being clutched inside a cage of Ataraxus' talons as hundreds of drakonati flew towards Azrael's palace. Or what was left of it, at least.

Less than an hour later Malovada came into view. It had already been reduced to ash from the riot where Erius had taken me captive, but it was the sight *beyond* it that had my jaw dropping.

A massive crater had replaced Azrael's palace. Now, only sharp, ragged remnants remained. And beyond that, an exodus of demons and the rest of Azrael's denizens were fighting their way through the barrier of Atratusian soldiers towards a towering black portal.

My heart leapt so far into my throat I choked on a sudden sob at the sight of a turquoise and gold drakonati that I knew without a doubt was Malekai. I squinted, desperately searching for Nakoa. We were still much too far away to see him, but the burning tug in my chest told me he was there.

My soulbound had crossed the realms and travelled to an actual hell for me.

FORTY-SIX

AZRAEL

Terrenea is a bizarre place. Infested with humans that seemed to have no concern for the land they inhabit—always biting the hand that feeds them, draining it of every drop of blood, gnawing at every bone until nothing at all remains. It's a compulsion I'm familiar with. Perhaps that's why I found myself drawn here so frequently. *Akash* knew it wasn't for my friends' suits. I already had thousands of them.

Giuseppe Tartini's *Devil's Trill Sonata* played softly in the background of Ettore's studio; a dear, very *human* Italian friend who also happened to have become my favorite tailor in the last forty years since I'd known him. The male was my only friend—even if he had no idea who I really was.

It seemed too bizarre a coincidence that he would unwittingly be playing a song that one of my *soulbound* had influenced in the composer's dream. *Mors...* with the help of his brother. *Somnus.*

Perhaps it was *Akash* giving me a sign to find him... Though I'd sworn—

"Preferisce il blu grafite o il blu notte, signore?" Ettore asked as he looked up at me with dark, almond-shaped gaze.

223

Do you prefer graphite blue or night blue?

Folds of skin creased his wide lids, peppered with moles across the puffy bags under his eyes that stared up at me from behind a pair of tortoiseshell spectacles perched on his bulbous nose. The male was impossibly young. Only 67 years. And yet, he was dying. *Soon.*

I could feel it. Like an unwelcome whisper on the nape of my neck.

I swallowed against the suffocating weight of sadness rising in my chest as I glanced down at Ettore from the mirror, attempting to force a smile onto my face to mask my heartbreak. My words came out softer than I intended in a feeble attempt to quell the emotion fisting my throat. *"Il blu notte, per favore. Grazie mille, mio caro amico."*

Night blue, please. Thank you, dear friend.

Concern flickered in Ettore's eyes, but he didn't acknowledge it. Merely gave me an affectionate pat on the back as he set down the fabric samples and hobbled towards his towering wooden, cubed shelves filled with bolts of fabric in nearly every colour and textile.

When he was halfway to the shelf, I felt a phantom of the sharp pain in his chest and left shoulder before he did. Before the stabbing pain of a myocardial infarction—the sudden and complete cessation of blood flow to one of the coronary arteries of the heart—registered in his brain.

Anger and sadness welled up in my chest like a geyser, ready to burst as his footsteps faltered. I *willed* myself beside him before he could hit the unforgiving wood floors and break any bones.

The gentle kindness in Ettore's eyes was replaced with fear as he clutched his chest and his lungs spasmed, unable to take a breath. I gently lowered us to the floor and cradled his stout body against mine. His hand trembled and reached for mine, squeezing with surprising strength that rapidly waned.

Ettore was a devout Catholic, so I murmured the Latin prayer of the dead to him, one he'd recognize and hopefully find comfort in.

"Requiem aeternam dona eis Domine, et lux
perpetua luceat eis."

Eternal rest grant unto them, O Lord, and let
light perpetual shine upon them.

My eyes swelled with tears as I held Ettore's gaze. *"Mi dispiace,*
vecchio amico. Il mio potere presiede alla morte, non alla vita".
I'm sorry, old friend. My power presides over death, not life.

Realization settled on his features. He'd always known I was
something *other.*

As he began to age, and I did not, he occasionally asked questions
and made subtle hints. I would explain to him in reductive terms
that I was not from this place or time. I showed him a few seemingly
spectacular feats but never dared to tell him exactly who or what I
was. It would have ruined our friendship otherwise. I'd learned that
too many times the hard way.

I'd been a patron of Ettore's since he first opened his business,
after my previous tailor, Vittorio Rossi, vacated his human flesh sack
and abandoned Terrenea for Avernus.

When the tension in Ettore's body slackened and his eyes turned
glassy, something inside me shifted. I'd never allowed myself to
grow *too* close to him. Another lesson I'd had to learn far too many
times to salvage the wreckage of my heart. Even so, I loved this man
despite my envy of him. He'd had a loving wife—I'd attended their
wedding thirty years ago—and loving children.

The things I wanted most in this world.

Love.

Some sickening melange of numbness, sadness, and anger
settled deep in my bones.

My head hit the shelf behind me with a *thud,* and I sat there, still
holding Ettore, as silent emotion tracked down my cheeks.

Fatigue began to wash over me. Initially, I assumed it was the shitstorm of my emotions. It was only when the fatigue grew so intense that I realised what it was.

Akash-fucking-damn-it.

Has she killed Ataraxus already?

When would this female's hunger be sated?

Within moments of embedding that rhyton in Mareina's chest, I'd begun to feel some semblance of my old self—energetic, power-ful, dare I say even hopeful—but every time there was a riot, and she would *devour* my citizens *en masse,* the fatigue would return.

I'd bargained with Ataraxus to take her off my hands, keep her well-fed *without killing anyone,* and thoroughly distracted. In exchange, he would get a plaything. Potentially even a mate. The fact he looked so much like Mareina's *chosen mate,* Malekai, had been wildly fortuitous and reassuring that she might not be inclined to kill him and escape. That she might, on some subconscious level, desire him. It all seemed a little too serendipitous to be purely coincidence, but... As Ettore would say, *"A caval donato non si guarda in bocca."*

Don't look a gift horse in the mouth.

"It's only been two days, Ettore. How bloodthirsty can one female possibly be?!"

Ettore's corpse remained silent. I groaned, slapping myself in the face with one of Ettore's meaty hands.

Fuck.

Fuck. Fuck. Fuck. Akash-fucking-fuck.

"I'm tired, Ettore. What I wouldn't give to trade places with you. You're a lucky man, you know that? Always have been. I mean, look at you."

Ettore stared back at me, his expression a mask of boredom. I huffed.

"You were far more compassionate when you were alive."

I sat there for several long moments and my fatigue only continued to increase, but I couldn't muster the willpower to get up and do something about it.

Eventually, Ettore's body grew cold and my ass numb. Wiping away the last of my tears on his perfectly starched sleeve, I bade his corpse goodbye and sent a prayer of love and gratitude to *Akash* that I'd known him, and that his soul would find peace in Avernus.

FORTY-SEVEN

NAKOA

Asterion, as promised, had reduced Azrael's palace to a 200-foot wide crater of scorched ruin in under thirty minutes. And now I could only pray that the very *fragile* and desperate plan I'd hewn together at the last minute would actually work.

We'd all nearly been destroyed along with it if it hadn't been for the female that had reappeared behind him in the portal. Her strange magic had the power to control emotions, and she'd succeeded in calming him with nothing more than the touch of her hand. She'd nearly died in the process, and I'd urged a few of my soldiers to take her back to the palace.

Shouts went up at the sight of beasts and creatures of all kinds beelining for the portal, some *folding* just in front of it to attempt to dive through.

Malekai roared orders at our soldiers above the building chaos *"Guard the portal!"*

Drawing his swords, he turned back to me—eyes suddenly widening in hope and recognition. I twisted to follow his gaze to witness the darkening of the skies. Not with ominous clouds, but *drakonati.*

Mareina.

"Go get her."

My gaze snapped back to Malekai's at his demand. The realization that followed them was like a bludgeon to my heart. Considering the state of our relationship, I doubted she would *want* to come with me. She might fight against me... But Malekai...

"She wants *you.* I'll guard the portal."

"I hate to break it to you, but there's no way you can guard the portal better than my drakonati."

The *weight* of a terrible magic manifested at my back, and I turned to find a subtle frown creasing Azrael's face at the sight of his decimated palace and thousands of our enemy soldiers. If anyone were to guess based on his expression alone, they'd assume he'd merely found a stain on a white shirt.

Azrael's four wings gracefully pounded the air to keep him hovering a few dozen feet before me.

"I tried. I really did, Nakoa. I *tried* to be nice. I tried to be fair. I tried to be considerate. And look what it's earned me."

His eyes dipped to the hole in the ground and the battle behind me for emphasis, raising mildly accusatory brows.

"I will happily open Atratus to your denizens so long as you return our *soulbound.*"

FORTY-EIGHT

AZRAEL

I felt nothing as I stared down at the scorched remains of my palace. I hadn't particularly enjoyed being there. I mean, it is *hell,* so I did try to avoid coming here. And when you're as old as time immemorial, you become rather desensitized to things.

Though what I did find upsetting was the sight of an entire league of my people—even if they were mostly demons—rushing towards the portal, desperate to escape this.

To escape *me.*

That and the fact that Nakoa, Malekai, *fucking Rumiel*—that male had always been a thistle in my cock—and a few thousand of Nakoa's soldiers appeared to be staging a coup.

How very droll.

On four wings, I hovered in the air a couple of dozen feet from Nakoa, heaving a longsuffering sigh.

"Mareina's solution has proven to be more than sufficient so she'll be staying put, I'm afraid."

Shouts and cries went up as Nakoa's army began to drop like flies. Guilt warred with righteous anger.

The sight of the gilded, cerulean drakonati decimating my people to prevent them from getting through the portal had regret piercing through me at what I feared I would have to do. I tugged firmly at the cord connecting his soul to his body in warning as I *willed* my Nephilim to *fold* between me and Nakoa and his army. I could feel their collective reluctance to do so, but they were bound to my will. All except Asterion—because he was something else entirely—and Rumiel, who I had given far too much freedom long ago.

Malekai's drakonati roared as it's hungry flames attempted to devor my Nephilim. I could feel the magic of those who perished leave me, weakening me as though it were my own magic.

Fuck.

As if returning his call, I hear the very distinct, magic-laced roar of Ataraxus in response behind me. I twisted to find what appeared to be *all* of his drakonati damning the skies behind me, only moments away.

Akash-fucking-damn-it.

My helplessness was paralyzing. If I killed *everyone,* I'd, in turn, be killing myself. Indecision and anger burned through me as I watched what remained of Nakoa's army slaughter my people in an effort to prevent my demons from breaching the portal and wreaking havoc in their realm. With each of their deaths, my power weakened further.

Nakoa had already somehow worked his way through so many of my Nephilim that within moments, he was only feet away from me. Drenched in blood, vengeance and fury burning in the twin black pools of his eyes as they locked with mine. Instinct had me reaching for the cord binding soul to body.

Within that split second, I attempted to sever it, blinding pain shot through me. The face of a dark male with silver eyes flashed within my mind as I tried to recover, and I summoned another onslaught of my nephilim as Nakoa leapt towards me, sword raised to relieve my body of its head.

With a few hundred nephilim pummelling Nakoa across the battlefield, I launched myself into the air, eyes scanning.

Get to Mareina.

I swivelled to find Mareina cutting her way through my nephilim at a speed my eyes could barely follow—but still remained well out of reach of Ataraxus, Nakoa, or Malekai. While she wouldn't have any memory of the latter two, I had no doubt she would follow them through the portal the moment she had the chance.

My breath caught a fraction of a moment later when my eyes snagged on the dark crimson shadow fighting in the opposite direction to guard her back.

She connected with her arcanum.

I was *thoroughly* dismayed at the sight. What could possibly be worse than one bloodthirsty and insatiable Goddess of Death?

Two of them.

Akash-fucking-damn-it-all-to-hell.

I could feel my own arcanum, Cerebus, howling to be set free, but I didn't dare set her free to meet Mareina's wrath. Cerebus was the only love I had left in my life.

I soared towards her just as Ataraxus' deafening roar pierced my ears. A preface to his flames engulfing me and being roasted like a bird on fucking spit.

Rude.

My rage was silenced by the hungry flames attempting to devour me as my wings propelled me forward.

I visualized his life's thread and *willed* my hellfire to consume it. Ataraxus' flames ceased, but I'm stunned to discover the tensile resilience of his life force. Or perhaps the weakening of my own. Ataraxus's wings gave out, and as I weaved away, he swiped out with his talons, scoring my back and wings. Again, I *willed* his life's cord to be severed as a rage tore from my throat at the blinding pain.

Crashing into the hazardous ruin of my palace, the battle behind us was now nothing more than a distant roar of violent death.

The ground shuddered beneath the collision of Ataraxus' body as I was skewered on a rogue metal rod sticking out of the detritus of my palace.

I gasped for breath that wouldn't come as blood spilled from my lips. My wings pounded at the air behind me, gradually inching me off the rod. My wings gave a final pound against the air, and I collapsed in a heap on a broken slab of marble.

The eyes of one of Persephone's fractured statues watched me as I laid there while my wounds healed. I could hear her voice inside my mind, admonishing me. My wounds couldn't heal fast enough, if for that reason alone.

I finally crawled to standing and made my way towards Ataraxus' motionless form, waiting for the sensation of his life force to dissipate, taking a part of me with it, but I realized there were too many cumulative lives and the magic of my people dying in droves to discern his. At the sight of his body gradually shifting back to its fae form, caused by the dissipating of his magic, I was satisfied enough to leave.

Such a fucking pity...

Now to find Mareina and end this.

As I returned to the skies, my eyes passed over the battlefield. The sight before me had dread sinking like an anvil in my gut. *Thousands* of dead drakonati, nephilim, demons, humans, fae, and the like were strewn across my land as far as my eyes could see.

This has to stop.

More than just *seeing*, I could *feel* my people dying as though *Akash* herself had put a fucking *syphon* on my power.

How were they all dying so fast? I'll be dead before they are at this rate.

A cloud of red caught my eyes as Mareina's magic devoured nephilim as it passed over them.

It was then I could no longer deny it was a mistake bringing her here.

Now the solution was no longer keeping her but *killing* her.

Persephone and Mors will never forgive you, the insidious voice of my conscience whispered.

They already want nothing to do with me, so what difference does it make?

The guilt already twisting in my gut was answer enough.

As if the mere thought summoned her *Akash*-forsaken *soulbound*, magic boasting the force of Odinson's Hammer, slammed me to the ground. Nakoa's magic gripped my lungs with an iron fist, and my blood vessels felt set to burst. Resisting the pain and power of his magic against the waning of my own sent me to my knees.

I *folded* away just before the blade of his sword could remove my head. Landing in the mud formed solely by spilled blood in the dusty soil of my land, I gulped breaths of air. Relief washed over me when I managed to sever the life threads of the soldiers nearest to me with ease. At the sensation of my ever-waning magic, I *willed* my sword, *Thanapheros,* into my hand—forged in hellfire and imbued with my death magic. Even a superficial wound would be lethal.

A tall, dark, slender male appeared, only a dozen feet away. Silvery power curled from him in waves as he passed his hand over the leagues of demons, humans, and other beings desperate to reach the portal. His silver gaze snapped to mine, and I felt his magic like an axe brought down upon the immortal tether connecting my soul to my body, causing me to stumble.

His words felt like the tolling of a death knell inside my mind.

"Only in death will you find freedom, Azrael."

The recognition of truth, an all too familiar and unwelcome sensation, pinched tight inside my chest as the male *folded* in front of me. Searing pain pierced my side, and I looked down in both shock and relief to see the male had merely plunged a dagger into my abdomen. I couldn't help but burst into laughter.

"If you think that tiny little blade is enough to kill me—

The male withdrew the blade, and it was then I noticed a dark, viscous substance dripping from the hilt. A substance *other* than my blood.

My lips parted in recognition as the chill of fear seeped through me.

The male's face splits in a terrifying grin.

"Mortsbane."

Intuition told me it was no coincidence at all that mortsbane was precisely what I'd dosed Mareina and Asterion with when I'd given them their dose of the River Obvilion.

The connection to my power was burning away like a strand of hair set above a flame. The male *folded* away just as I attempted to impale him with *Thanapheros*. Before I'm cut off from my magic entirely, victory swells in my chest as I conjure his life's thread and sever it.

My eyes frantically searched for his dead body as the ground rushed towards me, and I fell face-first.

Fuck, fuck, fuck.

My heart thundered in my chest as I waited for some soldier to notice me and finally end the stinking refuse of my life.

Instead, they battled on around me.

I'm just another corpse on the ground, I realized.

Like the answer to a prayer, Nephilim blood splattered my face just before a large winged body hit the ground beside me. Fresh blood pumped out of a gaping wound in the female's chest, empty gaze tilted heavenward. A puddle formed beneath her, gradually growing so large that it reached my face. I began to lick it up, knowing it would hasten my recovery.

In under a few minutes, I'd regained enough of my facilities to stand. I attempted to *fold* away but my magic was still well out of reach.

Thank fuck for you, I inwardly murmured to *Thanapheros* as I rescued it from the bloody mud and passed my gaze over the nephilim, demons, humans, orcs, lykos, humans, and fae. All lying dead and in indistinguishable piles.

Panic gripped me as I saw Mareina soar through the air towards Malekai's drakonati, guarding the portal as he charred what remained of the demons who hadn't yet managed to escape while several more buried daggers in his body to *climb* him.

Gripping my sword, I leapt, wings pounding and *Thanapheros* poised to strike as I dove towards her like an eagle, its prey. She was too distracted battling those on the ground to notice my descent from on high.

Relief and victory swelled in my breast as I closed in—her death so close I could fucking taste it.

I was only feet away as Malekai's gargantuan beast descended, absorbing my blow. *Thanapheros* split open his throat and chest with the ease of a ship's keel through the water.

The drakonati plummeted to the ground, crushing several dozen of my people beneath him. A tremor rumbled through the ground as Mareina's blood-curdling scream filled my ears. Nakoa's guttural roar in the nearby distance was barely audible.

Her mate.

I am truly every wretched thing Persephone has ever thought of me.

A spiderweb of gorges split the bloodstained soil as Mareina's magic burst from her in crimson tendrils that speared through my flesh and bone. Blood gurgled from my throat as I was lifted from the ground. Even so, I could feel the power of my magic and my life force repairing my body. Preventing my death.

My sight waned as my face disintegrated to reveal bone, and *still*, my magic continued to heal the wounds as quickly as they were made.

I realized then that I wished the healing would stop. For millennia, a part of me had longed for death, but never so desperately as now.

The silver-eyed male's words returned to me at that moment.

'Only in death will you find peace, Azrael.'

I couldn't help but observe in awe as I absently witnessed the survivors of battle running to escape the deep fissures splitting the land, stretching beyond the horizon; many of them disappearing within the gorges and falling into what took me a moment to realize was an open sky leading elsewhere.

Portals.

But how?

My eyes caught on the sight of Marenia's arcanum *glowing* in the center of her chest, just above where the rhyton I'd put there had been. Realization washes over me as I recognized the sensation of my lifeforce bleeding out of me, *into her.*

She's syphoning my power and shredding the barriers between realms with my power.

CHAPTER

FORTY-NINE

MAREINA

illing my magic to devour Azrael, I *folded* to Malekai, clutching onto the face of his drakonati form as a violent, choking sob left me. Icy horror bled through me like the rapidly cooling pool of his blood, soaking my clothes as I dropped to my knees beside him.

"No.... No, no, no, no..."

Malekai's body gradually shifted back, the glow of his lifeforce still faintly glowing in his eyes.

My words came out a tremulous whisper. *"You can't leave..."*

A corner of Malekai's mouth tipped up to gift me one of his dimples one last time. "I wish I'd spent every day telling you how much I loved you. Should have built you that little house near that thermal pool in Bein Sith Mór we loved..."

A choked sob burst free as I clutched his fighting leathers. "You always made me feel loved. You're the *only* one who ever made me feel loved. I'm so sorry I held us back... *All these years, all I ever wanted was you..."*

Malekai gave a subtle shake of his head. "He loves you too, Mareina... More than you know."

The light in Malekai's eyes dimmed like the fading glow of a dying ember. Glassy, vacant eyes stared back at me. My hands trembled as I stroked his blood-crusted skin, unwilling to believe he was actually gone. *"Please, come back... I can't... I can't do this without you..."*

I had no idea how much time had passed when gentle hands curled over my shoulders, pulling me away from the cold, lifeless body I'd glued myself to. I clutched tighter to Malekai despite the beginning of rigor mortis setting in.

My voice came out a hoarse croak.

"I will not leave him here."

Nakoa squatted down beside me, his own face stricken. The evidence of his emotion lay in pale, watery paths streaking the dried blood staining his face. Malekai and Nakoa had hated each other before I'd left, so the sincerity and fervor in his words took me by surprise.

"I wouldn't want you to."

I gradually nodded, the action causing the crusted, blood-soaked strands sticking to my face to peel away.

"I don't want to be here without him."

Grief spilled down Nakoa's cheeks as he knelt in Malekai's blood beside me, pressing a tremoring hand to my drakonati's cheek. There was a tenderness in the gesture that I'd never witnessed in him. Not even towards *me*.

Another wave of icy-cold fear washes over me as I scan our surroundings. While I found a few of Nakoa's *olana kah'hei* lingering on the battlefield... There was no sight of Ataraxus. And I know, despite having hardly known him, that he would never leave this place without me.

My words pay no heed to the terror coursing through me.

"Where is Ataraxus?"

Nakoa's jaw worked furiously to hold back the emotion I could see clawing its way up his throat.

"I found his—

Nakoa's words were cut short by grief. He didn't need to finish them. Helplessness and rage have my hands gripping the front of Nakoa's fighting leathers as if he were the only thing holding me in one piece. His arms came around me, and I sank against him, sobbing into his chest. My breath caught in realization... If they're dead...

"Their souls must be here then... In one of Azrael's realms?"

Nakoa's words somehow brought both devastation and relief. "I do not think their souls would go to any hell realm, Mareina..."

I glanced to where Rumiel stood beside the mangled heap of Azrael's body. If anyone will be able to find them, it's him. "We're taking him with us."

My breathing ceased at the pull of the tether in my chest, yanking my gaze away from Azrael. I twist in Nakoa's arms to find Ataraxus's still form lying prone on the ground where Erius knelt, weeping beside him, along with countless other drakonati. A guttering spark of hope in my chest had me *folding* to Ataraxus' side. As I laid tremulous hands upon his chest, that hope burst into a full-fledged fire in the gaping wound of my chest.

I could feel his soul still inside his corporeal body like I could feel the frantic drum of my own heart. Tears of relief peppered his face as I held his head almost in disbelief.

"He's alive."

FIFTY

MAREINA

The first place we returned to was Zurie's palace. It still felt too surreal to call it *my* palace or even Nakoa's palace. All of the surviving drakonati had accompanied us. Pomona and Famei took the liberty of getting most of them settled in a distant wing of the palace. Roderick, Lokus, Rayne, Vesper, and Val had all also survived and escorted an unconscious Azrael, slung over Rumiel's shoulder, to the dungeons.

It seemed impossible to me that Miroslav had apparently not survived. My mind seemed entirely unable to fathom such a possibility, and I could only attribute it to the fact that I couldn't even begin to emotionally process it while I was mourning Malekai.

Asterion was nowhere to be found, something that I vowed to remedy. As soon as Azrael woke. I had hope that he'd survived, was safe and somewhere where he would find his *soulbound...* and that one day I would be able to see my friend again.

Erius, joined by the alabaster female, stood beside Nakoa, and I, as Bohyun, our army's best healer who had apparently been promoted to chief healer in my absence, examined Ataraxus.

"His body has recovered from whatever wounds he sustained, so

I can't say exactly why he hasn't wakened. His lifeforce is there, but it remains... *faint.*"

I squeezed Ataraxus' limp hand in mine as if doing so might push some of my own life force into him.

"But he's not getting worse?"

Bohyun gave me a helpless shrug. "Not from what I can tell. Have you tried giving him some of your blood?"

I felt like a fucking idiot when the truth forced to reply *no.* Bohyun nodded, eyes drifting back to Erius. "Try... If the blood of even a *minori* wielder can sustain a sanguinati, then surely the blood of a god would expedite a drakonati's recovery... Not that I have *any* knowledge of the drakonati," she adds pointedly. "Do you not have a healer?"

Erius frowned. "They did not survive."

Bohyun's expression softened as she heaved a sigh and returned her gaze to mine and Nakoa's. "Considering the three of you are *soulbound,* both of you need to give him blood. Even if it's only a few drops... I'm guessing neither of you have fulfilled the bond either?"

I could *feel* the way Nakoa held his breath before I answered. "No. I haven't." Bohyun's gaze slid to Nakoa as he shook his head.

Bohyun looked annoyed by the answer, unable to hold back her commentary. "If I had found my *soulbound,* I wouldn't hesitate a single fucking moment."

My eyes narrowed at the female I'd known for at least fifty years, but I couldn't find fault in her words, even if they were insensitive. She turned to leave, parting on one final word, *"Blood."*

Silence fell. Erius and his female left, followed by the other few drakonati after they each took turns whispering a short prayer in Vassileon and pressing their foreheads to Ataraxus'.

For several moments, Nakoa and I only stared down at Ataraxus' ashen face. Now that we were alone, the emotion I'd been desperately holding back could finally be set free. Nakoa took me in his arms again as I maintained my grip on Atraxus. Nakoa's hand found mine and to my surprise, wove his fingers with mine *and* Ataraxus'.

"You're awfully calm about this…"

"Somnus came to me beforehand… And I can feel it too. The tether between us. I will not do to him what I did to you. And I vow to spend the rest of my days making up for the error of my ways."

My lament swelled anew. "You went to *hell* to save me. Started a *war* for me. You've made it up to me a thousandfold. If anything, I *owe you*. And if I hadn't…"

I couldn't bring myself to utter the rest without another sob wracking my body. Nakoa's hold tightens on me. *"Shhhhh…* There isn't a thing in this world I wouldn't do to save you, *lohane thili."*

FIFTY-ONE

MAREINA

After Nakoa and I had each given Ataraxus a few droplets of blood, lest he choke on the fluid he could not swallow, we made our way down to the dungeons. Azrael had regained consciousness and made no protest or plea to be set free.

And it only served to awaken my rage. I wanted him to fight back. I wanted *him* to attack me, wound me, cause my physical pain, *kill me* if only it would liberate me of this pain.

Azrael's eyes lifted to mine as my crimson magic flowed toward him like a mist pouring over the ground and climbed up his body. He didn't resist as my arcanum manifested and coiled around him.

My serpent constricted as her fangs sank into the flesh of his right shoulder. Azrael only shut his eyes, eventually grimacing when the pain became overwhelming.

My voice was like a whip cracking through the air.

"Do something. Have you no will to live now that you've taken every-thing *from me?"*

Azrael's gaze opened, and through my serpent, I could feel the cracking of his ribs, one by one, as she squeezed further. I could barely make out his words, though the sadness in his voice rang crystal clear, gaze flicking briefly to Nakoa. "Not... everything."

My words were little more than an inhuman growl. *"Bring them back."*

Azrael's expression tenses. "Them?" Realization filtered through the pain, widening his gaze before he shook his head, guilt and remorse lining his pained features. "I wish more than anything my power was one that brought forth life instead of death. That rare gift was left to my *soulbound*. Wherever she is."

Persephone.

All at once, my magic and my serpent left him.

A spark of hope lit my chest.

Somnus went to look for her.

Guilt and watery grief returned, clogging my throat like a fucking fist.

"And where is Malekai?"

Azrael gestured limply to the collar around his throat. "If you remove it, I can tell you."

I *willed* away the palladium without a moment's hesitation. I didn't bother to threaten him. If he tried to escape, he would fail.

Azrael's gaze grew distant, his features sinking further into despair. "... His soul is not in my domain."

His words are like the severing of a cord—that sets me free.

Not in his domain...

Ataraxus' words echo in my mind, *"... When a drakonati claims and bonds with another, the magic infusing their venom weaves itself into your magic, and thus your soul..."*

Hope and relief swelled in my chest as I reached out with my magic, scanning the whole of Avernus, the existence of which is a presence in my soul, like my heart within my body.

Like a spindle drawing blood from a finger, I felt a faint pricking sensation the moment my magic found Malekai.

Home.

My gaze snapped to Nakoa's, and I didn't miss the unmistakable hope widening his gaze. Nakoa gives me a single nod in under-standing.

I *willed* the palladium collar back onto Azrael's throat as I *folded* back to Avernus on beating wings. Instantly, I was drawn towards the mountains lying in the distance.

Is this where your soul has gone, tessari mú?

I let my eyelids fall as my soul carried me towards the male who possessed my heart. Icy wind whipped around me, and I opened my eyes to find myself standing in a towering cavemouth. The tunnel inside dripping with frozen, sickle-shaped icicles. Hope pounded furiously in my chest as I made my way inside, not bothering to glance back at the frozen wasteland behind me.

Ice crunched beneath my boots, and the sound of a beastly huff echoed in the dark recesses before me. I treaded deeper into the cave, *willing* a fire to illuminate my path. My heart stuttered as my eyes reached the furthest corner of the cave, where two glowing turquoise and golden orbs glimmered, each one nearly as large as my head.

A sob of relief strangled me as I *folded* to the space in front of him and threw myself at him. The frozen cave trembled as a wail of unmistakable lament rumbled through him, and a foreleg curled around me, pulling me into the warm space beneath his neck.

Part of how my father's after realm cleansed and repaid karmic debt was by causing the soul to experience all that they had inflicted upon others—whether it be joy and love, or pain and suffering. It could sometimes take hundreds of years before a soul recovered from the atrocities they had inflicted in the living realms. And Malekai, while his intentions weren't always malevolent... He had wrought death and destruction to countless lives.

Right beside me.

My time for penance would one day come, and I couldn't help but feel this was part of it.

FIFTY-TWO

MAREINA

Time passed at an indiscernible pace, and I only vaguely noticed that it went by quicker than my mind could follow as darkness gave way to light and light to darkness. I never wanted to leave Malekai's side again. It was only a matter of time before my worry for Ataraxus, still in need of my blood, and Nakoa reached a tipping point. My soul felt torn in three, being separated from them.

Coupled with the fact that my body had demands I could only deny for so long. I came and went, folding between Malekai's cave and my father's house only to use the toilet and shower when I began to grow weary of my own stench and to the bed chamber where Ataraxus *rested* so I could give him my blood and reassure myself he was still alive. Nakoa, to my dismay, remained elusive.

Until one day, I returned to Malekai's cave to discover he was gone. Panic struck me like a bolt of electricity as my magic scoured my realm to find his drakonati curled away in another cave in a distant forest I hadn't yet visited, but somehow knew because my soul was tied to this place as much as it was to the broken male in front of me. Malekai's beast groaned at the sight of me, nudging me back towards the entrance of the cave. My eyes squeezed shut against the pain. He wanted me to let him go.

I had responsibilities to attend to. Two *soulbound* that needed me. People, a kingdom, and a realm to care for. All of which were in the throes of turmoil after being breached by the malevolent beings formerly trapped in Vassileo. And I had selfishly remained here, desperately shoving away the constant nagging at the back of my mind. Yet here I was, clutching onto my beloved drakonati, who was trying to shove me out of his lair. My heart was shattering all over again.

"I told you. I can't do this without you," I whimpered as he gently tried to usher me to the cave's mouth. *"Please, give me Malekai. Change back. I need him."*

His drakonati replied with a great huff that blew my hair back. With another nudge, I stumbled back, feeling like a shunned canine.

Tears tracked my face as he held my gaze. I could *feel* his words.

Live your life, Mareina.

A shuddering breath left me. *"I can't."*

A huff that may have sounded like, *You can,* followed by another gentle nudge sent me another step away.

"Please, don't make me."

Malekai's drakonati gave a pained groan, tossing its massive head.

The gentle winds outside the cavern whirled around me as if trying to coax me out of the cave itself. Somehow, that breeze drew my gaze. The light of day shone bright, another glaring reminder that the world went on. Birdsong filtered in from a distance accompanying the sound of leaves whispering against one another on the breeze as the murmur of life beyond beckoned me.

Akash, when was the last time I'd felt the sun on my face.

A stone-hard snout nuzzled against me as a rough tongue the length of my arm licked me from head to toe. The scent of his saliva, so very near to Malekai's sea salt and embers scent, filled me with a sense of peace.

I curved my body over Malekai's drakonati's snout as my resolution to ignore my duties, *my life,* waned. I pressed my lips to his silken scales before whispering our favorite words against him.

Words I wished I had declared every day of the last 100 years and shown him just how true they were.

"I love you in this life and every life to come. Katadamna kaza."

FIFTY-THREE

NAKOA

For the last two weeks, I had taken residence in Mareina's father's house. Only surfacing to Atratus to spend my days beside my army, my *olana kah'hei,* and Rumiel fighting tirelessly to exterminate our newfound plague of demons. The moment night fell, I would return to Ataraxus' side to offer him droplets of my blood and pray that he would wake.

And, much to my absolute fucking dismay, the spare moments I found in between proved to be exactly when Mareina would show up.

I'd return to her father's to find the bathtub wet, watery footprints lining the floor, and her night-blooming rose scent perfuming the air.

Still, I knew that one day, she would return.

Despite the bone-deep exhaustion weighing me down after slaughtering demons all day and visiting Ataraxus to give him my blood, I felt the familiar call to return to Avernus.

My heart nearly stopped beating as my eyes landed on Mareina curled in a ball at the edge of the bed in the spare bedroom I'd taken residence in.

Freshly showered, still damp hair curled around her face, and her skin looked even paler than I'd ever seen her.

Our gazes held silently as emotion swelled in my chest, heart throbbing in protest at the fact I hadn't yet launched myself at her to simply *hold* her.

Worry tightened her features as she rose from the bed, taking in my filthy, blood-crusted appearance.

"Are you injured?"

The word came out little more than a breath. "No."

Her relief was palpable and that breadcrumb of love was enough to fill my heart to bursting. Emboldened, I strayed towards her, closing the distance between us to stand in front of her. I didn't dare taint the bed with my muddy, bloody fighting leathers.

"How is Ataraxus?"

My chest tightened to the point of pain. "Still unconscious, but alive."

Mareina drew in a deep breath.

"What happened with the Vassileons that breached the portal?"

"Most are dead. Or so we think. Though the ones that remain are... concerning. We've been working diligently to resolve the problem."

I watched the wheels of her mind turn as guilt settled on her features."I'm sorry that I disappeared. That I haven't been upholding my duties towards... anything."

"Don't worry. I understand. If anything had happened to you, I would have been the same."

My selfish heart gave a pitter-patter of relief when her eyes began to glisten. I longed to tell her how fucking sorry I was and how much I missed her. How much my soul longed for her, and life wasn't worth living without her. My lips were already forming the words, but as I took in the gauntness haunting her features and the pallid hue of the normally sun-kissed rosiness of her skin, worry for her took over.

The steadiness I forced into my voice betrayed my tortured emotions. "When was the last time you fed?"

Mareina shook her head. "I don't need to feed when I'm in Avernus."

I shook my head in disbelief but recognized forcing her to drink my blood would get us nowhere.

Instead, I sat her on the edge of the bed and lowered to one knee, curling a finger beneath her chin to raise her gaze to mine. Her eyes squeezed shut, tears slipping down her pinkening cheeks as her lower lip trembled under the weight of all that she had been through.

Her eyes peeked open as she drew in another shuddering breath, and I reached forward, curling my arms around her, pulling her against my blood-crusted chest before sitting cross-legged on the floor.

Mareina's body shook as she began to sob quietly against me. Grief burned my eyes at witnessing my *soulbound* so broken. The most powerful female I'd ever known wilted and bludgeoned by life. Again, oh-so-selfishly, my heart ached when she allowed me to see her at her most vulnerable. That she allowed me to hold her and touch her. *Console her.*

Her delicate fingers curled to grip my fighting leathers, pulling me against her. The action had my own tears finally slipping free as my heart shattered all over again.

"I miss him too, lohane thili."

Some hours later, I woke up from the dull ache forming at the back of my head from lying on the hardwood floor. Mareina was curled against my body, lying on her side, sound asleep. Carefully rolling to my side to face her, I wove my other arm around her and tucked her against my chest. A deep, soul-nourishing satisfaction poured through me when she gave a soft sigh and nuzzled deeper, burying her face in the center of my chest.

"You smell like stale demon blood," she whispered, "Lots of it."

A huffed laugh rumbled my chest. "I was drenched in it."

"Do you want to take a shower? And then we can crawl in bed?"

My breath caught before I managed to infuse my voice with every ounce of steadiness I didn't feel. "That would be a dream come true, Mareina."

The idea of sharing a bed with my *soulbound* again was nothing short of an answered prayer. I pressed a lingering kiss to the top of Mareina's head before shifting us so I could sit up.

Mareina's grip tightened on me. "Do you mind if I join you?"

My cock promptly thickened in response, drawing a silent curse from me. Overcome with the longing that the idea of her joining me inspired, I couldn't manage words to respond. Instead, I scooped her into my arms and carried her to the bathroom.

Willing the shower on, steam curled through the air as every nerve in my body lit up with anticipation. Outside of the sound of the running water, silence stretched between us as we stood mere inches apart, hesitating to undress. There was so much I needed to say to her. To apologize for. To express. But I recognised that now, was not the time to put any more emotional burden on her.

However, before I could step into that shower, there was one thing that I couldn't wait for an apology. "I have to apologize... I can't help—

Mareina's eyes dipped between us, and the ghost of a smile appeared on her lips. "I don't take your erections as a personal insult, *soulbound.*"

My heart squeezed to the point of pain at the endearment. The first-ever. The tension between us lifted a little and Mareina took the opportunity to *will* her clothing away. My eyeballs practically shook under the strain to *not* allow my gaze to fall upon her nude perfection.

She turned and stepped into the shower, taking my willpower

with her. My eyes landed heavily on the thick curves of her ass and thighs. I swallowed my groan, willing my fighting leathers away. My cock sprang forward, already hard as the fucking tile beneath my feet. I couldn't help but notice the way her eyes fell from my face to my cock, demanding her attention, and then *blushed.*

A deep groan escaped me as I stepped beneath the scalding hot water raining down upon us. Mareina reached for a bottle of cleanser, lathering a loofah before taking one of my arms in her hands and working it over my skin. Surprise illuminated the dark, hollow cavern of my chest, followed by the meeting of our eyes, something unspoken passing between us.

I'm sorry.

Mareina continued her ministrations, taking extra care as she worked over the sharp black armored protrusions that had formed over parts of my arms, shoulders, and legs when I'd made my transformation after our *altercation.*

I *willed* them away, slipping them beneath my skin, lest she cut herself on them. She gave a soft gasp. "I didn't know you could do that," she murmured.

"Only with the armor... The rest, I'd have to glamor."

I'd developed mixed emotions about my changed appearance. How the lush, dark feathers of my wings had been replaced with bat-like membranes. The thick, lethal horns that now grew from my head.

Before my transformation, I'd always kept the inhuman parts of me glamored, but now, I hadn't often bothered even though every time I looked in the mirror, I only saw a monster. I'd be lying if I said I didn't feel a pang of insecurity in front of Mareina. The thought had me willing away my horns, wings, and tail.

Mareina shook her head, searching my gaze and no doubt discovering all my insecurities. "Please, don't. I want all of you."

Sudden emotion clogged my throat. I managed a nod, bringing forth my tail, horns, and wings.

"What about the armor?"

I shook my head. "I don't want to accidentally cut you."

She reached for my wings, gently brushing the loofah over them. Every muscle in my body tensed. *Including the ones in my cock.*

"Is this ok?"

A tight groan escaped as I nodded. "Yes. It's just... intense."

Mareina remained still behind me for a moment before her fingers gingerly caressed a stripe up the length of my wings, and I swear to *fuck* I felt the beginning of an orgasm tingle at the base of my spine. My hips gave an involuntary thrust as I failed to stifle a soft growl. Her night-blooming rose scent thickened in the air, denoting her arousal.

This was becoming torture. A sweet, delicious torture but torture none-theless.

"Maybe we should just skip my wings."

The suggestion felt like shards of glass on my tongue because that was the last thing I wanted her to do when every stroke sent delicious currents of energy straight to my engorged, aching cock.

Instead of heeding my suggestion, Mareina continued the gentle glide of her fingers. Every muscle in my body coiled tight and trembled with restraint, only relaxing briefly when she stopped to shift in front of me. My cock slid against her abdomen as her hands coasted over the planes of my chest. Gradually working lower.

Before she could reach my cock, I snagged her wrists in my hands.

My voice dropped to a low, warning growl. *"Mareina..."*

She tugged at my grasp, and I allowed one of her hands to break free. I shouldn't have, but I did.

"Let me take care of you..."

She lowered a hand, brushing the loofah over my hard length and lower, even beneath my balls, before she knelt to scrub down each of my legs. The sight of her kneeling beneath me harkened memories of our nights together in my tent.

When she began to scrub my feet, my tail whipped forward and curled around her waist, lifting her back to her feet. All of my pent-up emotions and desire for this maddening female had every muscle in my body rigid and primed to strike. *Or thrust.*

I snagged the loofah from her hands as I pinned her arms above her head. My tail pushed her against the shower wall. Unable to resist temptation, I leaned forward to take in her scent.

"Akash, you smell like fucking heaven."

Both my arousal and emotion *burned* through me so fiercely my heart clenched and my eyes stung. My words were spoken through clenched teeth.

"Do you have any idea how much I've missed you, Mareina? Do you?"

Mareina remained silent as she pulled her hands free from mine before sliding them over my shoulders and my neck and carding her fingers through my wet hair.

"How every moment you were away from me, I felt as though my soul was fucking dying?"

Her haunted gaze held mine. "Four months passed in *hell* without you, and there was not an hour that would go by where I didn't think about you and—

Mareina's words stopped short as her voice cracked, and she was forced to draw in a steadying breath. "Even before Vassileo, when I was here with..." Her voice broke again as her eyes glistened. "With Malekai... I *still* longed for you."

Like the drawback of a wave upon the shore, my eyes searched hers, frantically scouring her gaze for sign of anything that might stop this cresting tsunami of agony. My jaw worked desperately to hold back the swelling of my emotion. "I'm sorry for everything I've done to hurt you, Mareina... I am beyond ashamed of how I treated you and tried to—

My words were cut off as Mareina tugged her hands out of my grip and covered my mouth. "Not right now... Please. I just need you to help me forget. Even if it's just for a few minutes. *Please.*"

FIFTY-FOUR

MAREINA

Nakoa's expression was nothing short of tortured as he held my gaze. My hands roamed over his thickly muscled shoulders before curling my fingers around his neck. I didn't miss the hope and fear infusing his words. "What would you have me do?"

Akash almighty.

Anything and everything.

Iron wings flapped in my belly as I gathered my courage. I knew he desired me. Our bond made sure of that, but after everything that had happened... I was still terrified of opening myself up to him. Perhaps most of all, because, next to Azrael, I couldn't ignore the fact that so much of this was *my* fault.

But if I had learned anything with Malekai... It was that time was never guaranteed, and I refused to waste a second more of it on fear instead of allowing myself to love and be loved. To give my soul what it *longed* for and demanded.

And just as my soul needed and demanded Malekai, I knew that nothing would ever change the fact that I would always feel the same for Nakoa. No matter what happened between us. We had literally tried to kill one another, and still, it had done very little to quell the soul-deep longing for him.

I rose to my tiptoes and pulled him down to graze my lips across his beautifully scarred cheek. *"I love you, Nakoa Solanis. Let me show you, please. Let me fulfill our bond."*

Nakoa's arms came around me, and in the next moment, the shower turned off, and our bodies were dry. The brush of his magic in doing so made every hair on my body rise. My legs instinctively curled around his waist as he lifted me off the ground.

Nakoa's lips captured mine as his fingers sank into the globes of my ass to the point of bruising. Our lips and tongues slid together and twined, each caress infused with an aching, soul-deep need.

As he strode towards the bed, his teeth nipped firmly at my bottom lip before sucking it into his mouth in a way that I felt in my clit. With every pass of his tongue and lips, it further coaxed open the floodgates of all our restrained emotions.

All the hurt, unhealed wounds, the lust and desire, the longing. How much we had missed one another. The love and need we shared all crested in a tidal wave, ready to obliterate our feebly constructed walls.

Tears burned my eyes as Nakoa laid me on the bed with shocking tenderness. He pulled back to take in the glistening in my eyes, and caressed my cheek as we both savored this moment. Squeezing me against his chest, he buried his face in the curve of my neck, breathing in my scent.

My hips oscillated against his, painting the thick length of him pinned between us with my arousal. "Please... I need you now." Nakoa's body tightened as he growled low and braced himself on his elbows on either side of my head. The cage of his body around mine was the singular thread holding together my sanity.

"I never told you how much I love you, *lohane thili.*"

My breath caught, as the memory of my dream returned.

"I wish I had, Nakoa."

Relief floods me as his lips and tongue devoured mine. His hips drew back, notching the head of his cock at my entrance, and he slowly began to push in. The action stole my breath. He was so *thick* that the further he sank into me, it felt as though the action shoved the air from my lungs just to make room for him. His gaze held mine all the while, drawing a hand to grip the meat of my hip before his thumb moved to my clit to lavish me with teasing strokes.

Keening softly, my nails dug into the flesh of his arms, hips thrusting upwards to capture more of him. He brushed his nose against my cheek as he murmured.

"I have loved you since the moment you threatened to cut off my balls with a dull, jagged blade, Mareina."

A surprised laugh bubbled out of me, cut by the pang of swelling emotion and the deep stroke of his cock.

"And there is nothing in this world or the next that could change that. With or without this bond, I will always love you, *lohane thili*. You are the air in my lungs, and without you, I have been fucking suffocating."

Helpless to the joy spilling down my cheeks, a tremulous smile spread across my face.

"No matter what pain or pleasure it earns me, I love every glorious facet of you, Nakoa, and despite how I may have tried to will it away, my love for you will never fade."

My eyes caught the dip of Nakoa's throat as he swallowed thickly, eyes glistening.

"Do you remember the fire? When you helped me save those humans?"

Nakoa huffed a laugh. "How could I forget? We nearly died."

"That was when I fell in love with you. Even if I couldn't bring myself to admit it. When we were laying on the ground watching that house burn after we'd managed to escape... I wanted so badly to hold your hand."

Nakoa smiled, slowly easing himself in and out of me as I adjusted to his formidable size and my pussy wettened with increasing arousal. His smile such a rare, awe-inspiringly beautiful sight that it stole my breath even as my channel gripped his thick length.

"I wish so badly that you had."

My smile waned. "I was too conflicted..."

Remorse takes over Nakoa's expression. "I grew to love him too, Mareina..."

I nod in understanding. I'd begun to assume as much, and I wished more than anything I'd been blessed with witnessing it.

Nakoa leaned forward to capture my tears. "We'll find a way, *maha loha.* All of us."

My throat tightened with grief, but I swallowed it back, moving my hips up to slide back down Nakoa's length. "Just help me forget. For now."

Nakoa sat back on his heels, holding me in place by my hips with his hands and his beloved tail, now fully regrown, came around to slide against my clit. His thrusts turned steady and deep as he leaned into me, licking the curve of my neck. *"May I?"*

"Akash, yes."

Nakoa's fangs sank in, and my back bowed in pleasure as a cry tore from my throat. Each pull of my blood was a sensation I felt directly against my clit. Between that and the caress of his tail, the firm strokes of his tremendous cock, the cries and whimpers drawn from me were enough to make my cheeks burn.

After a few, too-short moments, he withdrew his fangs and sat back against his heels. His heavy-lidded, reverent gaze made my heart soar. Truly, the sight of him was nothing short of breathtaking. From the thick black horns curling from his head, to the dark, membranous wings at his back, and the small dark plates of armor at his temples... he looked like a demon, if anything. Or perhaps some god of the underworld.

He used to call me his little nightmare, and it seemed too serendipitous not to be the deliberate workings of Akash herself that he would be my demon and tormentor, forcing me to acknowledge and heal the worst parts of myself. And I, his little nightmare, forced him to do the same.

All the while Malekai, for all his morally black ways, would always be my avenging and saving angel.

I wish you were here.

Grief and longing swelled in my chest, coupled with the overwhelming love radiating from me as the ecstasy of my body rose higher, all working together to produce catharsis. My orgasm rose in tandem. Every muscle and fiber of my being was set alight as the tether between us coiled impossibly tighter, even as my heart still longed for Malekai. *"I love you so much."*

Nakoa drew one of my legs up to his chest, angling my hips higher, thrusting his cock deeper, his tail never faltering in the teasing of my clit. Nakoa pressed his lips to my foot and licked a stripe along the inside of my sole, making me clench firmly around him.

"I love you, lohane thili, in this life and every life to come."

The words stole my breath, nearly identical the same shared between me and Malekai, but I was too far gone to speak of it.

Nakoa's strokes turned punishing as my pussy spasmed around him. The orgasm lighting up every molecule of my being felt like the birth of new stars, new worlds as something within us both changed. Transformed. Distantly, I realized it was the sensation of our bond finally being fulfilled.

His gaze held mine as his cock pulsed inside of me, filling me with liquid heat. Something in my chest, *our tether,* burst. Emotion and ecstasy coursed through us in synchronized, unending waves that felt as though my body was dissolving to meld with his.

"You're mine, Mareina. Say it. Tell me that you belong to me as I belong to you."

My heart clenched with the sweetest pain as our bond continued to both ignite and dissolve every molecule of our being until it felt as though I could no longer discern where my body ended, and his began. Tears streaked my cheeks in awe.

"I always have, *anim gemla.*"

Soulbound. The Aurialingan term for it. The same language Malekai so often spoke to me when calling me *tessari mú.*

I knew Nakoa understood that a part of me would always belong to Malekai, in both life and death, just as I would to him and Ataraxus. Not even time, the creator and destroyer of all things, could change that because love is enduring and eternal.

Nakoa's features tensed under the weight of his emotion, which I could feel barrelling down our tether. His eyes shut briefly as his strokes gentled. My watery emotion doubled its efforts at witnessing this powerful male come undone before me, physically and emotionally. Whatever walls had been between us had now been reduced to nothing.

Hope flickered within me at this new beginning for us. I could only pray that somehow Malekai and Ataraxus would be there with us.

FIFTY-FIVE

NAKOA

Something had changed. Not only between Mareina and I, but something else in the center of my chest. A pull that, at first, seemed inconsequential but eventually became unignorable. My Knowingness whispered to me who it was.

Malekai.

Mareina was still sound asleep beside me, the moons casting a soft celestial glow in the room. My eyes remained fixed on her, wondering if it was just a trick of the light or if she really was healthier after we'd finally fulfilled our bond. The dark circles under her eyes had disappeared, her cheeks were no longer gaunt, but full and rosy. Her skin practically glittered. And the expression on her face was more peaceful than I'd ever seen it. The sight filled me with so much love and fucking *relief* it stole my breath.

And as if that thread tugging me toward the pull couldn't possibly pull any tighter, my gaze dipped to where her hands and arms were curled sweetly in the burrow between my chest and hers and a mark on her wrist caught my eyes.

Gently, I took her wrist in my hand to discover a pink, raised scar bearing Malekai's name in curling cursive.

To my surprise, I didn't feel the burn of jealousy. Instead, it made me actually miss the fucker.

Carefully, I tucked Mareina's arm back against her chest and disentangled our limbs before pressing a kiss to her forehead.

I had a dead drakonati to visit.

Finding Malekai had been much easier than I'd anticipated. It was like a cord had been tied directly between the two of us. If I wavered from the path to him, second guessing my self, pain would flare down the bond until I returned to the proper course.

Just fucking like him to pull me out of bed when I'm with our mate.

A forest appeared on the silvery horizon, and like a beacon, my soul was somehow now connected, drawn towards a small clearing at the foot of mountains I had no name for.

An eerie stillness surrounded the cave as if everything that lived in the vicinity had fled to safer ground. I padded across the clearing on silent feet as the hairs on my arms began to rise. I could feel the flame of Malekai's magic beckoning me into the giant cavemouth, igniting hope and relief to fill the gaping hole of grief his death had left.

I willed an orb of light to illuminate my path, though my eyes could see just fine in the dark. The tunnel inside was cavernous, opening further into cathedral heights as I reached its end, where I found Malekai's drakonati. Seeing him reawakened my grief. The weight of it returning like a boulder on my chest.

The sadness in his glowing eyes was a mirror to my own. Laying on all fours with his head between his forelegs. Relief twined with grief escaped my eyes as I approached, laying a hand on the scales of his hide as he released a mournful groan.

I owed this male everything. My *soulbound—our mate.* My life. My Kingdom. Fear flayed me open as my mind flashed back to the heartstopping memory of Azrael descending with his blade poised to kill. The terror and impotence of being too far away to reach them in time.

"Thank you," I managed to whisper.

The drakonati huffed in response. Silence stretched between us before I finally took a seat on the ground beside a boulder a few feet away.

"We need you, Malekai."

Expression softened the curves around the drakonati's eyes as they lifted from the cave floor to mine, reminding me of a dog's expressive features.

"She's doing better now. Looks healthier. Less... traumatized."

A great sigh leaves the beast's chest, and his relief is palpable.

"So what happens now? Do you just... lay here? In this cave forever? Is this what the afterlife is?"

If a drakonati could look bored, it would be wearing the expression on his face now.

"Can you shift back?"

"No."

The unfamiliar male voice nearly caused me to jump out of my skin. I twisted to find a hulking, winged male standing only a few meters away. He frowned at me, stepping forward with a basket of...

Flowers?

"Lathrimos," the male answered without me needing to ask, "I'm the *protus archestratim.*"

Chief Archangel.

"I have helped your *soulbound's* father rule this realm for more millennia than I care to count... And I know your father, Rumiel. Though I haven't seen him in an age."

Lathrimos swayed the basket in front of Malekai's nostrils like a priest or priestess swings a thurible of incense. Malekai's nostrils twitched before inhaling deeply. The black chasms in the center of his sea green and gold eyes dilated wide in one swift leap, and something like a laugh, if a drakonati could do such a thing, rumbled in his chest.

"What the hells is that?"

Lathrimos glanced over his shoulder at me as he continued to sway the flowers in front of Malekai's beast's nose. Glittering, iridescent pollen drifted up from the basket as Malekai continued to breathe in slow, measured breaths, and that rumbling laugh vibrated through him and the ground beneath where I sat.

"Dendrata zou. It's a flower that normally only grows in *Lucidi Regorum,* your uncle-in-law's realm, but Mors convinced Somnus to let him grow a garden of it here... It thins the veil between *Akash* and ourselves. It enables us to reconnect more consciously with her Source energy, tap into her knowledge, and clear karmic debts and energy. Heal wounds..."

My brows lept, thoroughly intrigued. The drakonati in front of us rolled onto his back, feet peddling through the air whilst wiggling around like a dog in a field of flowers as that rumbling, drakonati laughter made the stone of the cave tremble.

The sound was contagious. The tension in my body eased, the weight on my chest lifted, all as I began to laugh, watching with no small amount of awe as this gigantic, fearsome drakonati *laughed.*

"Akash almighty. Is he hallucinating?"

Lathrimos' laughter beside me increased. "Well, I would think so. He just inhaled enough *dendrata zou* pollen to reduce an entire army to babbling toddlers."

My head tipped back with laughter that liberated my soul from the shackles of grief in one fell swoop.

Malekai's beast hummed and babbled in a strange drakonati tongue that I wasn't entirely sure the drakonati himself even understood. Laughter streamed from mine and Lathrimos' eyes as our gazes met. His laughter became high-pitched, and mine a silent wheeze.

"I've never seen a drakonati on dendrata zou before," he wept through his laughter, bending at the waist as he held his spasming abdomen.

The beast suddenly twisted back around, sending Lathrimos'

enormous body tumbling backwards onto the ground to avoid getting crushed. It only served to intensify our laughter to the point that I couldn't breathe.

If I don't stop laughing, I'm going to pass out from lack of oxygen.

As if to relieve me of this possibility, a warm and heavy snout suddenly thrust itself towards me and began to *nuzzle me.* My laughter cut off in shock, unsure if it, in his hallucinations, caused him to mistake me for a snack. From the look on Lathrimos' face, he wasn't entirely sure either.

A pink tongue the size of a baby whale snuck out and licked up the entire front of my body. The force of it even lifted me to my toes.

The drakonati *purred,* nudging me as if demanding to be petted. My eyes met Lathrimos' from over the top of the beast's head to find his brows sat just as high as mine. I tentatively raised a hand, stroking his scales, and the drakonati hummed with satisfaction.

"I've never seen a bond transfer like that before."

Suspecting this had been one thing, but hearing it confirmed from the *protus archestratim*'s mouth was another thing entirely.

"You're sure?" I asked, even though I already, intuitively, knew the answer.

"Somehow, when you fulfilled your bond with *Her Majesty,* the bond they share, though very different from your own, extended to you."

About a thousand questions rose to the front of my mind.

"So... He's also my *soulbound?*"

Lathrimos shrugged, shaking his head a little helplessly. "Something like that."

My hand stilled upon Malekai's scales, making him nudge me like a needy pup demanding more pets.

"Does that mean..."

My throat worked on an awkward smile... I mean... It's not like I could fuck a dragon.

"... That I'll *desire* him like I do Mareina?"

I'd already been wondering the same about Ataraxus.

Lathrimos gave a chuckle. "I don't know. As I said, I've never witnessed this before. Have you ever desired a male before? That would be a good indicator, I imagine."

"No... I've only ever craved a female's touch."

The male shrugged. "Well, there you have it... However, I imagine there might come a day when love leads you to make exceptions. I have rarely ever found anything to be absolute."

The drakonati gave a pained whine, drawing our gazes back to him. I watched as a glistening tear the size of my head swelled like a watery balloon in the corner of his eye. Malekai's drakonati rose, ambling toward the cavemouth in pounding steps.

Lathrimos and I followed him outside to see him take to the air on gargantuan wings.

Lathrimos sighed in relief beside me. "Well, that's progress."

"Progress?"

"Yes. Some people will spend an eon in the caves of Avernus mourning their past lives, buried beneath hundreds if not thousands of years worth of guilt from a lifetime of misdeeds before they're able to transform that pain into compassion. *Love.* Which is usually when they feel called to reincarnate."

His words managed to pry my gaze from the shrinking drakonati in the distance that my soul was now tied to.

Lathrimos' frown was pitying at best, as if he could see every sin I'd committed against another.

"No one is without their faults, and it is never too late to change and embrace the version of ourselves that we long to be."

I'd barely managed to thank the male before I flew back to Mareina with a speed and determination I'd only ever experienced when it came to her.

Only ever her.

FIFTY-SIX

MAREINA

The scent of burning ambers and sea salt filled my nose, jolting me awake. *Malekai.* My eyes burst open to find Nakoa pulling his clothes off before climbing back into bed. "You visited him."

Nakoa gave me a silent nod, as he lifted the covers and slid in beside me and tugged me against his chest. Love, relief, and *comfort* washed over me as I buried my face between the twin boulders of his pectorals. *And fuck if it wasn't one of the most beautiful things I'd ever experienced.*

All that was missing was Malekai... and Ataraxus.

I inhaled, drawing in Nakoa and Malekai's scents as deeply as I could, sending a flare of arousal through me.

"How was he?"

Nakoa chuckled against me, drawing my gaze to his.

"Hallucinating."

"What?"

"Lathrimos showed up. Gave him something called dendrata zou pollen."

My consciousness, tied to this realm and everything within it, helpfully provided an explanation. Realization and hope blossomed within my mind. "He's trying to help him shift back."

"He mentioned something about karmic clearing and reincarnating."

Pain lanced through my heart at the idea. *Selfishly.*

If Malekai reincarnated...

"It could be... Hundreds of years, potentially thousands before he returns if he chose to reincarnate."

An even more painful and selfish realization hit me like a fucking boulder.

"And he might meet his *soulbound*."

My hands trembled as I gripped Nakoa's arms, and he squeezed me tighter against him.

"I don't know that he has a *soulbound* outside of you. And me. And Ataraxus."

I drew in a deep breath, trying to calm myself as I lifted my eyes to Nakoa's."What do you mean?"

Nakoa's hand came up to caress my cheek. The action effectively soothed my tremors.

"Lathrimos said that I'm bound to him as well now. Since we fulfilled our bond... He wasn't able to explain it, but he said he saw a tether connecting me to Malekai."

My shock must have been blatant because another chuckle rumbled beneath my hands from his chest. A thousand questions rose in my mind, and I had no idea where to begin.

Nakoa's thumb coasted over my parted lips.

"I love you, *lohane thili.* In this life and every life to come."

A wellspring of emotion swelled in my breast. Again, he'd spoken the exact words that Malekai used to tell me. My brows drew together in confusion as my emotion swelled, and *fuck,* if I wasn't exhausted from weeping.

"Malekai and I used to say that to each other."

Nakoa leaned in and kissed the saline from my cheeks, murmuring against them. "I suppose it's all Kismet then."

His breath stole my words as my mind harkened back to Ataraxus' words. *"This is Kismet, Mareina…"*

My love for Nakoa swelled in my chest even as a part of me longed for both Malekai and Ataraxus. I slotted my mouth against his, tongue seeking. His cock was already hard, pinned between us. I curled one of my legs over his hips and thrust towards him, aligning his length with my entrance, dripping with need. Nakoa groaned against my mouth, carding his fingers through my hair, fisting a handful of it at the back of my head. *"Fuck, maha loha. You're soaked."*

My pussy clenched as I took him in shallow, teasing thrusts that squeezed against him. Nakoa allowed this for all of a few seconds before he pushed me onto my back, gripping my thighs and spreading them wide beneath him as he slowly thrust into me in deep, steady strokes. Sucking on his cheeks, he allowed a ball of spit to drop from his mouth to my clit, circling it with his thumb.

I was already so primed for him that it was the work of a moment before my pussy began to spasm around him. His name was a breathless moan on my lips.

"That's it, *lohane thili.*"

My back arched, and my eyes squeezed shut with overwhelm. *"Gods, Nakoa, yes."*

"Eyes on me, Mareina."

My orgasm reached its peak as my gaze returned to his. The tightness in my body slackened as waves of tingling energy washed through me like a cleansing tide. My heart, and our tether, pulsing as if with aftershock.

Nakoa's strokes turned hard and demanding as he fisted my hair to bare my neck to him. He inhaled deeply, and I felt his cock harden further. *"Look how your body sings for me, lohane thili. There's no part of you that doesn't belong to me."*

The wet heat of his tongue licked a stripe up the column of my neck before his fangs sank in. Time seemed to slow as something passed between our tether, and that sensation of being unable to discern where I ended and he began returned. It seemed impossible for our souls to twine further together than they already had, but the feeling was unmistakable.

When my orgasm receded, Nakoa's fangs withdrew, and he sat back on his heels. His gaze passing over me as he continued to thrust inside of me was a tangible heat through which I felt his reverence and love.

Nakoa bit into the flesh of his forearm and held the trickling wound over where we were joined. "There is nothing more perfect than the sight of you taking my cock and my blood."

His words, as deranged as some may find them, had my love and arousal soaring for him. My fangs lengthened, and without needing to be told, he braced arms beneath me—no fucks given for the blood staining our white sheets—and pulled me against his chest.

I titled my hips to counter his thrusts. My words were little more than a breathless whisper. *"Akash, you're so perfect for me..."*

His strokes slowed as he bared his throat to me the moment his cock began to pulse, filling me in hot spurts. I whispered against his throat before sliding my fangs into the corded muscle at the top of his shoulder.

"I love you in this life and every life to come."

"In this life and every life to come, lohane thili."

FIFTY-SEVEN

MALEKAI

The temperature of the sea was that of a warm bath. Whatever those flowers were that Lathrimos had brought me had created a mind-bending experience that started with me being catapulted through the realms, cradled in the universal arms of *Akash* herself and *tickled by cherubs.*

This took place *before* the veil between physical reality and the eternal lifted, and I was forced to bear witness to the connection between all things through *Akash.* To experience the gravitas of each of us being a micro-cosmic aspect of herself, to spiralling down the tether that linked me from Mareina to Nakoa to Ataraxus, to then purging the weight of a lifetime of slaughter and all the consequences and effects that spiderwebbed from that and into the lives of others.

If you had told me all of this occurred in the span of 150 years, I'd have believed you, but when I returned to my senses on a beach, with no recollection of travelling to, only to see the sun just barely beginning to rise... I realized only a few hours had passed.

Holy fuck.

I felt like I'd been reborn a different male. As did the drakonati within me. At some point, I couldn't recall, I'd shifted back, and the distinct sensation that I was still very much dead was something with which I hadn't yet come to terms.

Or the fact that I was now bound to Avernus.

Stranded.

Naked.

And not a clue as to how the fuck I could find my way home. To my female.

Our female.

Before I'd died, I had already been growing used to the idea that I'd have to share Mareina with Nakoa, but now a soul-deep satisfaction had blossomed in my chest at the idea of being bound to Nakoa, and even Ataraxus who *Akash* had revealed to me in full.

The fact that I would be *sharing* Mareina with them infused me with a sense of *rightness* and relief that she would be protected by two other formidable males who would protect her with their lives —*travel to hell and back just to save her.*

The tether between my two male counterparts endowed me with a sense of *brotherness.* Like I could trust these males with my life and that I would protect them with mine. Not that I had any idea as to how much of a life I actually had.

My soul reached out towards Mareina and then Nakoa to see if I could somehow summon them as I walked the shore naked and turned in a circle, eventually settling on the mountainous horizon.

The beat of my heart leapt into my throat when they appeared in front of me. A strangled cry tore from Mareina's throat when her eyes landed on me, and she launched herself at me, tackling me to the ground.

Laughter bubbled up, though it was cut short when I recognized the shaking of her shoulders as she sobbed against my chest.

"Oh, *tessari mú.*"

My heart ached for her, for how she must have mourned me.

Nakoa stepped forward, staring down at me. His scarred face and black eyes tense as he held his wings aloft to avoid the sand, tail swaying restlessly in the air behind him in vaguely feline way. The visceral force of his magic pressed upon me as though I could feel it in my chest before I realized I was also feeling a phantom of his emotion.

I clutched onto Mareina though I seemed unable to tear my gaze away from his. The scar on his upper lip pulled one side a little tighter than the other as a tense smile tilted his mouth. The glistening in his eyes had my heart cracking in two, and my hand reached toward him.

He stepped forward and knelt in the sand beside us, draping his long, thick arms over mine and Mareina's shoulders. My heart swelled to bursting.

Family.

This is what family feels like.

I'd nearly forgotten.

Mareina was the only person I was close enough with to consider family for over half a century since my mother was killed.

What a bizarre and incredible place the physical worlds could be. How fate could alter things in such a beautiful way, no matter how unforgiving.

This felt like a second chance. Even if I didn't deserve one.

Now that Mareina was in my arms again, a fucking bath was at the top of my to-do list. I couldn't help but wonder if I looked that filthy, *smelled* that filthy, or if Nakoa was just that intuitive, but the moment we *folded* back, he strode into the bathroom to run the shower.

Still carrying Mareina, I followed him inside and set her down. He turned to leave, and I felt the pinch of Mareina's longing in my chest as if it were my own. *Perhaps it was my own...*

My stomach gave a nervous leap as the word caught him at the threshold of the bathroom door. *"Stay."*

Mareina's breath stilled as Nakoa stopped, looking at us over his shoulder. Despite the unreadable mask shielding his expression, I could feel the pang of vulnerability bleed through the bond between us. His eyes met mine before dipping to Mareina.

"You wish me to stay, *lohane thili?*'"

Mareina gave him a watery grin, nodding. *"Please."*

Mareina *willed* away the paper-thin, white shift dress she was wearing and stepped beneath the shower. The sight of her nudity had my cock thickening, and by the time my eyes landed on the peaks of her breasts, pebbled beneath the hot water, my cock was already aching and jutting out like an extra extremity in front of me.

And I could see Nakoa, who had *willed* a blood-crusted pair of fighting leathers away, was having the same issue.

Shit's about to get weird.

For all the debauchery I had partaken in, in all my 250 years of life... I'd never shared a female with another male. Much less the female who possessed me mind, body, and soul.

Mareina's eyes lifted to mine as I stepped beneath the shower, sliding one hand up my abdomen to my chest. Nakoa returned to the shower, and she reached behind her to pull him against her.

Mareina's nervousness was palpable, and I failed to stifle a grin. With teeth and fang, she tugged on her bottom lip to hide her own smile as her eyes dropped to the ground but incidentally landed on my cock instead. I took her chin between my thumb and forefinger to return her gaze to mine. *"Tessari mú."*

Her lip began to quiver with her emotion like it was begging for the tenderness of my affection.

"You're different now..."

I nodded, caressing my thumb against her jaw.

"You won't be able to leave here... Not unless you reincarnate," she added pitifully.

"So long as you're with me, I don't care where I am."

She frowned. "I'll have to spend time in Atratus... And I don't want you stuck here. I want you to be free."

My eyes lifted to the male standing behind her like a giant sentinel.

"Which is one reason why I'm so grateful that you have two more *soulbound* to protect you when I can't physically be beside you."

Lament tracked her cheeks. I dipped my head to capture her lips with my own, and she instantly sighed, sinking against me. I stepped forward, crowding her against Nakoa so I could step further beneath the water because while I wanted *desperately* to be buried deep inside her—I wanted to do it clean.

Nakoa's arms curled around Mareina from behind as he pinned her against his chest, making her back arch and her full breasts strain forward. His head dipped to the corner of her neck, licking a stripe along its column at the same time his tattooed fingers teased her nipples. I caught the brief flash of his fangs lengthening before he sank his teeth into her. On a soft, needy gasp, her hips began to work against his. Her heavy-lidded gaze met mine and...

Oh, fuck... What was I supposed to be doing?

Bathing. Right.

I made quick work of scrubbing myself clean; all the while, Mareina's eyes remained locked onto mine as Nakoa fed from her. His free hand dipped between her thighs and began to gently stroke her clit.

I couldn't help but be taken aback by how *not* jealous I was. Before this, the idea of Mareina being touched by any male other than me, including her *soulbound*, made me murderous.

Instead, I felt nothing but love, lust, and *rightness*. Though there was some strange sensation lingering in the back of my mind. It took me a moment to realize that it was because *someone* was missing.

Ataraxus.

Not that his absence would cause me to falter.

Nervousness wound through me as I *willed* the three of us dry the moment I shut the water off.

Nakoa lifted his head from Mareina's neck and his eyes met mine, giving me a slight nod of encouragement before he swept her off her feet and threw her over his shoulder. A cry of both shock and plea-sure left her as his hand landed on the globe of a thick, ripe ass cheek. Her head lifted to meet my gaze, and there was a fucking *smile* on her face. The rare sight stole my breath away, just as it always had. Her hand reached for mine, and it stirred me from my stupor to follow behind them.

Nakoa gently set her on the bed as though she were made of glass, and I grunted my approval. Mareina's cheeks flushed, looking nothing short of awe-struck as she took in the sight of us towering over her at the foot of the bed.

FIFTY-EIGHT

MAREINA

I could scarcely believe what had occurred over the last hour.

Day.

I must *be dreaming again.*

Between Nakoa and I making peace with one another and fulfilling our bond, it had been one of the most beautiful experiences of my life. Right beside the event where Malekai and I finally allowed our own bond to become something so much more, as we had always yearned. The only thing tainting my euphoria was the fact that Malekai was bound to Avernus. Though at this moment, I refused to let anything soil the fact he was right here with me *and* Nakoa.

Before I'd left, they'd hated each other, and now, somehow... something had *changed.*

I felt like I was being given a second chance, and even though I wasn't entirely sure I deserved one, I wasn't going to let my chance at happiness pass me by. Again.

I could only pray that *Ataraxus* would be ok. That he would soon wake *and join us.* My heart throttled at the idea.

Nakoa and Malekai both hesitated as if they could scarcely

believe this wasn't a dream either. Our eyes danced between one another, faces cracking with a smile as laughter bubbled up.

Malekai and Nakoa prowled on hands and knees onto the bed as I laid back to receive them. Nakoa's tail curled possessively around my waist, turning me on my side and dragging my back against his front, just as a hand reverently cupped one of my breasts before teasing its turgid peak and drawing a soft sigh from my throat.

Malekai, laying on his side, with his cock pinned between us, held my gaze as his thumb whispered over my jaw. Without even needing to see the serious expression shadowing Malekai's face, Nakoa ceased his ministrations and waited. "You know there's a few things we need to discuss."

Oh fuck. I could feel the emotion swelling again already. I swallowed it back, refusing to ruin this moment and managed a nod. His eyes searched mine. "Namely, you making decisions without us. *Leaving us.*"

My defence, my reasoning, the last four months of fucking torture rose to my throat in another onslaught of emotion, but again, I swallowed it back. At my silence, Nakoa's tail tightened. I attempted to nod again, but Malekai shook his head giving me a pitying look through heavy-lidded eyes. "I think our female needs to be taught a lesson."

Malekai's turquoise and gold eyes lifted to Nakoa's, whose expression was as foreboding as I'd ever seen it. He grunted his agreement.

My heart fluttered in anticipation, and I *gulped,* suddenly feeling like prey.

"What kind of lesson?"

Nakoa's voice was all gravel and doom. "The kind of lesson that will further embed in your soul the fact that we *own* you. That ensures you *trust* us in *everything.*"

Malekai's expression turned downright devious. "That sounds fair, wouldn't you agree, *tessari mú?*"

Nakoa gave a thoughtful growl as he amended, "The kind of

lesson that would prevent you from making decisions again without us."

Malekai hummed his agreement. "Indeed... One that would ensure you never fucking leave our sides again."

Nakoa's claw-tipped fingers dug into my flesh, fingers tensing where they gripped me around my ribs as his hand collared my throat, forcing my gaze to his. "Perhaps we should start by binding you and gagging you, as I did before?"

My breath caught as memories of being bound and gagged, utterly vulnerable to his will, returned to me.

Nakoa inhaled deeply as he buried his nose at the curve of my neck as my arousal further intensified. Chest rumbling with satisfaction, his thick, steeled length gave a thrust, painting my back in precum as one of his hands came around to torture my clit with a teasing caress. Malekai gripped my jaw between thumb and forefinger. "You'd like that, wouldn't you, Mareina?"

My hips writhed against Nakoa's hand and his cock as my pussy clenched with need, turning my words to whimper. *"Akash, yes."*

Malekai leaned in and took my bottom lip into his mouth, biting until he drew blood that unleashed a growl of pleasure spread through his chest. *"You'll take your punishment like a good girl, tessari mú?"*

"Yes. I want you both to ruin me."

Nakoa and Malekai growled in unison as the latter took the top sheet and tore the fabric with his fangs before rending it between his hands, resulting in two strips of fabric. He bound my wrists with one strip before tying my ankles together, at which point Nakoa's attention to my clit ceased. I whined in protest, but Malekai cut me off with a growled command.

"On your knees, Mareina."

My belly twisted with nerves as my desire spiked higher. Nakoa drew away from me before guiding me to my knees and elbows.

"Knees apart," Nakoa added gruffly as he settled himself against the headboard, thickly corded legs on either side of my elbows. My pussy clenched as he spread his leaking pre-cum over the head of cock before stroking its length.

"*Fuck,* this pretty little pussy is desperate to be filled by us, isn't she?" Malekai growled, admiring the view from behind.

I wiggled my hips to entice him forward, but all it earned me was a swift smack on the thick curve of my ass. I felt the sting just as much against my clit, causing my pussy to spasm around nothing.

"I want you to lavish your *soulbound's* cock with attention while I make this ass nice and rosy. And for each second you manage to take him deep in your throat, I'll reward this needy, dripping cunt with my dick. Understood?"

My breath caught in my throat because this wasn't a side of him I'd seen yet. When I didn't respond, Malekai delivered a smack to my pussy that had me crying out.

"Misbehaving already? What do you say?"

"*Yes, sir.*"

Malekai rewarded me by gingerly caressing up my thigh and ass.

"*Good girl. Now swallow that dick.*"

Nakoa watched me with hooded eyes, fisting my hair in one hand as I took his dick in one of my own. I drew upon my saliva before spitting it on the tip of his cock and worked my hands over it to slide down his length. His growl-like purr hums to life in his chest as his hips punched forward. "*So fucking beautiful, lohane thili.*"

Before I could reply, Malekai's hand came down on one ass cheek, followed swiftly to the other. My flesh jiggled, followed by the sound of Malekai's deep hum of satisfaction.

My mouth closed over Nakoa's length, sighing my pleasure at his taste and the feel of his silken steeled length against my tongue. In tandem, my hands and mouth worked over him as Malekai continued to deliver smacks to my ass and pussy. When I finally pressed him as far as I could to the back of my throat, he began to count.

"*One, lohane thili.*"

Swallowed against him, I forced away my throat's reflex at the pressure of his enormous cock.

"Two. So fucking perfect.

Saliva began to pool in my mouth as I continued to bob against him, his cock still buried deep in the back of my throat.

"Three, four, five. That's it, *maha loha.* Be a good girl and gag on this dĩck so I can lick up those pretty tears."

I could feel the reverence in his gaze as he watched me and tucked a strand of hair behind my ear.

"Six. Fuck, look how greedy you are… "

I whimpered from around my mouthful of him.

Oh gods, I can't much longer.

A few more seconds ticked by as my throat spasmed around his length, demanding I take a reprieve, but fuck, I wanted a lot more than six strokes of Malekai's cock. Saliva began to leak from the sides of my mouth, dripping down the remaining half of his thick cock that had *no* way of fitting down my throat.

Malekai's hands alternated between firm smacks and gentle caresses as my clit throbbed with need for attention.

Nakoa's hand tightened the grip on my hair as his hips began to thrust in counter to the bobbing of my head.

I finally gagged, pushing away from Nakoa's length. Saliva stretched between us in thick strings as I panted for air.

Malekai's touch turned tender as he slid a single digit through my dripping slit to tease my clit. "Is that all you've got, *tessari mú? 12 seconds?"*

I resumed stroking Nakoa's cock as I gave a breathless reply.

"No, sir."

Malekai hummed his pleasure. *"Good girl."*

I wiped the saliva from my mouth and chin before lowering my mouth back to Nakoa's length, holding his gaze again to return lavishing his cock with teasing strokes and licking him from base to tip. *"I love you."*

Nakoa's breath caught in his chest as his gaze widened slightly with emotion. "In this life and every life to come, Mareina."

I twisted to look over my shoulder to find Malekai's lips parted as he stared straight at Nakoa upon hearing the familiar declaration. His throat dipped with swallowed emotion as he returned to teasing my clit, and his eyes met mine. My words, filled with every ounce of my emotion, strained to keep my voice from wavering.

"I love you, *anim gemla.*"

The broad plane of Malekai's chest swelled, and I didn't miss how his eyes glistened, reminding me what a fucking gift it was that we were here together. Nakoa must have seen it as well because, in the next moment, he was beside me, tugging my back against his chest as Malekai settled in front of me, tearing the binding at my ankles before gripping one of my legs beneath the knee to spread me wide for him.

Malekai drew his hips back to align his cock with my entrance as his free hand wound my hair in his fist and tugged my head back to meet his gaze. *"I love you in this life and every life to come, tessari mú."*

The head of Malekai's cock breached my entrance and slowly pushed further, stretching me and filling me with the sweetest pain as I keened unintelligible curses.

Nakoa grunted his approval as he watched Malekai's cock settle all the way to the hilt. Nakoa's voice turned to gravel as he barred his forearm around my waist to hold me in place for Malekai. "You belong to us, Mareina."

My body had already begun to coil tight and tremble with an approaching orgasm.

"Oh fuck, I'm not gonna last 12 strokes."

Malekai withdrew until just the thick, flared head of his cock remained before slamming all the way back in. When I gasped my pleasure, Nakoa stole the opportunity to tilt my parted lips further towards him and spat into my open mouth. His fingers squeezed my jaw, preventing me from swallowing, before turning my head back towards Malekai. He didn't miss a beat and gifted me a ball of spit on the flat of my offered tongue. The sensation filled my heart to bursting as I swallowed them down. Before I could dwell on my satisfaction, a bottle of oil appeared in Nakoa's hand.

My breathing stilled. The only occasions where someone had taken me *there* had been in the Erosyan Temple, and it hadn't been with my consent. Anxiety twisted in my gut even though I didn't want him to stop, and I realized I wanted him to replace those long-buried memories.

Nakoa and Malekai's motions stilled as if they sensed my anxiety.

"Nakoa, I..."

"I know, *lohane thili*... Do you want me to stop?"

I shook my head, core clenching needily around Malekai's length, making him grip my hips all the harder.

"No. I want you both."

"You're sure?"

"More than anything."

Nakoa's lips part on a grin against my cheek. "My Queen is so strong. And so greedy."

Malekai's husky laugh was cut off by a groan when my pussy gripped him tight. His response was collaring my throat, drawing my gaze back to his. "Such a good girl, taking both our cocks." He brought his mouth to mine in a bruising kiss that turned tender. Nakoa's fingers began to massage oil against my puckered entrance, gently working a finger in, causing the ring of flesh to tighten against him, making Malekai groan into my mouth as his strokes deepened.

"You were made for us, Mareina. Just as we were made for you. We're going to fill every pretty little hole you have so fucking perfectly."

I was beyond words at this point. Nakoa sunk two fingers inside me as his tail worked against my clit in tandem to Maleka's firm thrusts. My pussy began to clench, and Nakoa withdrew as Malekai stilled. "Don't cum just yet, *lohane thili,* or that pussy and ass is gonna clench so tight I'll never fit."

Oh gods, I didn't think I could hold it back.

"Hurry, please... Please, please, please."

"Fuck, I love when you beg," Nakoa growled as he began to push his oil-slicked cock into me.

Malekai hummed his agreement as slowly slid back inside of me. "Mmmmm, we shall have to endeavor to make her do it more often."

I whimpered as the head of Nakoa's cock pushed into that taut ring of muscle, and he collared my throat with one hand.

"Breathe, *lohane thili.* Let your body relax and give yourself over to us. You're right where you belong."

I took a deep breath, exhaling slowly and willed my body to relax; to settle and become languid between them, all the while my heart clenched tighter with the love I felt for them. The action drew Ataraxus to my thoughts. *Gods, how would I fit all three of them?*

I cried out a curse, nails sinking deep into Nakoa's forearm as he pushed forward inch-by-tantalizing-inch while Malekai caressed my cheek and held my tortured, euphoric gaze. *"You're so fucking beautiful it hurts, tessari mú."*

My heart burst with emotion at his words. Words that I'd so recently feared I'd never be blessed with hearing again. My emotion was swift to breach the dams of my eyes. *"I love you. So fucking much."*

Malekai licked up each of my tears. "To death and beyond," he murmured against my lips before his tongue gently stroked mine as his calloused fingertips teased my nipples. Nakoa's tail returned to caressing my clit. My keening was muffled as Nakoa settled deeper and deeper until he reached the hilt. I felt like I could barely breathe. *"Oh gods... It's too much... Hurts—so fucking good."*

Neither of them had moved, and already my pussy was fluttering with orgasm. *"There's our good girl,"* Nakoa purred against my neck as he began to move slowly.

My body felt like it had burst into a sea of glittering stars, fluid and rising and crashing wave after wave. Malekai's hips slid forward, punching the air from my lungs intensifying the sensation so much it stole my breath.

With deep, steady thrusts and the fullness of both of them being rooted inside me, it pressed fiercely against pleasure points I hadn't even realized existed. Liquid heat began to leak from me as I whimpered helplessly against them.

Malekai felt it first, drawing back to gaze at the fruitful evidence of their labor and, as if in sync, Nakoa's tail retreated from my clit to give him an unobstructed view. "*Oh fuck, tessari mú.* Is this perfect, pretty, little pussy gushing for us?"

I managed to whimper and nod, tears streaming. Nakoa leaned back, lifting my left leg to peer down between us as the last of my cum trickled between us. A growl resonated between us as he admired where the three of us were joined, and his hand gently caressed the globes of my ass. "Tell us who you belong to, *lohane thili.*"

Nakoa and Malekai's strokes remained synchronous, drawing ungodly noises from me in between my keening moans and whimpers. Malekai licked his thumb and rubbed it back and forth to tease my clit. My pussy immediately clenched tight again as more fluid gushed out of me. "Say it, Mareina. Tell us who you belong to."

A tremor worked through Malekai as his eyes briefly rolled in the back of his head. Nakoa went rigid behind me; claws dipping into the flesh of my hips. I reached up to card my fingers through their hair, gripping them tightly and pulling their faces nearer to mine.

"Yours. Always and forever, in this life and every life to come. To death and beyond."

Nakoa hummed his pleasure as he sank his fangs in the curve of my neck. Malekai groaned, slanting his mouth over mine. Knowing that my body still needed time to adjust to accommodating both of them, the pace of their thrusts remained steady and slow, all while Malekai continued his gentle ministrations upon my oversensitized clit.

Within minutes, another liquifying yet gentle and lingering orgasm overtook me. Nakoa followed me over the edge, filling me with his cum. His arms wove tighter around me and his purr started up again.

Nakoa's fangs released me, licking up the blood dripping from the puncture wounds. I arched my back into him, caressing his cheek as I captured his lips and offered him my soft moans.

Malekai's hips stuttered, drawing my gaze, and I found all my awe, admiration, and love mirrored in those eyes. Emotion clogged thickly in my throat. *'I love you, Kalini,'* he whispered as his cock pulsed inside of me.

My voice wavered as I gave him a tremulous smile, ready to break on my building tears.

"Katadamna kaza."

CHAPTER

FIFTY-NINE

NAKOA

What a bizarre turn of the tides. If someone had told me that I'd be sharing my *soulbund* with another male, I'd probably have gutted them for even daring to speak the words. Now... I wasn't entirely sure I would have it any other way. Though it felt like we were treading upon new, fragile grounds, daring to build something new. Something unfathomably precious.

And I found myself constantly worrying about someone new.

Ataraxus.

And I silently vowed that we would visit him tomorrow and sent a prayer that he would recover from whatever it was stealing his consciousness.

When I woke, some hours later, it was still only early evening. Mareina's head lay on my chest with a leg draped over mine. Malekai was curled on his side against her with his large hand curved over the swell of her hip. I peeked down to see her eyes closed, lashes faintly kissing the apples of her cheeks, and her breathing even. My heart pinched at the gorgeous sight of her.

It also felt startlingly intimate to see Malekai in a sleeping state, his expression peaceful. I realized then that I'd never seen him at peace until now.

As if reading my mind, Malekai's eyes opened in that exact moment. A beat later, he carefully disentangled himself from Mareina and silently rolled over to climb out of bed. His gaze dropped to the floor as if suddenly realizing that he didn't have any previously shed clothes waiting for him there. Perhaps Mors wouldn't mind sharing. Likely not, considering he was currently suffering the amnesiac effects of drinking from the River Oblivion. Malekai peered over his shoulder at me with a silent question.

Malekai followed me out of the room as we padded towards Mors' bedroom. We strode directly towards a door on the far side of the room to discover his wardrobe. Constructed of elaborately carved dark wood, it was filled to the brim with clothing in every fashion, boasting surprising pops of color I'd never have assumed the God of Death would fancy. I opened one of several drawers to discover a style of soft, form-fitting undergarments with a stretchy waistband I'd never seen before. All of which were in a tremendous variety of patterns.

"He seemed kind. I can't imagine he'd mind lending clothing to one of Mareina's mates." Malekai's words sounded, if anything, as if they'd been spoken to reassure himself as he opened a few other drawers, sifting around beyond what was necessary to gather borrowed clothing.

I couldn't help but feel a little pang of jealousy at the admission. "You met him?"

"Briefly. Yes."

Before I could ask any other questions, Malekai's snooping resulted in the discovery of a wide velvet-lined wooden drawer boasting coils of rope, silk ties, masks, nipple clamps, a remarkable variety of butt plugs in every shape and size, and other sex toys I didn't even have names for.

Our brows lept with mild surprise as we stared down at the God of Death's treasure trove. Malekai took a short breath, hesitating to ask the very question running through my mind. "It would be... *wrong* for us to borrow these to use on his daughter... Right?"

I grunted in affirmation. "Without a doubt..."

Neither of us moved and simply remained staring as our minds whirled with opportunity. Malekai gave a thoughtful hum.

"... So very, very wrong."

My eyes caught on a sealed box. "Unforgivable, really."

Malekai's gaze followed mine. "Twisted beyond measure."

As if drawn by some unknowable force, my hand found its way to the entirely new, unopened box.

"What're you two doing?"

Malekai and I both yelped, jolting around to face Mareina, dressed in nothing but a *soiled* white sheet.

Malekai's and my response came in unison. Our voices were the epitome of innocence. *"Nothing."*

Malekai cleared his throat. "Just borrowing some of your father's... clothing."

Mareina's eyes narrowed with distrust, her expression only softening as she took in our nudity. "... Right."

Mustering nonchalance, I turned and carefully closed the drawer of Mor's box of butt-hole pleasures and plucked out pairs of undergarments, trousers, and shirts for myself and Malekai. I hadn't brought a change of clothing from the palace and wasn't inclined to pull on gore and sweat-crusted fighting leathers. Malekai shifted to take them, and we both stifled conspiratorial grins when our eyes met, silently communicating that *soon*, we would come back and find out what was in that fucking box.

Mareina stepped up behind us, now seeing nothing amiss in her father's closet. "Hm. I don't know why I expected his clothing to be less... extravagant."

"I imagine when you've been around as long as he has, you collect all manner of things."

Mareina snatched a pair of ~~stolen~~ borrowed undergarments, the pattern of which I hadn't yet noticed. *"Are those eggplants?"*

Our eyes met, chuckling, just as a knock sounded from the entrance of Mor's bedroom.

Malekai and I were still nude when we turned to find Lathrimos standing in the doorway. Still, Mareina called him in, tightening the sheet around her body.

"Lathrimos. Lovely to see you."

The male was so large he seemed to dwarf Mors' enormous bedroom. My brows leapt when Val appeared just behind him. The two of them exchanged sheepish grins.

Well, well, well. What do we have here?

Val's brows leapt as he takes in the state of our undress. *"Well,* what a delicious picture you three paint. I'm so happy ta see ya'all're playing nicely now."

My eyes narrowed as I caught Val's eyes lingering on both Mareina and Malekai.

"Is there something I can help you with, Valerius?"

Val cleared his throat, eyes darting to mine. "Apologies, *Your Majesty.* I just thought you might like to know that your ehm... Zurie and Keres are at the palace."

I waited to feel some form of emotion at the news my mother hadn't died. It never came.

"Is everything ok with Ataraxus?"

"Still asleep, but otherwise healthy, according to Bohyun."

I grunted my disappointment. As much as it pained me to leave Malekai behind so Mareina and I could visit Ataraxus, his absence, and fragile state was an incessant cloud darkening the back of my mind.

"Well, thank you for coming. I appreciate you going out of your way. Pomona wasn't around to spare you the trouble?"

A muscle in Val's jaw ticked, sparking my anxiety. "She's staying with your mother. Miroslav has gone missing."

My heart seized. The male was so aloof and nigh-unkillable I'd merely assumed he'd *folded* back home.

"There's been no sign of him at all?"

Val shook his head. My eyes dipped to Mareina as her gaze grew distant before she shook her head. "I don't feel him here…"

I *willed* on the borrowed clothing as Malekai did the same, stopping short as realization darkened his expression.

"I'll fold you to her," Mareina offered, her features lined with worry. I nodded my reply even as my eyes returned to Malekai. His chest heaved, hands fisting at his sides to force away the tremor working through his hands. My heart squeezed with empathy. I couldn't imagine being trapped here, forced to worry about Mareina and Malekai. Mareina pressed her hands on his chest.

"Azrael is trapped in a dungeon, wearing a palladium collar—
Malekai shook his head, gaze lifting to mine. "So was Zurie."

CHAPTER
SIXTY
MALEKAI

This was going to be fucking challenging. Only a few minutes had passed since Val, Mareina, and Nakoa had surfaced to Atratus, and already I was pacing a hole in the fucking floor.

What if Zurie frees Azrael as he freed her?

Lathrimos had remained with me and was now frowning as he watched from the still *doorless* entry of Mors' home.

"There has to be a way."

Lathrimos' frown deepened, still mourning the absence of his best friend. "For?"

"What would happen if I were to try and leave Avernus?"

Lathrimos' face paled as if the mere idea is born of nightmares. "It is forbidden."

The only way I was able to keep the volume of my voice below a roar was to speak through clenched teeth. "Azrael could be killing the only two people in this entire world that I love. Even *if* Zurie's synchronous visit to the palace is merely a coincidence—there *will* be other occasions when they will need me to protect them. I will *not* stay here for the rest of eternity *praying* for their safety."

Lathrimos' face hardened in a way that enabled me to see him through a different lens. "I don't think you understand… If you cross that threshold between Avernus and Bellorum… You could become something else. Something *other*. You have a body in this realm. An immortal one. If you try to go to the living realm, your soul would remain here but it would be set adrift. Like a ship without a captain or an anchor. And *this* physical form…"

I held my breath as Lathrimos scrubbed a hand down his face. "You would become a soulless monster driven solely by an insatiable hunger. The people and things that matter to you now will be nothing compared to the need you have to feed. Blood will become your sole source of sustenance."

My eyes narrowed with doubt. "So you're saying I'll become a sanguinati?"

The curling of Lathrimos' lip told me I'd just said something monumentally stupid.

"You'll become a demon. The worst of their kind. A *Syfaro Vescor."*

I gave a noncommittal grunt. "Never heard of him."

Lathrimos rolled his eyes. *"A soul-eater."*

Ah. Right.

Perhaps it would be better to try and entertain some other options. I didn't know much about them because they were such a rare entity, but what I had heard and seen in illustrations or paintings was… *unsettling.*

I'd nearly been prepared to dive through that threshold.

Still…

Lathrimos strode over to me, wearing a compassionate look as his gigantic hand landed on my shoulder. "She's a Goddess of Death. She'll be fine. They wiped his memory with the River Oblivion… there's no way Azrael would be able to overpower her or Nakoa without the memories of his magic."

"Do you have a library? Did Mors, I mean?"

Lathirmos' eyes narrowed with suspicion. "Why do you ask?"

I glared back. "You already know. Humor me."

After a longsuffering sigh and a few long moments of internal deliberating, Lathrimos finally relented.

"There's one at the palace."

"Palace?"

"Mors moved out of it after he married Soteira and built this place... 600 or so years ago."

"Does anyone reside there now?"

"Palace staff. Some of Mors' friends, if they haven't all chosen to reincarnate already."

"Does Mareina know?"

Another nod.

"And she doesn't have any interest in living there?"

Lathrimos gave me a guilty look. "Nakoa only knew of this place, and he came frequently searching for her... I think she..."

Realization washed over me. My precious *tessari mú*. She must have been so heartbroken and torn.

"She was waiting for him..."

Lathrimos shifted uncomfortably as though the very idea of discussing Mareina behind her back made his skin crawl.

"Would you mind showing it to me?"

Lathrimos huffs. "You might want to shift into your drakonati form, though. Otherwise, I'd have to carry you."

I gave a thoughtful hum as if I were actually deliberating which was the better option.

There was no fucking way I was going to risk shifting into my drakonati form and getting stuck in it again.

I failed to stifle my grin as an image entered my mind of Lathrimos soaring through the sky whilst carrying me in his arms like a bride.

Lathrimos' jaw drops. "You *are* joking?"

SIXTY-ONE

MALEKAI

Lathrimos grunts through his laughter as he hefted me into his arms. "Gods, you're a big bastard." That causes my laughter to renew. "Hey, you offered. Though, I think even if I wasn't terrified of being unable to shift back from my drakonati form, watching you struggle to carry me like a damsel is well worth it."

Lathrimos' wings gave a powerful beat, lifting us into the air and several more to keep us there before we're finally soaring through the air. Silence descended between us for several moments as we glided beyond the meadow surrounding Mors' humble home towards the mountains in the distance.

Admittedly, our journey was a highly welcome distraction from my worrying about Mareina, Nakoa, and Ataraxus since I was apparently fucking trapped here. Though I dared not vocalize my complaints, lest the universe somehow realize that my being able to share some part of life with Mareina wasn't supposed to happen, and it was indeed *too good to be true*. My heart squeezed with gratitude for the male currently hefting me across Avernus.

"Words will never be enough to express my gratitude..."

His gaze shifts to mine, offering me a sad smile. "It wasn't entirely selfless. Avernus was bound to fall apart with her in that state. And probably Bellorum with it if her *soulbound* was left to his own devices."

I give a thoughtful but noncommittal grunt as my thoughts return to Mareina and my stomach gives a familiar churn of anxiety. As I've done a thousand times before, like when Mareina was a soldier in Zurie's army or her Royal Irae, I repeated a familiar mantra in my mind to calm myself.

Mareina is the Goddess of Death and she will not be felled.

CHAPTER

SIXTY-TWO

MAREINA

After briefly *folding* to the palace to drop Val off, Nakoa and I came straight to his mother's. Though leaving so swiftly when Ataraxus was still unconscious had tension winding knots in my chest. Leilani, Nakoa's mother, was already waiting for us outside with Pomona when we arrived, presumably having already anticipated our arrival thanks to her skills as a seer. Her face was splotched with red, her eyes puffy as if she'd been recently weeping. A choked sob escaped her when her eyes landed on Nakoa.

My heart squeezed painfully tight at the sight of Nakoa taking his mother in his arms and holding her against his chest. I could only imagine what she had been going through, considering Nakoa hadn't spoken to her since before we'd overthrown Zurie, and he'd realized she'd hidden the fact that Zurie was his birth mother. And now, with Miroslav, her *soulbound,* missing, potentially even *dead,* no matter how unfathomable, it was remarkable she hadn't shown up at the palace herself.

Pomona threw her arms around my neck. "I'm so fucking relieved you're back." I squeezed her back, eyes suddenly stinging.

299

When she pulled back, the concern in her eyes made my gut sicken with anxiety. *She doesn't know I found Malekai in Avernus.*

"How are you?"

I gave her arm an appreciative squeeze. "Better... He's in Avernus. With me."

Pomona's eyes went round, her jaw-dropping in realization for a moment before saline swelled in her eyes, and she threw her arms around my neck. "*Oh, praise Akash.*"

I rubbed soothing circles on her back, the action soothing both her and my own freshly healing wound. Leilani and Nakoa filled my line of vision, and I let Pomona go to give Leilani a hug that she accepted gratefully, stroking my hair.

My words lacked the conviction I'd hoped to muster. "We'll find him, Leilani."

Leilani's fingers dug into my tunic as she held me tighter, losing a shuddering breath. "You need to go."

I froze before slowly pulling back.

"To Ataraxus."

Leilani opened her palm, and a vial of dark blue, glimmering fluid appeared. "It will induce a coma-like sleep. It is for both you and Azrael. Atraxus' soul is somehow tied to Azrael's."

Nakoa's hand slipped into mine as my throat squeezed tight. "But how? And why would inducing a coma fix it?"

"You need to find their souls. There is a haemorrhaging of Azrael's magic. When he attempted to kill Ataraxus, somehow, Ataraxus managed to survive by attaching his life force, his *soul*, to Azrael. And Azrael is dying, as you may have already noticed. You need to heal him."

My heartbeat echoed in my ears as her voice grew distant. Whatever anger I would have felt at the news that Azrael had also attempted to kill Ataraxus was drowned out by the fact that my *soul-bound's* life was tied to one of the most wretched creatures in existence who was *dying.* The consequences of Azrael's death would be catastrophic.

"I still don't understand... Why would *I* be able to heal him? All I know how to do is kill."

Leilani's grey eyes searched mine as the darkness veiling them lifted like a cloud revealing the moon.

"That is because you have only come to know one aspect of your power."

I frowned, anxiety twisting my stomach in anticipation—of what I didn't know. "I am a Goddess of Death. What more is there to know?"

Leilani's head tipped back with laughter. When her gaze returned to mine, unmistakable excitement shone in her eyes.

"Oh, my darling, you are so much more. You are a Goddess of *Rebirth*."

I KNOW THAT WAS A BIT OF A CLIFFHANGER...

Fear not—Blood of Two Crowns is now available on Kindle Unlimited and Amazon.

Want some free NSFW art?
All *signed paperbacks* (they're only a few £s more) ordered on ChiaraForestieri.com come with free 5x8" NSFW art prints printed on 400 gsm (thick gallery quality) silk paper.

Get exclusive sneak peeks into my upcoming works, events, giveaways, and by signing up to my monthly newsletter at: https://www.chiaraforestieri.com/epistle-sign-up

or

Become an exclusive content subscriber at chiaraforestieri.com where you'll also get access to tons of perks (free NSFW art prints, merch, free signed copies of all my new releases, exclusive ebooks (Goddess of Origin, The God of All Good Things, & more)

I KNOW THAT WAS A BIT OF A CLIFFHANGER...

Follow me @authorchiaraforestieri on Instagram to stay up-to-date
with all my upcoming releases like:

Book Three of Hallowed Fates
Spring 2025

The Captive Witch & the Unborn Palladin
2025

Nox: When Darkness Takes Form
now available only on chiaraforestieri.com

HOLY FUCK, THANK YOU.

Words cannot even begin to describe the gratitude I have to you for giving my work a chance. **I poured my heart and soul into this one y'all.** I mean, I always do, but somehow this one just hits different. I also feel like Mareina's emotional journey thus far has been parallel to my own. I'm *well* familiar with feelings of unworthiness and have dealt with tremendous depression and crippling anxiety—and have only somewhat recently turned that around by learning to love and accept myself. For me, personally, meditation has been utterly life-changing, but that's all I'll say about that. Don't wanna get all preachy or ruffle anyone's feathers, but I would like to add that if you are suffering from emotional distress, adverse circumstances, etc. here are some **free** resources for those who may be in need and live in the UK, US, Canada, & Australia:

<u>United Kingdom</u>
    Victim's Support (UK) 08 08 16 89 111
An independent charity dedicated to supporting victims of crime and traumatic incidents in England and Wales.
    Anxiety UK

HOLY FUCK, THANK YOU.

03444 775 774

Flexible, online peer support groups, therapist-led anxiety management courses and Art for **Anxiety** Relief (AfAR)

Campaign Against Living Miserably (CALM)

0800 58 58 58

Suicide prevention charity on a mission to help people end their misery, not their lives.

MindOut

mindout.org.uk

Mental health service run by and for LGBTQ+ people.

No Panic

0300 7729844

Provides a helpline, step-by-step programmes, and support for people with anxiety disorders.

Sane

0300 304 7000

Offers emotional support and information for anyone affected by mental health problems, including a helpline.

UNITED STATES

Crisis Text Line

Text TALK to 741741 to text with a trained crisis counselor for free, 24/7

National Alliance on Mental Illness

800-950-6264, open M-F 10am – 10pm ET

PTSD Alliance

888-436-6306

contact@ptsdalliance.org

American Foundation for Suicide Prevention

Simply dial 988 or visit them online at suicidepreventionlifeline.org

For Veterans, dial 988 and press 1 or visit www.veteranscrisisline.net

No Panic

Helpline Number 0300 772 9844

Available everyday - 10am - 10pm (365 days of the year)

No Panic specializes in self-help and offers the following services:

- Recovery services
- Pen pal programs
- Advice and support
- Confidential helpline
- Recovery programs
- Raising awareness programs
- Self-help behavior therapy
- Literature
- Social events
- Online or via telephone conferencing
- Recovery groups

Canada

The Listening Ear

Everyday from 3 pm-3 am

(517) 337-1717

The Listening Ear is dedicated to providing free, compassionate and confidential support over the phone.

LGBT National Hotline

888-843-4564

Suicide Crisis Helping

Simply dial 988

Certified Listeners Society

visit certifiedlisteners.org to chat for free with a trained volunteer.

CLS offers free, confidential, and non-judgmental emotional support to individuals struggling with emotional challenges related to anxiety, depression, stress, and loneliness. CLS provides trained volunteers who offer a safe and supportive space for individuals to express their feelings and concerns.

Canadian Resource Centre for Victims of Crime
Everyday 1:30 pm-9:30 pm
(613) 208-0747 or 1-877-232-2610
or CRCVC.ca
Victims and survivors of crime, their friends, and families can call or reach out via our texting service, and live chat system.

<u>AUSTRALIA</u>

FriendLine
1800 424 287
7 days a week
Supports anyone who's feeling lonely, needs to reconnect or just wants to chat online with one of their trained volunteers. All conversations with FriendLine are anonymous.

Lifeline
13 11 14, <u>text 0477 13 11 14</u> or <u>chat online.</u>
Provides 24-hour crisis counselling, support groups and suicide prevention services.

Beyond Blue
1300 22 4636
Aims to increase awareness of depression and anxiety and reduce stigma. If you or a loved one need help, you can call 24 hours/7 days a week or <u>chat online</u>.

MindSpot
1800 61 44 34
Free telephone and online service for people with anxiety, stress, low mood or depression. It provides online assessment and treatment for anxiety and depression. MindSpot is not an emergency or instant response service.

About the Author

Originally from the US, Chiara Forestieri is a single mother of two [not-so] tiny little love muffins (an 18-year-old and a five-year-old, as of 2024) who spends her days taking care of her small family, practicing Brazilian Jiu-Jitsu and Muay Thai [with the grace of a failing inflatable tube man], pouring her heart and soul into creative and entrepreneurial endeavors, such as this book. All with varying degrees of success, of course. Ranging from 'Well, at least no one died' to 'Have you lost your mind?'

Currently, she lives in wonderful London, praying desperately for sunshine and warm weather. While many of her prayers have been answered, this one is often not.

Some of her favourite things (outside of family and friends) include:

Her Kindle
Brazilian Jiu-jitsu
Muay Thai
All things nature and wilderness
Animals
Clean sheets (*drool*)
Dirty humor
The sea (her home)
Hot-warm-and-squishy freshly baked cookies
Sun

Kindness
Cuddles
A fiery hearth
Pyjamas
Oh, and love. Love, love, love. :)

Wanna see more of your favorite characters? See excerpts from upcoming books? Or just general juicy, steamy, romantasy content?

Follow the journey instagram! :)
@authorchiaraforestieri